Dear Amy

Congratulations on winning the Goodreads Giveaway! Now no one can ever say you're not a winner!

In this second novel of the Sessions University series Thomas and Zoltan again find themselves in the middle of events that

A Matter of Circumstance

threaten the university, themselves and their families. Thank God Mark Berger is there to help them.

I hope you enjoy the novel!

All the best and may you enjoy a wonderful 2022.

THE SESSIONS UNIVERSITY SERIES

BOOK II

A MATTER OF CIRCUMSTANCE

A Novel

NELSON COVER

Epigraph Books
Rhinebeck, New York

A Matter of Circumstance: A Novel © 2020 by Nelson Cover

All rights reserved. No part of this book may be used or reproduced in any manner without written permission from the author except in critical articles or reviews. Contact the publisher for information.

Paperback ISBN: 978-1-951937-41-6
Hardcover ISBN: 978-1-951937-42-3
eBook ISBN: 978-1-951937-43-0

Library of Congress Control Number 2020909651

Book design by Colin Rolfe

Epigraph Books
22 East Market Street, Suite 304
Rhinebeck, NY 12572
(845) 876-4861
epigraphPS.com

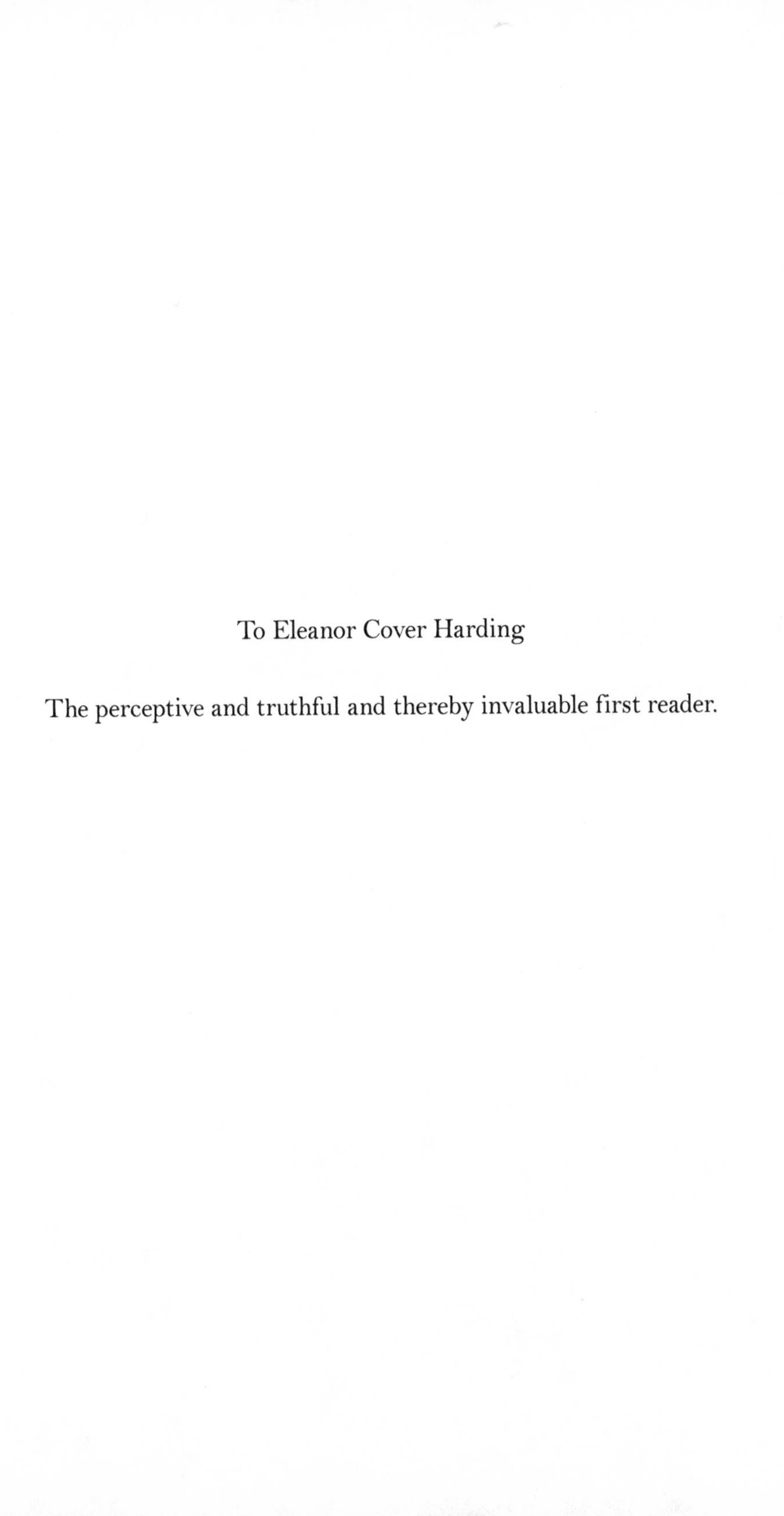

To Eleanor Cover Harding

The perceptive and truthful and thereby invaluable first reader.

I

The Big Guy

SEPTEMBER AND THE new academic year at Sessions University had begun on a sour and worrisome note, creating the strong impression that last year's troubles and the danger they posed for each of us remained.

Inside our antiquated administration building the air was stale, hot and stuffy, laced with outgassing, the HVAC system undoubtedly confused by the prior cool evening and today's Indian-summer relentless heat.

I had turned my desk chair around and was staring out the sealed window of my office in the Communications Department, looking past the driveway and the parking lot, where the trees in the woods were utterly still. The sky was its lightest blue and cloudless. Students drove slowly in the parking lot, scanning for open spaces. Others rushed to their new courses, faces transfixed with uncertainty.

I was thinking, daydreaming really, about how our difficulties had begun almost exactly twelve months before. Not an anniversary I cared to remember but one, given the current cover-up, I could not forget.

The phone behind me rang—small, short rings indicating that the call was from inside the university, the signaling of its never-ending bureaucratic needs.

I turned, sighed, reluctantly picked up the receiver. It was Wentz. President Jack Wentz. Even now, this reality was difficult to grasp.

"Thomas, you got a minute?" Since his promotion to interim president and now, only last week, to president, his normal slick manner of speaking occasionally betrayed some sign of the pressures he was under through a hint of breathlessness.

"Sure."

"Good. Come up to my office, will you?"

"Okay."

As I took the elevator to the third floor and walked down the several hallways to the president's office, presided over by the redoubtable gatekeeper, Ms. Bemis, I reflected that whatever he wanted to see me about must be important. He had been appointed officially at the board of trustees meeting the previous Friday. Our regular meeting was this coming Thursday. If he wanted to see me in person now, rather than wait for our normal meeting, something was up.

So, the board of trustees had done it. They had made the big guy president, promoting him from interim to the real deal. While I knew from experience that Wentz was a brilliant practitioner—some, especially the faculty, thought his appointment a travesty given his well-known propensity for vulgarity, his nasty habit of making insulting personal comments in the guise of humor, his girth and used-car-salesman manner and dress. However, the facts were that he was hands down the most capable and experienced choice, carrying a portfolio of success after success from his progressive management of the College of Continuing Education, as its dean, to his role in the founding of our Beijing Center and now our new Brussels Center.

Further he had been groomed by our superstar former president, Bryan Q. Fitz-Hugh, who was still held in high regard, having secretly escaped a major scandal at Sessions, and who was now undersecretary of state for the European Union. Wentz was the devil the board knew, a familiar face among a crowd of candidates who were strangers. More than that, he could keep a secret, and his elevation amplified the likelihood that he would forever continue to do so, an important consideration when the subject arose of the prior year's very suspicious suicide of our provost, Samuel Kravitz, shortly after he had secured a vote from the Faculty Senate to conduct an independent audit of university finances. Many, especially the family, suspected that provost Kravitz had been murdered.

Ms. Bemis sat as usual on her substantial derriere behind her massive, paperless desk and, as usual, looked through me as I entered the waiting area. Clearly, I was not only beneath contempt but beneath even existing. Today she wore a heat-relieving mass of jade-green gauze. Her inch-long, stiletto nails were painted to match. Jade-spangled earrings hung from ears accentuated by her shorn head.

"The president called and asked that I see him," I told her, feeling as always, a childlike helplessness in her presence.

She betrayed no hint of acknowledgement, save a flick of a sidelong glance tinged with dislike, as if a house fly had just flown into her peripheral vision and threatened to land on a freshly baked pie.

Dutifully I sat on the hard-as-rock, university-seal chair by a table with university pamphlets arranged in a fan and felt as if I was back in the school principal's office. As usual, I began to fantasize about her life outside the administration building and what things might look like under all that gauze. Lord have Mercy.

Ten minutes passed before the president's door lock sounded. The door swung open and Wentz stepped out in shirt sleeves in parting conversation with our new provost—tall, blow-dried black hair, immaculately dressed, yes-man Don Powers.

I stood, noting that Ms. Bemis acknowledged none of our presence. The Jade Sphinx.

Wentz saw me.

"Ah, Dr. Simpson …" he greeted me with false joviality, mocking my PhD. He then turned back to Powers.

"Dr. Powers, I believe you two have met previously," he joked, including Powers in the mockery. "But let me formally introduce you to the 'untouchable' Dr. Simpson, our director of university and campaign communications."

Powers smiled his empty smile, his reaction to almost anything.

"Untouchable?" I asked as I stood.

Wentz gave a pig-like snort, his small black eyes fixed on me as he looked for the effect his comment was having. "Oh yes. You and I have not had a chance to talk, Thomas. Glad you could spare the time just now," he said with just a hint of condescension. "But one of the pre-conditions of my new promotion was that I understand in very explicit terms that you and your pal Zoltan are hands-off employees of mother university until the end of time."

Zoltan was my best friend, a cancer research scientist at the medical center, a giant of a human being, a virtual uncle to our children, a reprobate of Hungarian descent whose normal on-the-edge-of-going-berserk countenance frightened those who did not know him.

"Really?" I looked between him and Powers and could tell by Wentz's sardonic smile and Powers's expression indicating he would welcome being anywhere but the present situation that Wentz's comment had some seriousness to it. Was this what he wanted to see me about?

Powers made a parting mumble. His exit was so swift he seemed to vaporize, as if he were a character in a Road Runner cartoon. Wentz motioned me into his office with a jerk of his head and we walked in.

It was the same office as when Fitz-Hugh had inhabited it with its thick Persian rug to cover the original parquet now flimsy with age and deteriorated underlayment, its oil paintings of campus scenery hanging on mahogany-paneled walls, its splendid view of the lower quadrangle. But it felt devoid of spirit and life, a feeling accentuated by empty shelves on the left where once Fitz-Hugh's various honors and grip-and-grin pictures with dignitaries at important events had resided.

Wentz took a seat behind the beautiful partners desk that had been Fitz-Hugh's but sat in a new double-wide office chair to accommodate his corpulence. His jacket was on the chair back behind him, his rolled-up sleeves revealing large, white, dark-haired arms. A new Omega had replaced the cheap afterthought watch he had worn previously.

He had obviously sought professional advice about his appearance. Which brought up the thought of Mrs. Wentz, Florence, whom I had never heard of until her name showed up in the information the president's office supplied for our drafting the announcement of his appointment. Until now I had thought Wentz was single and a wastrel. The latter was certainly true as in the past he and our capital campaign consultant, Frank Lusby, had been known for their carousing—who knows where and with what. Perhaps Florence, whomever the hell she was, also had something to do with the upgrade.

The onyx pinky ring with its side diamond was gone. The cheap acetate and sharkskin suits had been replaced by wool in muted colors. Wentz, however, was one of those guys who could never pull off anything remotely conservative, and he was still wearing a God-awful paisley tie with his new dark-grey suit.

In an instant his used-car-salesman façade melted away, leaving a very large, serious, saturnine man looking me straight in the eye. Chilling. I had not seen this side of Wentz before. Even during his interim appointment, he had been all palsy-walsy.

"We have a problem."

"Yeah?"

"The Kravitz family has hired a private detective agency. As you might expect, given Joan Kravitz's independent wealth, they've hired the best, and of course, the most expensive, the Blaylock Agency, to investigate Provost Kravitz's suicide to determine exactly what the hell happened out there in the park that night, whether in fact it was a suicide."

"Oh shit."

"That's a succinct summation, yes."

The scandal that Fitz-Hugh had escaped had featured wire transfers of anonymous multi-million-dollar gifts from clandestine foreign sources to the ongoing capital campaign. We now knew that he had used the funds to partially finance Sessions's international center in Beijing and the new center in Brussels, the beginnings of his ambitious vision of making Sessions The Global University.

The founding of these centers and their international education and exchange mission was completely legitimate, despite clandestine funding. The problem was that a plan was also being coordinated by Fitz-Hugh's assistant Ursula Mueller, with his knowledge and support, to appoint several scholars and fellows in each center who were US spies—the plan being to have Sessions University international centers operate in part as black ops outposts.

That Fitz-Hugh was an amorous friend of the Secretary of State, Madam Secretary Greta Hauser, with whom he graduated from the Harvard Kennedy School, only made matters more complicated, not to mention more suspicious.

I had, through the unforgiveable behavior of having an affair with Ursula, unwittingly been caught in the middle of all this. Kravitz, in his jealousy at having Fitz-Hugh chosen as president over him and in his zeal to unmask him as a fraud, had with his Faculty Senate victory come too close to the truth and as a consequence had lost his life. I did not want to be next. I assumed Wentz now knew perhaps more than I about the whole mess, but I was not about to ask him, nor was he about ask me all the particulars about what had happened, especially the so-called Kravitz suicide.

"How'd you find this out?"

"Initially, Lusby."

Two months after Wentz's interim appointment, Frank Lusby had returned from rehab to again manage our multi-billion-dollar capital campaign, the Campaign for Progress. Within days he had the lowdown on everything going on at the university.

"In fact, I met with several of the Blaylock principals late yesterday, and we agreed that Ms. Bemis will coordinate their interview appointments. I figured this was easier and faster and gives us a little control, gets them out of our hair ASAP and lets us get on with our lives.

"When it's your turn just tell them what you think is…," he paused momentarily, choosing the next word carefully, "appropriate. Keep your response factual and to the minimum. Please refrain from repeating any gossip or theorizing about what happened to our esteemed former colleague. The fact is that we do not know. Bad enough that the family and we have to go through this. Let's not make it any worse or more complicated than it needs to be. Of course, from a communications standpoint we want a total blackout."

"Jesus, okay …. You have any thoughts on what they already know and where this inquiry will lead?"

Wentz shrugged. "They play things close to the vest, as you might expect. Hopefully their inquiry leads nowhere."

"Yeah. Lord, I hope so."

There was an awkward pause while we both considered the requirements of escaping unscathed from this new inquiry. It felt like there would be risk at every turn. And then my mind drifted to another concern that had been bothering me.

"So, let me ask you something, since we're on the subject. I keep wondering whether our government just went ahead and embedded spooks in our new international centers anyway. How would we know?"

Wentz sat back in his chair which creaked under the shifting of his mass. He thought for a long moment, then shrugged. "It's not as if the idea hasn't occurred to me, Thomas. We're vetting the hell out of our new appointments at Beijing and Brussels. But the truth is, we wouldn't know. We have to take their word for it."

"Their?"

"The secretary of state, Madam Secretary, and Bryan."

"But they're the ones, presumably, who hatched the whole scheme to begin with, stemming from their quote 'friendship'."

"Yeah, not real reassuring, is it?"

For the first time I began to appreciate the challenges Wentz faced in his new appointment. Where was last year's wiseass, funny man, jokester now that things weren't so damn funny?

"Okay," I said and decided that it was safe to return to his earlier comment, "If you don't mind, could we clarify your thought about me and Zoltan being 'untouchable'?"

His smile returned, amusement at his earlier joke. "It's true," he told me. "One of the conditions of my employment, as put to me by our board chair and vice-chair, is that I'm to leave you and Zoltan the fuck alone." Our board chair was Fritz Johnson, a top-flight Texas attorney who had made his fortune in the boom and bust of the Texas oil business. The vice-chair was Mark Berger, an erstwhile Jewish Bostonian multi-billionaire alumnus who had strangely become a close friend of our family and Zoltan over the last year.

"That would piss me off if I were you."

Wentz shrugged, turned more serious, "Well, I thought about letting it piss me off. Then I thought about the fact that you and Zoltan can keep your mouths shut."

"True. I share most everything with Zoltan, but that's as far as it goes."

"Cover-ups are hell. We don't need any more complications or looking over our shoulders at the past. Full speed ahead into the future. That you're loyal to the university and to me, that's all I require, Thomas. That and doing an excellent job, which I know you'll do." Wentz began chuckle. It had bit of boorishness and a touch of nasty to it. "So, no problem."

"Good," I said. My comment sounded to me as if I was relieved, but that is not at all how I felt. What I felt was a creeping, almost overwhelming, anxiety tinged outright with the fear that this was all going to catch up to us.

I was halfway to the door when Wentz said, "Oh, one other thing."

I turned. "Yeah?"

"You didn't hear this from me, but I got a call from Harold Ramis."

Ramis was the director of the medical center.

"He says your boy, Zoltan, is onto something big. Probably just dumb luck. Just thought you'd want to know as your buddy may not be allowed to say anything about it."

"Okay. Thanks. I appreciate your sharing that."

"No problem."

II

A Bit Like Infidelity

AT FIVE O'CLOCK, following my meeting with Wentz I walked over to the university club to resume in the new academic year Zoltan's and my practice of sharing an after-work drink.

As seemed to happen every summer, we had meant to see one another frequently but had not—Zoltan in his new lab managing his researchers, and me shuttling our son, Tommie, around to his special needs day camp and teaching our daughter, Sarah, how to drive. So, now, finally we would have a chance to catch up.

The walk through the campus was pleasant. Yes, it was hot, my suit coat slung over my shoulder as I took in the beauty of our university, the normalcy of undergraduates hanging out in the quadrangles with friends, footballs and frisbees being tossed around, their dogs joining the action.

I inhaled welcome fresh air full of humidity and heat, the scent of fresh-mown lawn. The sun warmed the tight muscles in my shoulders and back. A gentle breeze brought a hint of a cooler evening. Even the smell of the reflecting pond seemed pleasant as I passed by Stewart House, which had been the president's residence before the Fitz-Hughs, with grade school daughters, declined to live there. I wondered whether Wentz would. That seemed unlikely.

I thought back to my life as an associate professor of communications, before Fitz-Hugh saw the right stuff in me and, with Ursula, seduced me into joining his administration. It seemed a long time ago now, a year later. I missed my old office, the slow pace and routine of the academic calendar, my department head—the lovely, curmudgeonly, often befuddled Howard Calhoun.

The club's air conditioning was on full blast. The place was crowded. New academic year, new membership, everyone was thirsty on a day like this. As I entered the bar area, I was struck by the curious circumstance that all the tables were occupied except those surrounding our usual gathering spot. I felt a smile come to my face.

It was apparent that Zoltan's immense size; his mustachioed, unshaven, Hungarian countenance; the coils of grey-black hair springing from his head; his slovenly dress of rumpled jeans and a worn-out sport coat; and his normal axe-murderer expression had once again silently compelled the other patrons to seek comfort elsewhere.

An empty university-seal glass of remnant ice, undoubtedly from a first vodka, and a scattering of bar snacks from small glass bowls were on our table.

"Got a head start, huh?"

Zoltan looked at me with mock suspicion. "These days no one can count on big administration star being on time."

"Oh, fuck you. You're just a greedy pig," I told him as I signaled our waiter to bring me my customary beer.

"Oh, I greedy pig? Speaking of, how Jabba?"

"Jabba?" I heard myself say in a half-startled laugh. "The Hutt? Oh, you really like to live dangerously. I'd keep that comment to yourself, as funny as it might be. Your great friend is now our commander-in-chief." The fact was that Zoltan and Wentz shared a mutual antipathy.

Zoltan gave a dismissive shrug. He had no intention of taking my advice. *Why should he*? I thought, his existence being one large and long lifeforce testament to his ability to prosper while being utterly politically incorrect.

I sat in the opposite chair and Zoltan and I grinned at one another as my beer, his second vodka and new bowls of bar snacks arrived. Then I continued, "To tell you the truth, I honestly don't know how Wentz is. Certainly, I can see that he's under a lot of stress, but other than that, I'm really having trouble reading the guy."

"Yes. In my mind I see big lard ass walking on tightrope over swamp full of crocodiles. Vision make me smile a lot."

I laughed. "Yeah." Then I paused, reflecting. "How is it that our esteemed former president, Fitz-Hugh, could lie outright to you. You'd know it and like him anyway, be completely charmed. Yet with Wentz, even when he's telling you God's own truth, you feel like he's lying to you."

Zoltan took a large swig of his new vodka. "It one of life's great mysteries, yes?"

"Yeah, right … so, I learned some very interesting things at my meeting with Wentz today."

"Yes?"

"First off, that our chair of the board, Fritz Johnson, and the vice-chair, our friend Mark Berger, as a condition of Wentz's promotion told him that you and I were hands off."

"That what? Crazy. Unnecessary, yes?"

"That's what I thought. Might just piss Wentz off, but he seems okay with it. Just wants our loyalty. Or maybe Johnson and Berger know something we don't?"

Zoltan thought this over for a moment. "No. Those two just making sure nothing else go wrong. They hundred-million-dollar lawyer and multi-billionaire. They not get that way ignoring details." He took a swig of vodka and began trying with his massive fingers to extract pretzel loops from the small bowl between us. He looked up at me as pretzels scattered onto the table. "So, how family?" he asked with great interest.

"Everything's changing," I told him. "We cut a deal with Sarah to skip her last two years of high school and enter the Sessions Center for Gifted and Talented Youth. She started there over the summer in advanced languages. I not only needed to teach her to drive, but she needed a car to get to tutoring and mentoring sessions and summer school classes, so I gave her my beater of a commuter car and took over Janet's old BMW—you know, the one I fixed up for her last winter."

"I thought Sarah want to go away."

"Yeah, she fought us all last spring about having to stay at home but eventually relented with the deal being that if things go well here for the next year she can transfer elsewhere. Given Tommie's continual disruption and distraction, she's determined to get the hell out of our household. But otherwise she's terrific, same old charmer and good sport."

"Umph. So, how Tommie?"

"I wish I knew. He's entering some new phase. His whole obsessive fascination with fire engines, fire stations and fire itself seems to be fading. He's not spending nearly as much time down in the basement with his Tommie Town village and his collection of fire engines, but instead he's up in his room on his computer playing virtual games, doing other stuff, won't really let you into what he's up to. At least he hasn't set anything on fire lately."

Last year Tommie had inadvertently set one of his toy fire engines ablaze on the stove top burner on Mark Berger's remarkable cruising trimaran sailboat as well as set our basement on fire.

"How Janet?"

I felt myself shrug unpleasantly, as if I was trying to toss off the burden of our present uncertainty. "I don't know. We're not really connecting that well these days. I'm kind of worried about it. Don't know what to do. She's withdrawing a bit."

"Hmmm … that not good. Her patient … what his name?"

"Dr. Compton."

"Yes. His suicide and Kravitz, those last year upset her."

"Yeah, I think maybe people like her become psychologists thinking that they can understand and maybe even control the world better, and of course both those thoughts are fallacies. You're bound to get disappointed and disillusioned…. So, should I ask how your family's doing?"

Zoltan made a dismissive wave of his hand, "Ack, the same.

Ungrateful, spiteful—both Frida the shrew and Anna the college senior who think democracy suck."

"Maybe Anna will think different as time goes on."

"I don't know. As parent, I worry."

"All of us parents worry. That's the lead item in our job description."

"Yes, true. But you not seen, you not know what I know, what happened to Hungary in Second World War and after, what happen when not democracy. My Hungarian parents be turning over in their graves at what Anna think. So, I stay away from Anna. Just hand over money. It all bad. No good come of anything I do."

"Shit. Sorry man.... Are you and Kristina still an item?" Last year at the dedication of The Beijing Center he and I attended in Washington, he had met the associate dean of the School of Foreign Service, and they were now in a longstanding romance.

"Ah, yes. It get better and better. I go to her place in Washington and we take in opera middle of the week. She come here for weekend or I go there. It good. Amazing I meet a beautiful Belarusian who love opera as much as me. This week we see *The Magic Flute* at Kennedy Center."

"So, something else, as I was on my way out of Wentz's office, he told me something about you."

Zoltan raised his eyebrows. "Yes?"

"He said I didn't hear it from him, but that Ramis said you were onto something big."

Zoltan's eyes widened. He looked at me directly, very serious, worried, a complete sea change from his prior expression.

"I not tell you because Ramis tell me not to tell anybody. Then he go blab it." He threw a hand up, a gesture of frustration. "Plus, it hard to explain and we just start next phase. But the head of the cancer institute and Ramis, they get very excited."

"Try me."

Zoltan moved forward, speaking quickly in almost a whisper, his hands moving expressively, "Over summer we create treatment for mice we give cancer tumors. Treatment have combination of agents that stimulate T-cell immune reaction to cancer cells and oncolytic virus, virus modified to attack cancer cells."

"Very cool."

"But you know what amazing?"

"No."

"We expect maybe it would help reduce cancer in tumors but it did much more. Thomas, it work amazing. We inject it in tumor site and it not only work there but it stimulate T-cell response, and T-cells and virus work together to go kill cancer cell motherfuckers everywhere in mouse body. In most cases cancer gone. No one ever see rates of remission, lasting remission, like this. Most times nothing work on these cancers. Cancer outsmart everything, adapt. Then we give these mice this treatment and in a couple weeks their cancer gone. It kind of a miracle. Everybody amazed and freaking out at medical center, think maybe we on way to creating cancer vaccine. Telling me to keep my mouth shut. Medical center lawyers now involved in getting patents. So, we apply FDA for fast track for Phase 1 trial with humans and that just start. But I don't know what to do, who owns rights to what. Who to talk to. No one telling me anything. I the one who think of all this, but I think they want to rob me of discovery."

"You know, I told you a damn year ago you needed to have an attorney look over your agreement with the medical center."

"Yes ... I fuck up."

"Well, on one hand, that's fantastic news, but I can see why you're worri ..." In my peripheral vision I sensed someone approaching our table. I turned. It was Frank Lusby. Since returning from rehab he had been a ghost, the door to his office closed, perfunctory greetings and goodbyes at meetings, silent participation, he and Wentz huddled together in the president's office. He looked remarkably better, had gained weight, his complexion was almost that of a normal person save the pock marks on his forehead from a car accident long ago.

"Buy you guys a drink for old times' sake?" he asked, his voice now less smoky, his enunciation crisp and clear.

"Well, Goddamned, yes. Have a seat, Frank. It's really good to see you." I felt like Frank and I had been through the wars together, because in some respects we had. Lusby had been the keeper of the university's deepest and darkest secrets, the anonymous international wire transfers and the ever-growing tens of millions of clandestine money being deposited in and being taken out of the capital campaign's unrestricted account, Ursula's role as the coordinator of the US black ops plan for our international centers, Fitz-Hugh and our secretary of state's liaison relationship. He had figured all this out more or less on his own, and it was literally killing him, which is one reason why he began confiding in me. He had to unburden to someone, and he knew I wouldn't talk.

He still had not figured out the one secret only I knew and would never disclose, even to Zoltan, that Ursula was Fitz-Hugh's and Madam Secretary Greta Hauser's daughter, given up for adoption as an infant and then reunited with her birth father as his assistant and with her birth mother as an agent. No wonder her loyalty, no wonder her service to our government and its Department of State.

Lusby sat down and when our waiter came, he ordered another round for us and a Dr. Pepper for himself.

"How are you fellas?"

"That not important," Zoltan waved a hand dismissively, "How Frank Lusby?"

Lusby considered this question, moving his head in a philosophic gesture, "Well, this beats dying, I guess, which is where I was headed."

"Yeah," I agreed.

"Of course, I hadn't realized how much I'd anesthetized myself to everything. Now life is kind of strange. I have all these emotions, sensations, reactions, thoughts and realizations. Interesting trip. But I'm still here, still on assignment and I gotta tell you, it's nice not being in the middle of a disaster. Last year I felt like we were all manning deck chairs on the Titanic."

"Man, you aren't alone in that," I assured him.

"Titanic still afloat," Zoltan observed. "How family?"

Lusby shrugged, "Dysfunctional."

We laughed.

"We're working at it. I had a chance when I was home after rehab to bond with our stupid cocker spaniel, so when I arrive back from assignment now, she doesn't bark at me."

"Well, that's a big improvement."

"And our daughter Elizabeth's got a job that's forcing her to tone down the Goth stuff."

"Yea, Frank."

"But I actually came over here to tell you guys something."

We both looked at him. "Oh shit," I heard myself say. I knew where he was going with this.

Lusby shook his head slowly, a bit sorrowfully, and let out a long sigh, "Yeahhh, well … look, you need to know this. The Kravitz family has hired a private detective agency, the Blaylock Agency, reputedly the best one around."

"FUCK!" Zoltan exclaimed emphatically, causing a number of patrons at other tables to look our way. Some looked very concerned, others frightened, still others irritated.

"Cool it, man," I told Zoltan. "Yeah, I'm sorry. I just found out from Wentz myself and hadn't had a chance to tell you." I turned back to Lusby, "This is never going to go away, is it?"

"Nope," Lusby said seriously, bringing his hands together, "A bit like infidelity."

"Oh Jesus, thanks."

"Sorry," Lusby said, and he meant it.

I motioned to him with my hand, "That's okay. Undoubtedly, you're right."

"Well, just be ready, 'cause I know they're going to be interviewing everybody. They're getting set to interview Wentz, and then Ms. Bemis will be setting up interviews with relevant staff."

"Yeah—that's what Wentz told me."

"How you know this?" Zoltan asked Lusby.

"'Cause they just interviewed me earlier today."

"You could have turned them down," I commented.

"I've got nothing to hide, and I know nothing."

"Very convincing."

"I can be when I try."

"You think they believed you?"

"Ummm, hard to say. I doubt it. I also think they've interviewed that babe of a reporter who likes you so much."

"Emily Sayzak. Ohh geez, I hope she doesn't start stalking me again. And she doesn't like me. She likes what she thinks I might know."

"You tell her she can stalk me."

We laughed a bit nervously. None of this was funny.

"Why would the family do that?"

"Anger, frustration. They fired the attorney Fitz-Hugh and the university hired for them. Saw through him being a holding action and not really acting in their interests, although that's what they were told he'd be doing. Then they explored a civil suit, but it quickly became clear there's not enough to go on. Who the hell would they sue? No one knows what happened in the park that night. So, in their frustration I guess this is a next step."

"God damn," I heard myself utter. "I mean, do you guys ever think about the fact that Ursula was undoubtedly a US agent and somehow was involved in killing Kravitz, a US citizen, to keep some acronym agency's covert plan secret? Now what would happen if Blaylock figured that out? What happens then?"

Zoltan shrugged. "You typical naïve American. In Russia, Europe, Asia this kind of thing happen all the time. Here too. Whatever happen, US just want to figure out a way to keep it all contained. Don't necessarily have to kill everyone. Too messy. Too suspicious. They have shown us, though, what they willing to do. Now hope to just keep us scared. If Blaylock find things out, they become part of cover-up one way or another. Kravitz family still in the dark."

"God damn, you think so?"

Zoltan shrugged. "Logical. Yes?"

Lusby nodded. "Yeah, that sounds right. We just have to live the cover-up every day for however long it takes for it to go away."

"Jesus."

We all paused, ruminating.

Finally, Lusby said, "Yeah, so could I interest you guys in attending the same reception at Stewart House for deans and department heads that you attended last year? It'll be toward the end of the month."

"That's where all this trouble started. Last year you wanted to bring Zoltan and me into the orbit of the president and that resulted in my meeting Ursula. The only good thing that happened is that we also met Mark Berger. Why invite us this year?"

"You mean, what's the catch? There really isn't one, except that it would probably help our new president to be surrounded by a supportive senior administrative officer and member of the president's executive committee, that being you, and having a future Nobel Prize-winning research scientist present certainly wouldn't hurt."

"A WHAT?" Zoltan asked loudly.

"Oh, I heard that you're onto something big."

"SHIT!"

The patrons at other tables now uniformly turned and stared at us, fear and anger on their faces.

"You really want to get our asses kicked out of here, don't you?"

"I just beginning trial and they tell not to tell anyone. I tell no one what going on and yet whole world know. This suck."

"Yeah," Lusby commented. "Get used to it. By the way, your buddy, Mark Berger, will be there again. Now that he's vice-chair of the board, it's even more important that he attend."

"Well, there's one good reason to be there. That damned guy saved all our collective asses last year, and he and our board chair, Fritz Johnson, did it brilliantly behind the scenes and no one has a clue that it was them."

The fact was that Johnson negotiated Fitz-Hugh's departure

and new position with the Department of State while Berger brought in a team of his auditors to clean up the books and wire the clandestine money back to its original sources, replacing it with his own anonymous gift of over $25 million. For all the board of trustees and the rest of the university and world knew, Fitz-Hugh had been chosen for a remarkably important government position which necessitated Wentz being appointed as interim.

Zoltan took a final swig of his vodka and set it down on the table hard. He looked at me. "Okay, we go again to this reception and fuck with them, just like last year."

We left the club together and went our separate ways. Lusby undoubtedly to AA. Zoltan, who was not a member of the club, shoved some bills into my hand as we walked out the door. Given that he and Frida had never managed to get divorced, he was paranoid about her finding out anything about his assets, most of which he kept in cash in his bottom bureau drawer. So, he made all his life transactions with hard currency, leaving no paper trail. Just another idiosyncrasy of my crazy friend. He was headed back to his lab to survey the day's results. I strolled to the university's lower parking lot, enjoying as pleasant a walk leaving as I had arriving, when the all too familiar sound of certain footsteps came from behind me. I felt my eyes close and shook my head. God damn it, Emily Sayzak.

I turned. She was dressed in a dark blue skirt that set off her small waist and nice hips, white blouse. She carried the usual reporter's shoulder bag. As she closed the distance between us, I took in her skinny legs; her thick blond hair; her small, long, pleasant face that was a bit offset, red lipstick on her coquettish mouth.

"Hi, Dr. Simpson," she said, waving.

I just looked at her. "Well, now my day's complete."

"You miss me?"

"Not at all."

She thought about my comment, half-grinned. "Actually, I kinda missed you. I must like stonewalling and rejection."

"I wouldn't want to disappoint you."

"So, do you mind if I walk with you for a minute or two?"

"Of course, I mind, but you're going to anyway."

"You're getting to know me, aren't you?"

"Ahhhh, Jesus …"

"I'd like to get to know you a lot better."

"Oh yeah. That's what you always say."

"So, what do you think of this inquiry by the Blaylock Agency?"

We began walking toward the lower parking lot.

"How the hell do you know about that?"

"They interviewed me yesterday," she confirmed.

"Oh." I shrugged. "From the family's point-of-view it's understandable. I can't say I'm thrilled that this tragic event keeps taking on a life of its own."

"That's because there's something that happened out there in the park that's not being disclosed, don't you think?"

"I don't think anymore. Just take things one day at a time."

"Yeah … I can see why you might want to do that."

"What did you tell Blaylock?" I asked her.

"That I was being stonewalled at every turn."

"Hmmm …. Okay, that's at least honest I guess."

We had reached my car.

"That's a nice little convertible."

"Thanks."

"You should take me for a ride sometime."

I knew she wasn't just talking about the car, but playing stupid has always been one of my strong suits.

"Oh, right. Why don't we put the top down and drive all over the Sessions campus, taking care to pass the administration building a couple times." A warning light went off in my brain somewhere that told me to never tell her that Bryan Fitz-Hugh had threatened to fire me if he ever saw me in her presence again. First of all, she would think that was really terrific; second, she'd ask why.

"That would be fun."

"Right. Look, Emily ..."

"Oh my God, you called me by my first name."

"Ms. Sayzak. Can't you get on with your life? Give this a rest?"

"No."

"I don't even know why I ask."

"Because if we could ever get to the bottom of all this, you and I could actually ... well..."

"I'm going home to my wife and children. It was not good to see you."

"Thanks, Thomas. It was not good to see you either."

"*Damn.*" Sitting in the driver's seat, I slammed the door shut, turned the ignition key, quick shifted into first as the engine started and drove off.

III

Blaylock

EARLY MORNING IN my office Wednesday the following week, I was staring out the window again, trying unsuccessfully to focus on small, subtle changes of color in the woods, sipping bitter, chlorinated, university-issue coffee. I was escaping from the demands of press releases, publication deadlines, media events, broadcasts, and interdepartmental squabbles and trying to come to terms with my upcoming appointment with a detective from the Blaylock Agency. Ms. Bemis had informed me about the appointment on Monday, no other information forthcoming. I knew better than to ask.

Damn. They had gotten to Wentz. I was sure he had given them the big Buddha act. Sitting there in his double-wide chair, hands folded across his chest, feigning polite ignorance to all the questions, deflecting attention to others (like me) who might have better insights, throwing me the hell under the bus.

At 9:30 a.m. exactly, the detective from the Blaylock Agency walked in. I turned, stood, mumbled a neutral hello.

"Dr. Simpson?" she asked.

"Thomas," I corrected, smiling an empty smile, then felt compelled to tell her. "In the university's administration a PhD doesn't count for much."

She ignored my comment. "Alicia McDonald. Thanks for seeing me. This shouldn't take too long."

She was tall, blue eyed, long legged, angular—her lustrous, champagne-colored hair parted in the middle, flowing over her shoulders. I reflected that in her youth it must have been white blond. She wore a well-tailored, black pants suit; white blouse; and sky-blue scarf. Very businesslike. *The ice maiden cometh,* I thought, and suppressed a small, nervous smile. I had expected some shadowy slimeball guy in a trench coat. Now I didn't know what to expect.

I motioned her to the chair in front of my desk. Sitting, she placed her black leather business satchel beside it as she pulled out a small digital recorder. She pressed the on-button and placed the recorder on the edge of my desk closest to her.

"I hope you don't mind my using this. We interview so many people and sometimes it all begins to run together, plus I can't write nearly as fast as some people can talk."

"Not a problem," I told her. *Hell,* I thought, *it might as well be a Goddamn handgun that she's going to ask me to shoot myself with.* I found myself wishing there was a ball-peen hammer in one of my desk drawers, imagining what satisfaction I'd have smashing the recorder to smithereens.

She swept her hair back over her shoulders, crossed her legs, rested her arms and looked at me. She was one cool woman, beyond confident. Name a perfume after her and it would be Breath of Arrogance or perhaps Scent of Suspicion.

"For the record, could I ask you to state the date, time, your name, occupation and relationship to former provost Samuel Kravitz and to his family?

"Sure." I gave her the date, looked at my watch. "9:34 a.m., Thomas Simpson, director of university and campaign communications. Before his passing, Provost Kravitz and I were members of the president's executive committee under former president Bryan Q. Fitz-Hugh. We have no personal relationship with the family except that my daughter Sarah was a sitter for their grandchildren last year."

"Thank you," she said officially, then paused as if some distracting and nagging thought had just crossed her mind. "I don't usually begin these interviews this way but let me ask you something. How do you like working here?"

"You mean here at the university?" I asked, puzzled.

"No, in this building."

"Oh," I laughed lightly. "I hate it."

"For starters, it's an architectural nightmare."

"Yeah," I agreed, "A bastardized Georgian travesty."

She laughed. A delightful, pealing, appreciative laugh. I found myself wanting to hear it again.

Okay, I thought, *she wants to put me at ease.* Internally, my guard went up even more, my stomach turning with anxiety, but at least this banter might make getting to the inquisition a little easier.

"Not only is it ugly, but its interior smells … like a mix between new carpeting and a catalytic converter or something. I mean, that's a nice view," she motioned with her head at the window behind me, "but being sealed in like this I would feel like I was a fish in an aquarium, looking out at the world, swimming in indoor air pollution."

"Umm-hmph," I replied, thinking to myself, *Damn, how many times have I thought and felt the same way?* Her resonance with my personal reflections and that she was direct and articulate unsettled me further.

She paused, looked directly at me, not unfriendly. "As I'm sure you know, we've been hired by the Kravitz family to investigate his death last year, his so-called suicide…" She paused again. "So, Thomas, what do you think happened?"

My mind was scrambling, "I have no idea. It would seem to be a suicide, that would seem to be the conclusion of the police."

"Hmm …," she mused. "Is it possible he might have been murdered?"

I forced myself to keep my mouth shut. I could feel myself clenching my jaw.

The silence between us was deafening.

"I'm sorry," she said finally, airily with a wave of a hand, "I'm getting ahead of myself. The Kravitz family likes you and your family a great deal. You've made a very nice impression on them, particularly Sarah."

I didn't like it at all that Alicia McDonald would bring my daughter into the conversation. At the same time, I knew she was doing it intentionally to underscore the stakes involved.

"Um-hmm," I replied.

"So, they thought perhaps you might be a helpful person to interview regarding his death."

I looked at her as blankly as I could, noticing distractedly her long-fingered hands, lack of any rings, manicured nails, a small mole on her neck.

She watched me and stifled a small smile. Her foot began a twirling motion that reminded me of the tail of a cat right before it pounces on its prey.

"The first question that keeps coming up with the family is what would he be doing sitting in his car in the park on a twenty-two-degree evening in the middle of winter?"

The foyer in Ursula's apartment that night flashed into my consciousness. Dressed in a black thermal outfit, she was getting ready to go for a jog in twenty-two-degree weather when I had never known her to jog before. A New Year's resolution, she said, shocking me by pulling a small Glock from the drawer of the table near the door, placing it in a custom-fitting holster in the small of her back, telling me that the Glock was for her protection, that she was an expert marksman, that shooting was her sport at MIT. Her nonchalant *au revoir* at the elevator door. Later in the administration building while we worked to help Fitz-Hugh deal with the crisis of Kravitz's suicide, I had acted as if I had stumbled and felt the Glock still firmly in place under Ursula's jogging outfit. The police then reported that Kravitz had killed himself with a pistol with the serial number filed off. Just another of the facts about his suicide that did not add up. What the hell then was Ursula doing out there?

"Why was he in the park?" I mused. "I've asked myself that same question a lot. Damned if I know. Maybe he figured that was the most private place he could go to kill himself."

"It just simply doesn't fit," she rebutted. "He was a man of consummate ego and self-absorption, not one likely to take his own life. All our background checks and interviews reveal that he was also a dedicated family man. So, no secret assignation for sexual reasons likely, especially given the weather. Unlikely that he went there for the winter scenery. Doesn't fit his personality. This is a man who adhered to a rarely interrupted daily routine. Normally at this time of day he would have been home working in his library on his collection of rare books. No, Thomas, the most likely reason was to meet someone who had information he wanted."

"Isn't that a bit speculative? I mean, look, Kravitz secured a significant victory with the Faculty Senate vote for an independent audit. But almost immediately he suffered a major humiliation at the board of trustees meeting where they listened to his concerns but then simply went on to the next order of business, ignored him to his face. For all his erudition he was a driven man, beyond jealous that Fitz-Hugh was chosen over him, plus he felt that Fitz-Hugh was aiming to eviscerate the humanities."

"You knew the provost. As I've noted, he was not a man to fall into despair."

I thought about what she said. She was right. I reminded myself again to open my mouth as little as possible.

"It's rare that we have an open-ended client assignment. Our job is to investigate until we come up with the most likely and plausible truth. We're not the police, none of what we discover will likely be adjudicated in a court of law, unless of course a crime has been committed. We simply want the truth for the family's sake."

Involuntarily, I rolled my eyes. We both knew that the family could do whatever they wanted with whatever information Blaylock came up with. They might very well take it public, take it to the police or to higher authorities without a single thought about consequences.

If the assumption I had discussed with Zoltan and Lusby the previous week was correct, that Ursula was part of a clandestine operation that was responsible for Kravitz's demise, then how far would US operatives go to continue the cover-up of their failed covert plan to place spies in Sessions's international centers, a scheme that if the dots were connected could directly implicate the secretary of state and our former president? They had already murdered the provost. I had not been comforted by Zoltan's observation that they would just try to keep us scared and somehow make Blaylock part of the cover-up. It seemed all too easy an explanation, given Kravitz's death. So, where exactly would they stop now? A sickening dread began to spread through me. They had certainly accomplished their objective with me.

"Our job is to pursue likely scenarios, Thomas. We think that someone offered Kravitz information, perhaps on the university's finances, and lured him to the park for a handoff."

I just looked at her. What was driving such speculative thinking and the confidence she seemed to have in it? Perhaps it was just bravado or bluffing. Perhaps they would never reach any certain conclusions.

"Wow," I said with a touch of disbelief, shaking my head. But I hated that she could very well be right. Ursula could have offered him inside information. That's all it would have taken to get him there.

"So, let me ask you this," Alicia continued, "what was Ursula Mueller doing, where was she that evening, just before Kravitz died?"

I felt myself jump at the mention of Ursula's name. "How would I know?" I blurted. *Uh-oh*, I thought, my stomach clutching with anxiety.

"You'd know because you were there in her apartment about an hour before Kravitz's death. You were there for about fifteen minutes, and then she left on foot out the front entrance before you left out the back-alley entrance, got in your car and drove off."

I thought, *Damn, these guys are pros.* Obviously, they had reviewed Ursula's apartment building's security tapes. I thought fast. The truth, or as close as you can get to it, is always the best defense.

"We had all just returned from the board of trustees meeting. I had left early, directly after my presentation. I hadn't been able to catch up with her during the day, so we arranged for me to stop by so she could fill me in on the rest of the meeting. I wanted to get her impressions as well as her thoughts."

"That's it?"

"That's it. Fifteen minutes."

"Where did she say she was going?"

"For a jog."

"In twenty-two degrees?"

"Yeah, New Year's resolution."

Alicia laughed. "That's some powerful resolution."

"Yeah," I agreed, shaking my head.

"What did you think she was really up to?"

"I hadn't a clue. Ursula is very much her own person with her own agendas. Not one to ever let you in. Frankly, given the weather, I was more worried about getting home on time and not ending up in a ditch somewhere."

"Hmm …. Tell me about your relationship."

"We were colleagues." I thought, *You know I'm lying, but it's none of your damn business.*

"I see. You wouldn't be protecting her?"

It was my turn to laugh. "Ursula can take care of herself. She does not need any help from me."

"Do you think she might have been involved in Kravitz's death?"

"I don't know."

"Did Kravitz have any enemies?"

"Not really. I mean he and Fitz-Hugh's relationship was certainly adversarial. Kravitz felt Fitz-Hugh was underfunding the humanities and questioned where the money for expansion into international centers was coming from."

"Where was it coming from?"

"How would I know? You know, we do have a $4.5 billion campaign underway. There's a $150 million pledge that's been made for the Beijing Center. I'm sure you're going to interview folks in the comptroller's office, if you haven't already. Ask them. But, I mean, these kinds of internal frictions go on all the time." I thought to myself, *You lying fuck.*

"Could Ursula have been involved with Kravitz?"

I laughed again. "Hell, no."

"Why?"

"Figure it out. He hated Fitz-Hugh, her boss."

"She was close to Fitz-Hugh?"

"Very devoted."

"Could she have been involved with him?"

"You're really grasping at straws, aren't you?"

A look of frustration crossed her features. "Perhaps I am," she said, "but one never knows until all the information is at hand. I appreciate your time."

A wave of relief passed over me, along with the slightest perverse and knuckleheaded regret that our interview had not been more productive for her.

She turned off the tape recorder, put it in her satchel, rose, took a step towards my desk and reached over it to shake hands. Her hand was smooth and firm, her fingers strong and supple. "Thomas, it was a pleasure meeting you." Beautiful eyes.

"Likewise."

She turned, picked up her satchel, put her arm through the shoulder strap and whisked out of my office.

Watching her go, I felt the overwhelming need for a strong drink or drinks, wishing that Lusby still had a bottle of George Dickel Private Reserve in his bottom desk drawer. I sat down and played back the interview in my mind, hearing myself lying or covering up at every turn, on one hand feeling miserable but also reassuring myself that I had let nothing slip that could blossom or boomerang into consequences for my family, my colleagues and our university. The whole situation, my role in it and everything related to it felt wrong. Maybe, I thought, I should burn in hell yet I was also peeved at the invasive nature of the whole inquiry. Worse, beyond all this I was troubled by something else. Alicia McDonald.

IV

Smart

THAT EVENING, AS I drove up the s-curved, tree-lined hill bordering our neighborhood, I pondered again why everything that had seemed so right originally about our moving there had turned out to be so wrong. How was it that our house was not our home, that our neighbors were not our friends, that our neighborhood had no sense of community and was filled with a bunch of second-rung wannabes more interested in social and career advancement than in any genuine relationship, insincerity being the only means of exchange?

It had all seemed so good—right location, what we thought were the right schools, near the river and a park, neighborhood Olympic pool, wide streets, attractive houses, even cut-throughs from street to street to allow walking without being in roadways.

Now it all seemed to Janet and me to be a cheap masquerade—from the quality of construction, which was too much all about appearance with shortcuts in material and workmanship taken behind the facades, to the community activities and gatherings that were empty of any real commitment, warmth or good will.

We felt a bit foolish, as if we had been tricked, and now we were stuck, trapped, because after much searching we had found the rare school that actually was right for Tommie, the alternative being to send him away. Trapped, because even though in my new position I was making three times what I had as a professor, my existence as an administrator, my "untouchable" branding notwithstanding, felt totally insecure. Sessions University might well be built of beautiful brick and stone on solid ground—but, given its recent history and an ongoing cover-up, it was a house of cards.

I parked the car in the garage. Sparky, our rescue Dalmatian, was yapping a greeting before I even came through the door, and she circled me excitedly as I walked through the laundry room into the family room. I patted her head and looked around. Her adoption a year before in reaction to Tommie's endless yammering about needing a "fire engine dog" had actually turned out well, thankfully, as she served as a welcome buffer and distraction to all our necessary efforts to deal daily with the machinations of our younger child.

The family room was empty. Last year Sarah would've been there watching her cool kids' show. The house seemed deserted and strange without her presence.

Janet walked in from the kitchen with two glasses of white wine, handed me one. I surveyed her in a glance. Still my brown-eyed, honey-blond-haired wife—but preoccupied and distracted, worry lines on her forehead and around her eyes. I felt my heart sink a little.

"Where's Sarah?"

"She called. Staying at the library to study. I ordered Thai."

"Okay. I know what staying at the library meant for you and me."

"She is a teenager."

I sighed, "Yeah, she's awful young to be hanging out over there."

"She's awfully mature for being so young."

"True. I guess we have to trust her, at least until she screws up."

"Yes."

"Where's Tommie?"

"In his room. On his computer, I'm sure."

"That figures. So how was your day?"

Janet considered the question. "Grotesquely normal."

"Hmm ...."

"How was yours?"

"Complicated, as usual. Not worth talking about."

There was a descending pounding on the carpeted front hallway stairs to our bedrooms. Over the summer Tommie's feet had grown, so now they were totally out of proportion to the rest of him and responsible for the noise.

He turned the corner, bursting into the room, hell-bent on his way to the basement and Tommie Town. I noticed Sparky quickly skirted behind Janet, having been tortured as Sparky the Fire Dog too many times by Tommie, who despite all our protests, threats and punishments had kept tying a toy fire hat around her head and a child's Superman cape to her collar.

"Whoa, cowboy!" I called to him. "Where are you going in such a hurry?"

He stopped in his tracks, aware of us for the first time, turned, ran up to me with his uncoordinated gait, his arms pinched into his body, hands randomly waving about and gave me his usual oddly over-affectionate hug, grasping me around my waist, looking up at me with his beautiful china-blue eyes, his eyelids with their long lashes blinking spasmodically, his fine featured face ticking slightly, his behavior that of a child half his age. "Dad, I'm going to Tommie Town."

"Yeah, what's the hurry?"

"I don' know."

"You going to play down there? You haven't done that in a while."

Shrug, "I don' know."

"Okay," I said, not knowing how else to react.

"Thanks!" Tommie said, turning and shouting over his shoulder as he lurched into a run toward the basement door and then pounded down the stairs.

I looked at Janet and shook my head. "Weird."

"Yeah …."

"Well, let me go see what the hell he's doing down there."

I headed down to the basement, taking a couple of well-appreciated sips of wine while Janet went into the kitchen to set the table for dinner.

Tommie Town was built on plywood laid on sawhorses and took up about a third of our basement. It was an extended village with two fire stations, a railroad with a model train, some painted plaster on screening hills, and lots of little trees and shrubbery, model buildings, a general store, shops and houses, a warehouse, populated by lovely plastic townspeople—a father/son project that had been completed primarily by me while Tommie pantomimed tasks without really accomplishing anything. But the town had at least turned out well, with a turn-of-the-century, country look to it.

Tommie kept his collection of fire engines under the sawhorses and rotated them in and out of the two firehouses depending on whatever imaginary scenario he had for a particular day. Fires were simulated by a flashlight with orange clear plastic over the lens, which worked effectively, at least in Tommie's imaginary world. That's not to say that we didn't have fire extinguishers tucked away all over the house and that anything that could actually set a fire, including the antique magnifying glass that he had used to set a real fire in Tommie Town the previous spring, was under lock and key.

But Tommie wasn't playing with his fire engines. Instead, he was standing in front of Tommie Town, looking at it thoughtfully, like some intergalactic god might. I stood for a moment watching him, thinking that our own neighborhood was probably about as fake as Tommie Town and that, with the way things seemed to work in life, perhaps God also had Asperger's syndrome. That would explain a lot.

I walked up and stood beside him. He barely noticed.

"What are you up to, man?" I asked.

"Oh, I'm playing this computer game where you build towns and cities, and it made me start thinking about how Tommie Town might work if it was, you know, a real town."

"Oh, interesting .... So, you're through with playing with your fire engines?"

"Dad, that was when I was a lit-tul *kid*!"

"Oh, and what are you now?"

"I'm in middle school now. That's, like, totally different."

"Oh, okay. You're three weeks into middle school. So, now you're getting into technology?"

"Yeah, it's really interesting. I'm learning *so* much."

"Great, so have you learned that you've got more homework now?"

"Yeah …, Dad?"

"Yeah."

"You sure know how to kill a mood."

"Oh, thanks."

"I'm going upstairs. I paused my game."

"Okay. Dinner will be here shortly, I guess. Thai."

"Thai! Okay!"

He half ran in his awkward way and thumped up the stairs.

I went upstairs, found the morning paper on the kitchen table and joined Janet in the family room where she was reading her book club novel. Truth was, I just looked at the paper without reading, replaying again my meeting with Alicia McDonald.

Soon enough, our delivery dinner arrived about the same time as Sarah, who breezed in from parking her car in the drive as Tommie, alerted by the doorbell, came pounding down the stairs.

"*Bonsoir, papa,*" she greeted me on my way to the kitchen.

"Hey, Sarah," I greeted her over my shoulder, "How was your day?"

"Tutoring, mentoring—pretty much the same. The classes, pretty intense. You don't get too many stupid jerkoffs in upper level languages, which is great. French is getting a bit *passé*. I'm looking into Asian languages to see what I might want to try next. We're all going to get taken over by the Chinese anyway."

"Really," I said as we sat down at the kitchen table, "Somehow I'd missed that headline."

"Oh, from the inside out. They'll infiltrate us."

"Hmmm."

We sat at the kitchen table and passed containers around.

"Honey," Janet said to Sarah, having overheard our conversation, "You could always continue with European languages. There'd likely be lots of job opportunities for you after college."

"Yeah," I added. "Multinational companies. They all have European divisions. Could be a lot of fun."

Sarah waved a hand dismissively, "I'll think about it."

Tommie was busy stacking large amounts of food on his plate. I imagined his feet might somehow grow another inch overnight.

"Hey Dad," Tommie said through a mouthful of Pad Thai. "When's Zoltan coming over? We haven't seen him forever."

"We've talked about that recently. We'll figure it out."

"Can he bring Kristina," Sarah asked. "I really like her."

"We'll talk about that too."

"So, Tommie, how was your day?" Janet asked.

Shrug. "Okay." He turned to me.

"Dad, I need a much more powerful computer. I need…" and he rattled off a stream of tech jargon about RAM, gigahertz, gigabytes and processors that I had not a clue about.

Janet and I looked at each other with the simultaneous realization that his computer was becoming the new Tommie Town.

"What are you talking about?" I asked him. "How do you know all this?"

"Dad, when it comes to this stuff, I'm smart."

I'd never heard anyone use the word "smart" in connection with my son before, let alone himself. Descriptions of Tommie in his new school were couched in the politically correct jargon that he was a "unique" and "differenced" learner.

In public school where he had been bullied, he had been "obsessive," "troubled," "in his own world." Teachers in both settings would go to great lengths to skirt the elephant-in-the-room word, the word "stupid," by using terms like "challenged." When we came to the mutual conclusion with the public school that Tommie could not continue there, they of course said he had "special needs."

Then there was the word that came from the other kids, the

worst word in the world, "retard," which never failed to drive Tommie into a paroxysm of anger.

Now, in the school we had found for him last year, Schossler Academy, they seemed to be onto something and to understand the challenges to learning and behavior that Tommie presented. Not that his grades were any better. Last year he had barely passed any subject because he never paid attention to anything outside of his own obsessive fixation on fire trucks and all that related to them, a subject about which he had encyclopedic knowledge.

"Okay," I replied and looked at Janet who gave me a direct look and a puzzled shrug.

"Hey," Sarah said, "Did you know they're saying that Dr. Kravitz was murdered last year? I thought he committed suicide."

"He did," I said, looking at Janet who now stared down at her plate. This was not a good subject.

Sarah seemed oblivious. "How do you know?"

"Um ...." I recalled the day I took Sarah over to the Kravitz house for her first job keeping watch over their grandchildren. Joan Kravitz the quintessential PhD grandmother—cultured and a bit disorganized, their mansion, their attractive pianist daughter Natalie and her two children, their standard poodle Marcel (a play on Proust's first name). Then the memorial service at the university's chapel, Samuel Kravitz II's angry questioning of his father's suicide, wanting anyone there to tell him what really happened that night, the stunned silence that had followed. Tragically awkward.

"Well, I only know what I read in the papers, honey. There is a lot of uncertainty, which is why I'm sure there are rumors out there. But to this point no one's come up with anything, including the police, so ..."

"It just seems weird. What would he be doing in the park on a night like that? They're such a nice family. It's so sad."

"Yeah ...."

I looked at Janet and saw a small tear begin to trickle down her face. She rose quickly, took her plate to the sink, turning and wiping at her eye with her free hand. I looked back at the Sarah and Tommie. They had not a clue. How could they be so damn perceptive about so much and yet miss what was going on with their mother? Their mother was someone in another realm for them, a symbol of sympathy, empathy, and caring—but in their own little insular, self-absorbed teenage and middle school world they missed seeing her as a real person.

I took another sip of wine. Is this what my life had come to, living a lie and hating every minute of it? Seeing everything but not knowing what to do about it or how make things better? I'd talk to Janet later. She would rebuff me, not let me in, admit to being troubled but provide no answers and not many clues.

I watched as Janet came back to the table, grabbed her glass of wine and headed out to the family room and her book. Would she even be reading or would she just be staring at the printed page like I had earlier?

I stood, "Okay, kids, let's clear the table and put the dishes in the dishwasher. Tommie, it's time for homework. No more games."

When they had gone upstairs, I walked out to the family room, sat down on the couch, turned and faced Janet. "Hey …"

She turned, put her book down, looked at me.

"Are you okay?"

She stared down at the table for a moment then looked up at me and said, "No, not really."

"What's wrong?"

She thought about my question. "Everything and nothing. My daughter's practically grown up and doesn't need me anymore. Our son's too obsessive to provide any meaningful interaction. My clients—it's difficult to tell whether they actually make any progress. Then there's Dr. Compton's suicide last year. I tried so hard to help him and he defied me at every turn. Then the provost. I feel so damn helpless. You?" she shrugged. "I'm just feeling lost."

"Well, I'm here for you."

"No, you're *not*," she said forcefully with shades of bitterness. "You haven't been here for me ever since you moved over to the administration building for your new position. You walk around this house in total preoccupation and distraction most of the time. It's like you're having an affair with your damn job."

I felt myself literally gulp and tried my best for a quick recovery. "Janet, I try. You don't seem to notice. You're getting harder and harder to please. You're numb to everything. We all love you."

Janet looked at me blankly. Sparky, sensing something was wrong, came up to her, took small licks on her fingers and looked at her face.

Tears rolled down her cheeks.

"Maybe you need some help we can't provide?" I asked, knowing the moment I said it that such a question to one's psychologist wife would go in one ear and out the other. How do you convincingly tell a mental health professional that they need a professional's help?

Janet rose, patted Sparky on the head and walked out of the room toward the stairs.

I looked at Sparky. "Shit …."

V

Guardian Angel

When the elevator doors opened in the atrium of the administration building I spotted Zoltan pacing back and forth outside the entrance, the security guard at the door inside eying him with worried hostility, hand on his nightstick.

We walked toward Stewart House and the reception for deans and department heads. The afternoon was sunny, crisp and cool. From the trees surrounding the walkways yellow, orange and dark-red leaves drifted to the ground. The distant sound of leaf blowers interrupted the tranquility.

"I really wish we hadn't agreed to do this," I told him as we passed by the entrance of the Farr Botanical Garden, a multi-colored parade of chrysanthemums lining each side of its curved wrought iron entrance.

"Yes, this last year where you first meet Ursula."

"Don't remind me."

"And Kravitz."

"Jee-sus, you have gift for saying the wrong thing, don't you?"

I thought of the conversation I had joined at this same event last year of Kravitz and my department chair Howard Calhoun—Kravitz interspersing his comments with foreign phrases, a well-known habit, irritating to those of us who were not multi-lingual, as they discussed possible curriculum choices for the next semester.

His whole persona and our numerous interactions came

flooding back: his large elegant head atop his small frame, his perfect enunciation in many languages, his jealous contempt for Fitz-Hugh because Fitz-Hugh had been chosen president over him, his vigorous—even viperish—defense of the humanities in the face of Fitz-Hugh's vision of Sessions becoming The Global University, his wife Joan's inherited wealth, their lovely mansion in Hampton Park and his remarkable library in a separate wing housing his collection of over seventy thousand rare books. When I had arrived with Sarah for her job sitting the grandchildren, he had taken me for a tour, lectured me on the dangers of working for Fitz-Hugh, calling him a "charlatan, carpetbagger, carnival barker of a president."

I sighed a long sigh.

"Berger?"

"Yeah. Well, that worked out."

"You hear from him?"

"Yeah, a couple of calls over the summer just to say hello and find out how the family's doing. It's still amazing that a guy like him would become our friend."

Zoltan shrugged, "Like he say, he like real folks, like us."

We climbed the marble stairs and Zoltan pushed through the massive mahogany door to the large, high-ceiling foyer with its black and white tiled floor and the same scene as last year—except on closer inspection, obviously, everything had changed.

Deans and department heads from different university and medical center divisions were cloistered in small groups, the sound of garbled conversation bouncing around the open room.

Off to the left, Lusby was steering Wentz from one group to another. I was struck by the stark contrast to the year before when Ursula, sleek and attractive, with her professional manner was seamlessly gliding Fitz-Hugh around. Then groups lit up as he brought to them the prestige of his position, his surprisingly adept knowledge of their particular discipline and their current challenges and opportunities, plus his ability to converse intelligently on almost any subject.

Now, with Lusby leading Wentz it was all a bit standoffish. The fact was that the faculty saw Lusby as "the henchman," even during Fitz-Hugh's tenure, and they still saw Wentz as a common operator. I watched Wentz trying hard to interact but receive emptiness in return. I sure as hell was not joining them, no matter how much Lusby wanted me to.

Except, who was this woman beside Wentz? She was petite, well-dressed, conservatively, in a dove-grey straight skirt and demur cream silk blouse, simple gold jewelry, light-brown styled hair. There was an appealing enthusiasm about her.

I watched as she interjected herself into the conversation. As she spoke, deans and department heads male and female looked down on her, but then, as she went on something remarkable happened. They began to smile. Initially the smiles were cynical, condescending, even contemptuous. They so wanted to dislike this woman. But then, within a few sentences their smiles changed, became more genuine, brightened as they discovered they liked her. You could see Wentz and Lusby also begin to smile, to relax a little as a real conversation began.

It occurred to me that this was the mystery woman, Wentz's wife Florence, who unabashedly, in her lovely motherly way was breaking down the battlements of intellectual snobbery.

I had to meet her.

"Are you seeing what I'm seeing?" I asked Zoltan.

"Yes. Wentz's woman, she Glinda."

"What?"

"Glinda, good witch of the south."

"What are you talking about?"

"From *Wizard of Oz*. I read it to Sarah and Tommie when they little."

"Oh." I immediately felt guilty that Zoltan had read a book to them that I had not. "Let's check her out."

"Yes. I need good fairy dust for my research."

"Oh, shut up, will you?"

"It very interesting Jabba married to witch. Could explain a lot. They belong maybe in theme park?"

"God damn," I told him, as we walked toward them among a group I recognized as being from the humanities.

Lusby saw us coming. Clutching a Dr. Pepper in both hands, he had pitted out his suit. Luckily, and perhaps as a cautionary measure, it was dark blue.

When we arrived, Lusby introduced us to Mrs. Wentz, "This is Thomas Simpson, director of university and campaign communications and his good friend, Zoltan Vastag, who runs a cancer research lab at the medical center."

She reached forward and took my right hand with both of hers. Her accent was southern, South Carolinian if I had to guess.

"Oh, Thomas—Jack and I are so proud of the job you're doing. You've had such a positive impact on Sessions. You've put us *on the map*."

"Well, thank you." I looked around and found the group nodding approvingly. I was certain that they did not actually approve but that Florence had cast some magical spell upon them which caused them all to nod their heads simultaneously. This was damn interesting.

"Now where are your children in school?"

"Actually, over the summer our daughter, Sarah, became a student at Sessions's Center for Gifted and Talented Youth."

"Oh, that's wonderful. You must be so proud."

"She takes after her mother," I noted with false modesty. "And our son, Tommie, is at Schossler Academy."

"Oh yes. I'm sure they are doing a good job by him. That is a very fine school."

Damn, I thought, she is certainly politic. I hated talking about our children and their education. I didn't view it as anyone else's business, especially Tommie's situation. But there it was, right out in the open and getting everyone's beaming approval.

She released my hand and turned to Zoltan. "Zoltan, I've just been hearing from folks about your very important work. That's fabulous what you are doing to help cure cancer."

I saw Zoltan clutch and catch himself from exploding, suck it up and say to her, "Thank you so much, madam," while he struggled to contort his face into something other than a wish to kill. Completely, hilariously unsuccessful. Even Lusby started to crack up, as did the whole group.

Florence Wentz was brilliantly oblivious. "You're so modest," she commented. "I've often found that the more successful people are, the less they want or even care to draw attention to themselves."

"Oh," Wentz commented, thoroughly enjoying this exchange, "That describes Zoltan perfectly. A paragon of modesty, and I might add, couth."

Everyone chuckled while Zoltan could be seen drifting into a slow burn. Normally he would have retorted with an insult directed at Wentz's obesity. Now with Florence present, he had no choice but to take the insults. Plus, somehow, Florence took the edge off everyone and everything and made it all okay.

"It's been such a pleasure meeting you," I said. "Zoltan and I have to catch up with a colleague at the bar. Please excuse us."

"Of course," Florence replied. "I'll so look forward to seeing you all ah-gain."

We excused ourselves and headed toward the bar where we knew Berger would be hanging out.

"Wentz's woman may be good witch." Zoltan told me. "He still bastard asshole."

"Yeah."

In the dining room, club bartenders were serving drinks from a large portable table covered with a white tablecloth. As we suspected, Berger was standing off to the side with his scotch.

Instead of the boat clothes and threadbare jacket that he had worn to last year's reception, having just come from his sailing trimaran *Calypso Too* in the harbor, he was dressed in an expensive three-piece, blue, pin-striped suit. He had even had his orange mustache that went from ear to ear as if from the 1800s trimmed up a bit and his greying black hair close cut.

He saw us, smiled and said, "Howaryah?" in his Boston accent as we reached him, moving his eyebrows up and down over the frames of his thick, black, center-hinged, ovular eyeglasses.

"Better for seeing you."

"Same ol' bullshit, Thomas, huh?"

"I meant it!"

"What wrong?" Zoltan asked, fingering the lapel of Berger's custom-tailored suit. "You not look like derelict."

"Ah, I've been at a damn meeting with some Chinese who want to buy some of my hotels. They ain't gonna get 'em. Plus, damn Jean Claude stole my boat outta the harbah so I got no place to hang out except the Intercontahnental."

The fact was that after Ursula had suddenly disappeared last year, I later learned from Berger, to my surprise, relief and regret, that she had set sail for Europe with Berger's maritime captain Jean Claude on Berger's trimaran.

"But I'm glad I bought that place," Berger continued, referring to the Intercontinental. "Ownahship has its privileges, I've discovered. But it means I gotta look a little respectable, although this is overdoin' it. Just kidding about Jean Claude stealin' the boat. It's fine by me that it's in the Med. I can fly over and use it anytime I want. Come spring he'll sail it back to My-yami. But right now I got a very serious problem." He held up his empty glass of half-melted ice cubes and a sliver of scotch at the bottom and made a helpless gesture with his other hand.

"Ah, I fix that," Zoltan said. He took Berger's glass, took two steps to the crowd around the bar and uttered a low, guttural, "Muuuuve." There was a brief turning of heads and then a rapid clearing of space, allowing him to place an order for the three of us.

We watched as the intimidated bartenders rushed to fix our drinks, the displaced deans and departments heads staring up at

Zoltan with "who the hell is this big, mean-ass son of a bitch" expressions, Zoltan oblivious to their displeasure.

"He's an effective mother-fucker, iddin he?" Berger commented.

"Yep. Sometimes unfortunately effective."

"Yeah, I can see that."

Zoltan turned and handed me my beer, then brought Berger his new scotch, while he held onto his own vodka.

"So, Zoltan," Berger said, "I hear you're onto a major discovery."

"CHRIST!" Zoltan exploded in part with the pent-up frustration from our conversation with Florence Wentz.

The crowd at the bar jumped, one of them spilling a drink on the other, both cursing loudly.

"Maybe we oughta wandah off to the foyah," Berger suggested.

"Oh yeah," I encouraged.

We did just that.

"So, let me ask something, Zoltan," Berger said as we stood in a corner. "All this goes down and you actually come up with somethin' big. What's your cut?"

Zoltan looked acutely embarrassed. "I do not know," he said, with a touch of dejection.

"Hmm…, jus' what I thought."

"Mark, no one's telling Zoltan anything about how be shares or benefits from his discovery should it turn into something. What should he do?"

"Ah," Berger said, "I asked the question because I got some concerns here.

"First, Zoltan, it just so happens that I've heard about this attorney guy who's apparently the man to answer these kinds of contract and intellectual property questions. Understand, of course, that I have no direct business or personal relationship with him, so my helping you out like this represents no conflict of interest to my service on the board of trustees," he said as he moved his eyebrows up and down knowingly. "Give him a call."

He reached into a side pocket and pulled out a piece of white scrap paper with a name and number scrawled on it and handed it to Zoltan, his hand looking tiny and wizened next to our friend's.

"No mention of my name. This gentleman happens to be clairvoyant so he may already know who the hell you are. Hell, he might even be interested in talking with you."

"Berger, you are guardian angel," Zoltan replied with an awestruck tone, looking closely at the slip of paper.

Berger nodded. "Second, more important, we got a serious challenge here. Our friend on the board, Stanhope Barrett, CEO of Allogenic Technologies, is going to be all over this and want to inveigle a sweethart deal. *Au contraire.*

"I will make sure he gets his ass handed to him should that happen. And it will happen. If you guys hear or see anything that smacks of trying to influence or buy folks off, you need to let me know.

"Sessions is gonna be assaulted by suitors, all the big pharmas and then some, all wanting to pahtner with us to develop this discovery, should it pan out, into a proprietary therapy, drug etc. We're talkin' many billions of dollars of profits over possibly decades. We'll get the best deal from a level playing field. At least that's what I'd hope, that they all bid against one another. No sweethart deals. Got it?"

Both Zoltan and I nodded. I was sure that Zoltan felt like I did, that when it came to these kinds of concerns, we were in way over our heads

"Berger, you in the miracle-working business, yes?" Zoltan asked.

"Not every day. That's for fucking sure.... Hey, so look, I hear too that the Kravitzes have hired a private dick firm."

"You've been talking to Lusby," I guessed.

"Yeah, so unfortunately I know so little about what happened that I'm not worth interviewing." He moved his eyebrows up and down again over the rims of his glasses.

"What do you think's going to happen?"

"Ah, I'll keep my own counsel on that for now. Let's see how it all plays out. Maybe it'll just fade away."

"I drink to that," Zoltan said and downed his vodka. "We have another round?"

"Good idea, my man. Then I gotta go. Dinner with a 'friend.'"

"Ohhh-kay."

Zoltan retrieved another round and when we had finished our drinks and bringing one another up-to-date with our lives, Berger headed out the door and we followed him, except on the way out I ran into my former department head Howard Calhoun, talking with Provost Don Powers. Zoltan excused himself to talk with his colleagues from the medical center, while Berger made his way out while shaking a few hands.

Powers saw me coming and also excused himself. After our recent exchange with Wentz, who could blame him?

Howard, with his unruly white hair and ever-present eczema on his neck, beamed at me. His brown eyes were, as always, small and distorted behind his glasses. "Thomas," he greeted, "it is so good to see you. We miss you." We shook hands.

"Yeah. New regime is keeping me way too busy."

"I can't believe the board has made that reprobate jackass president."

"I'm having a little trouble with it myself, and I've got to work for him."

"Come back to the Communications Department, Thomas. You can have your old position back. We have some bright new folks who could use your mentoring."

"Oh Lord, I think about that all the time, Howard, but right now we can't afford to. Now that Sarah's in college and even with some merit scholarship monies, tuition remission provided to staff and her living at home, it's not cheap—plus, to be honest with you, we don't know where Tommie's going to end up. He may have to go away to school at some point at a huge expense."

"That would be tragic."

"No question. It would kill Janet."

"How have you been?"

I shook my head, laughed a hollow laugh. "It's difficult to know. I have trouble enough just coping on a day-to-day basis."

"Hmm…, yes, I understand. It's all a perfervid rush to nowhere, isn't it?"

"Yeah…," I agreed. "Well, let me go. I need to catch up with Zoltan."

"Okay, Thomas. All the best."

"Thanks," I said with some feeling because coming from Howard, I knew it was completely and deeply sincere.

"Stop by the department, will you? We'd love to see you."

"That would be great." I felt badly that I so routinely avoided seeing Howard and my former department. I couldn't exactly put my finger on why, but it just felt extremely awkward to even think about going over there.

I found Zoltan. He excused himself from a group of scientists, and we walked out together, Zoltan headed to the front gate to catch a cab downtown to his lab and I to the lower parking lot. As I walked, I pondered why the idea of visiting my former department was so awkward and felt almost off-limits. I faced the hard fact that, no matter how much I spoke wistfully to the contrary, I would never return to academia. The truth was I was now a member of the administration and did not belong in my former world. Over the last year I had become a communications professional. It was as simple and as complicated as that. In my new profession, despite all its travail, I felt a real sense of achievement and a growing professionalism for which I was being rewarded handsomely. No matter how much I yearned for and had affection for my old career and lifestyle, the fact was, it had been rapidly becoming a dead end. These realizations, the clarity of them, took me a bit by surprise.

Janet's old Bimmer convertible was waiting for me in the lower lot. I thought about how last year, in an attempt to cheer her up following Dr. Compton's suicide, I had the car brought back to life from under the dust and boxes piled on top of it in the garage, trying to revive some spark of joy and remembrance of our younger days together. It hadn't worked. So, now it was mine, a very sweet driving machine with antiquated electronics that I supplemented with my cell phone.

I put the top down and cruised home, thinking about what I had learned that day and, as usual, about the mystery of where it might all be going. I thought briefly about Ursula, who, having left Berger's *Calypso Too* captain, Jean Claude, was now reputedly working in the German embassy, a position afforded by dual citizenship. I caught myself shaking my head and shut those thoughts down.

VI

Encrypted

On a mid-October morning in my office I had been in my chair no more than a moment when my cell phone buzzed. Zoltan. An unusual time of day for him to be calling. I put down my university-seal mug and picked up the phone from top of my desk.

"Hey, what the hell do you want?"

"Ah, I interrupt B-M-O-C."

"Where did you learn that—Big Man on Campus?"

"Kristina call me that at certain times."

"Oh, that's way more than I needed to know."

"Janet never call you that?"

"Not these days. It's tough being Big Man on Campus when the campus is closed."

"Oh, I sorry. That terrible."

"No kidding."

"Thomas, things happen. We must talk."

"Yeah? See you at the club?"

"No, too public. I tell you what. We keep talking about my coming for dinner. Want to see Tommie and Sarah and Janet anyway. I be there at seven. Can walk dog in neighborhood later and talk."

"Okay, I'll let Janet know."

"Yes, that good. Maybe we cheer up Janet? Anyway, things happen yesterday and already today—very unusual. I talk with lawyer. I get strange call from a—what you call her? Ah yes, execcu-tive re-cruit-ter."

"Headhunter?"

"Yes. She hunting my head."

"Yeah? I'll be interested to hear about that. See you at seven."

"Yes."

"When you come over, I can also tell you all about Wentz's first executive committee meeting. Due to commence in an hour."

"Umm, see what bullshit Fatso putting out today."

"Yeah."

I hung up and then, thinking, slowly rotated my chair to look out my window. After a minute or two I turned back, picked up my phone and called Berger.

He answered on the first ring. "Hey, Thomas. Howareyah?"

"Okay, I guess. Where are you?"

"Bahston."

"Good. Zoltan's coming over for dinner at our place tonight to talk about being approached by a headhunter. We may want to give you a call."

"Hmm, yeah. I'll be around. One of my guys there, he's going to talk to you. You have a meeting coming up today?"

"Yeah, president's executive committee at ten thirty."

"Okay, he'll be there. See him afterwards. Good man. Very trustworthy."

"Okay," I said. I could tell just from the vibe of conversation that Berger did not want to discuss what this was all about.

"Take care, Thomas."

"Sure."

At ten twenty I headed up to the president's executive committee meeting in Wentz's office. Thankfully, Ms. Bemis gave me an almost imperceptible nod to enter. Proof that today at least, I existed. She was decked out in an autumn outfit of russet orange with matching nails and earrings that cascaded in ever-larger, orange, plastic triangles almost to her shoulders. She was so mean-faced that I pictured trick-or-treaters running from her front door in terror when she opened it. Whaaaahhhh!

Inside the president's office, it was a different scene than when

Fitz-Hugh had presided. First, Wentz was already there. He had pulled his double-wide chair over to the head of the table. Fitz-Hugh had always been late, keeping us waiting uncomfortably and then breezing in and launching into his usual brilliant, charming and persuasive monologue. We were there to rubber stamp his initiatives for which he had carefully, behind the scenes, already made all the preparations. Now Wentz waited a bit impatiently for all of us to arrive. Good that I was not the last person.

Harold Ramis, the head of the medical center, was there in a medium-grey, three-piece suit; white-on-white shirt; red bow tie; glistening, bullet-shaped head; and bushy, grey eyebrows—light glinting off his titanium-framed glasses, the perfect model of the master clinician. In the past he had positioned himself directly to Fitz-Hugh's right. Now he was sitting at the other end of the table. A subtlety, but no, I immediately wanted to know what this was all about. People, like dogs, were set in their routines, would take the same seat at the same meeting every single time. You changed your seat, there was a reason. What was it? Opposition? Not likely. Wanting to appear independent? That was more like it. Why?

Lusby was sitting in his usual seat to Wentz's left. I took my usual seat next to him. He nodded at me, rolled his eyes toward Ramis, gave me a quizzical look and made a small shrug. He had picked up on the change too.

Bernie Reve, in his trademark dark suit, was on Wentz's right. Bernie was the chief fund raiser for Sessions, the vice president of advancement, a man with the Top 100-plus prospects of our ongoing $4.5 billion Campaign for Progress, who hid his deep insecurities with a charming and fun persona, comfort food and drink.

Don Powers sat in the middle right, his expression a mask of feigned alert interest.

Berger's lead auditor/accountant, a young, serious dweeb with a bad haircut and a large black briefcase scurried in last. He appeared to me as if he had somehow been beamed in from an early 1960s high school yearbook, perhaps as the captain of the debate team. Cluelessly, he sat in the chair that Kravitz used to occupy. I glanced around. Everyone looked awkward as hell. I had yet to get his name.

It all felt like a much smaller and more disjointed committee than last year because it was. Wentz had chosen not to appoint an assistant to take Ursula's place, thereby keeping total control of all initiatives and information relating to his presidency, using different departments to handle any projects. He had also decided that the attendance of our director of public relations, John "Fine Fine" Fein, was not necessary now that I was Fein's supervisor. Fein, a desperately ebullient, clueless and semi-competent staffer, had been nicknamed because his response to any inquiry about the status of anything, his health, a project, the weather was an unconvincing, "Oh … fine, fine!"

Wentz looked around at each of us before he spoke. It was difficult to know what he was thinking, but he was all business and, in this mode, he came off as almost baleful and threatening.

I thought back to last year's meeting just before Christmas where Wentz had been cutting up with a Rudolph the Red Nosed Reindeer tie with a red lightbulb on Rudolph's nose that he could flash at inappropriate moments. My how things had changed.

Wentz cleared his throat to bring the meeting to order. "As some of you have discovered, my office is coordinating appointments for the Blaylock Agency, which has been hired by the Kravitz family to investigate our former provost's death," he said with the hint of breathlessness I had noticed earlier. "For those of you who have been interviewed, my thanks. So far, I haven't heard that there will be any arrests."

We chuckled at the joke, ass-kissers one and all.

"Our next board of trustees meeting will be held at the School of Foreign Service in Washington in the second week of December. This will be the perfect occasion and venue to focus the board on Sessions University as The Global University. We'll be staying at the Tribone Hotel, courtesy of our board vice chair Mark Berger, who owns the place.

"I'm counting on all of you to make a hell of a good impression, underscoring what each of your divisions is accomplishing overall, particularly relating to our global university theme. Please have a six-month summary progress report for your division to me by the end of the week for inclusion in the formal board report. Once I've reviewed them, they'll be sent out in advance by mid-November. The Special Events Department will be handling all the logistics with the School of Foreign Service and with the hotel.

"Thomas, in particular I want you to layout the communications plan for the coming year. Focus on the continuation of The Global University theme, the opportunities offered by our presence in Beijing and Brussels and progress with the implementation of the enhanced communications plan that they heard about from you last year.

"Let's go around the table. Give me a couple of sentences summary of what you'll be reporting. Don?"

Powers put his hands in front of him, fingers touching one another, smiled his worthless smile, "You will recall that last year former president Fitz-Hugh, with the board's approval, made a $2 million allocation from the Campaign for Progress's unrestricted account to the humanities. Let me report that it has really breathed life into the humanities and quelled any discontent."

Fitz-Hugh had made the allocation directly after Kravitz's death, a blatantly manipulative preventative to assure no further opposition from the Faculty Senate regarding university finances. With Kravitz's demise and the allocation, the Faculty Senate's focus had turned to other more typical concerns and dissatisfactions and with nothing major to drive its agenda had begun meeting irregularly.

Wentz commented, "Don's been very smart about how he's chosen to administer these funds. He's required departments to make their case for increased funding through submitting directly to him a five-year departmental plan, budget and, would you believe, summary impacts. Of course, these summary impacts are to include each department's proposed international initiatives via Beijing and Brussels. Not only has this encouraged actual planning from that herd of cats, but it's stifled the infighting that would have occurred if he had done something egregious like form a committee to make such decisions. Now they can all just hate you, Don, rather than each other."

Powers smiled his benign smile. He was so Goddamned self-satisfied I wished I could somehow sneak under the table, stick a match into where his shoe top met the sole of his Cole Haans and light it, anything to produce a genuine reaction.

"Bernie, how are things going with the Campaign for Progress?"

Reve brightened, smiling, "Despite all this year's transitions, we're actually knockin' 'em dead," he said, rubbing his hands together gleefully. "Two $100 million pledges from alums in New York and Chicago, an endowment pledge of $50 million in company stock from Allogenic Technologies thanks to Stanhope Barrett, our board member and Allogenic's CEO, and a smattering of other $10 to $25 million gifts. Our board chair, Fritz Johnson, and I have initiated conversations with our vice chair, Mark Berger, about his gift to the campaign. As you may know, he made a very helpful unrestricted organizational enhancement gift of over $25 million last spring."

Bernie paused for a moment, looked at me and then around the table. "I actually have a bit of confession to make about our vice chair, Mark Berger, and let me add that's it's important that you keep what I'm telling you today in complete confidence," he said, looking at Neil, who was without a reaction.

Everyone else, I noticed, was now at full attention.

Bernie continued, "You'll remember that last year we estimated his net worth to be between seven to eight billion.... Well, we fucked up. The more we've researched him, the more we keep discovering his and his entities' involvement in other major US and foreign companies, often through limited partnerships which are simply a manner of disguising his involvement. So, we realize that in the past we just were seeing the tip of the iceberg, so to speak. Fact is, Mr. Berger is worth upward of fifteen to twenty billion, and even that estimate may be conservative."

He shrugged, "You know, wealth research is something of an inexact science, so we'll keep at it, but for now Berger is surfacing as our most wealthy alumnus, actually our overall most wealthy prospect."

I found my jaw had gone slack as I tried to reconcile our erstwhile, bohemian friend with the billions Bernie was referencing. In a conscious effort, I shut my mouth.

"So," Reve continued, "I want you to imagine what Mark Berger could do for Sessions if properly motivated. He's a cagy son-of-a-bitch, but we'll persist. Thomas, if you ever have any thoughts or ideas to share with us along these lines, feel free to give me a call."

"Sure," I said evenly. I'd already explained to both him and Lusby that our relationship with Berger was purely and genuinely friendship and that to go beyond that would be completely inappropriate; but like good hunting dogs on a scent they persisted in pursuing every possible path.

Wentz continued, "Let me introduce you to Neil Wexler, who is assisting the comptroller's office. Neil?"

It occurred to me that Neil had probably been working at Sessions since last spring when Berger would have assigned him to the controller's office, but this was the first time I was even aware of his existence.

I looked over at Neil the dweeb. Same nerdy expression. Reve's comments about Berger, his ultimate boss, had obviously been heard but would remain confidential. I could see both why Berger trusted him and why he would advance in Berger's many businesses.

From his black briefcase he pulled out a set of a thick financial reports. He passed them around the table and told us in his flat, constricted voice, "Here's the latest report we made this week to the board financial committee for your review. I think you'll find it to be transparent."

I watched as those around the table passed the report to one another and set it in front of them, each of them looking at it as if it were a lead-lined container of plutonium. The board finance committee consisted of Mark Berger, chair, and Fritz Johnson as its only member, with Jack Wentz and Don Powers as ex officio members. Whatever any of us around the table knew about Sessions University's recent finances, it was enough to know we did not want to have any further knowledge of them.

"Thomas?"

I reported on the upcoming events and communications, where now I was simply inserting Wentz where Fitz-Hugh had been, literally writing the script the same. Wentz knew he could pull off at least passable performances even though he had shown me no real interest or commitment to the philosophy underlying our university's direction. For him it was all about the appearance of business as usual as the cover-up continued.

"Harold," Wentz asked Ramis, "What's new at the medical center?"

Ramis's bearing became almost military, "Well," he told us, "The word's now out about this new trial being conducted by Professor Vastag and its potential for the discovery of a cancer vaccine."

He glanced my way momentarily.

"Fortunately, we were able to get the various national and international patent applications on his discovery filed before anyone was the wiser. As you may know, once a discovery gets into the public domain that significantly impacts its ability to be patented."

Now I knew why he had cautioned Zoltan from saying anything. Why Ramis felt the need to tell everyone about it and risk the patents was simply a reflection on his need to be the big shot. I wondered what would have happened had Zoltan been savvy enough to file his own patents before sharing his discovery with the medical center. I found myself shaking my head.

"I thank all of you who were aware of his initial findings and the beginning of a Phase 1 human trial for keeping quiet over the last several weeks."

I looked over at Lusby and watched a small, cynical smile cross his features. Our eyes met. He nodded his head at his note pad, where I saw he had just scrawled, "Blah, blah, blah."

Ramis continued. "The implications of such a potential world-renowned discovery have created a literal stampede to our doors. We have over thirty pharmaceutical companies wanting to know more, wanting to partner with us in taking this discovery to market, should it pan out. Of course, this Phase 1 trial is underway, so we really have nothing more to tell them. They all keep asking the same questions day after day, so at this point we've circled the wagons and are simply sending them a generic paper on his research findings to date and keeping them at arm's length. It's important that he be allowed to conduct this next Phase 1 without interruption. Until we have some results from human tests, we're all in the dark."

"We need to be very careful about how we handle this in the future," Wentz commented. All of us around the table nodded sagely, like the puppets we were.

The rest of the meeting deteriorated into discussions of minor jurisdictional and departmental concerns until mercifully it came to an end.

Neil was waiting for me with his big black briefcase in the hallway outside Ms. Bemis's office.

"Hey, Neil," I greeted him. We shook hands. His was cold and sweaty.

"Mr. Berger asked that I talk with you," Neil told me.

"Yeah, he mentioned that."

"Could we uh, take a walk?" His request was made even more awkward by his nerdy voice.

"Um, sure," I shrugged. This was all a bit strange.

We took the elevator down to the atrium, walked outside, Neil leading with a heavy stride, the heels on his black, tie shoes sounding on the flagstone walk and then the asphalt drive. We began our stroll turning right and then right again so that we were walking toward the back of the building. Neil obviously knew where he wanted to take me.

He cut across the campus drive toward the university's auditorium that stood at the base of the lower quadrangle and onto a paved walk behind it that took us through a wooded hill, a walk that I knew eventually exited onto a street running parallel to the campus. Neil seemed intent on his task, offering no small talk or any reason for why we were on our little jaunt.

Once we were no longer in view of any of the university buildings, Neil stopped and turned to me. He reached into his briefcase, pulled out box a bit smaller than a woman's shoe box wrapped in brown paper and handed it to me.

"What's this?"

"I do not know."

"Ohh-kay."

"Mr. Berger emphasized that you were to open it in a secure place."

"Secure?"

"Yes. That's what he said. He said also that you and I should not be seen together again except, of course, in meetings."

"Weird. Okay. Thanks, I guess."

"I'm walking back to my office. You wait here for a time."

"Geez, okay."

Neil walked away with his heavy stride and clomping shoes, a young man in a hurry. To what?

I waited a few moments and then walked back to the administration building slowly, taking in the woods, the crystalline blue sky between the trees, the colors of fallen leaves, the bright red of sumac, the lovely smell of it all—moist and dense, tannin, earth, moss and ferns. I thought to myself, *I need to take walks on campus more often.* I had not been on this walkway in years.

Back in the office, I was making my way distractedly through the rest of the day, the box shoved into my briefcase, fighting a burning desire to close my door and open it but at the same time counseling myself that it would better to do that once in my car, when Frank Lusby walked in, carefully closed my door and sat in the chair fronting my desk.

"You noticed Ramis today? Different seat, a bit of a different attitude?"

"Yeah," I acknowledged.

"What do you think's going on?"

"I haven't a clue. But, yeah, I noticed."

"I've got a sixth-sense feeling that he and Wentz are up to something."

"Yeah?"

"They're both acting suspicious. I've seen it now a couple times, not just at the executive committee meeting. Wentz has a private line in his office and a couple times, as Ms. Bemis has sent me in, he's been on it, back turned to the door, talking in low tones, don't know why but I'm sure he's taking with Ramis."

"I thought you and Wentz were asshole buddies."

Lusby looked at me with the expression one takes on when having to explain the obvious to someone clueless, "Well, we were. But that was then, seems like a century ago, last year. This is now. Lord knows we caroused back when he was dean and I was under the influence but now that I'm sober, I tend to see him in a very different light. Plus, he's changed. The presidency has turned him into a more-or-less serious motherfucker. Not like he's exactly fun to be around. I see him now strictly as my client. I have to get along with him, but it's not my job to protect him. I work for the good of the whole damn university."

"So, what do you think's going on?"

"I don't know. But I'm going to find out. My suspicion is that it's got to relate to Zoltan's discovery and the pharmaceutical companies who are falling all over themselves to get into bed with us, but that's just conjecture at this point. Do me a favor, let me know whether you see or hear anything that might be part of their dealings. Okay?"

"Sure."

Lusby stood, gave me a small half-salute, turned, opened my door and was gone.

When five o'clock came around I breathed a sigh of relief, grabbed my briefcase and walked to my car while on the lookout for Emily Sayzak, who thankfully did not make an appearance.

Once in the car, I started it and rolled down the windows to get some air circulating, then reached into my briefcase for the package Neil had given me, tore off the wrapping paper and opened the cardboard box inside. Nestled on all sides by a cushioning of brown packing paper was a row of six cheap cell phones, burners.

"What the hell?"

Tucked beside it were a folded copy of instructions on how to use each one-time use phone and a small note, scrawled unevenly on a bit of white scrap paper, a bit larger but resembling what Berger had handed Zoltan at the faculty club. It read, "Word is, they're listening to us. Use this when you need to talk. It's encrypted. Destroy this note. Destroyed each phone after one use."

I felt my face turn a fiery crimson as I recalled my conversation with Zoltan that morning about Janet's campus being closed.

"God damn." I heard myself mutter in a whisper. "Those motherfuckers."

I shoved the note in my suit pocket for later feeding into the garbage disposal, put the box and wrapping paper on the passenger's seat and the six phones and instructions in my glove box and headed home.

VII

Zoltanamas

LONG LATE-AFTERNOON shadows cast themselves across the streets of our neighborhood, the trees still colorful, new piles of raked leaves lining each side of the road in preparation for county pickup. I parked my car in the garage, threw Neil's box and wrapping paper into the trash bin in the garage corner and headed into the house.

The family room was empty. My daily reminder of Sarah's new maturity. Why did she have to grow up? I would not have minded if I had spent the rest of my life finding her there watching her cool kids' show every time I came into the house. In her absence Sparky, excited to see me, was at least a reasonable substitute.

Janet was in the kitchen fixing dinner for Zoltan and our family, a glass of wine on the counter already poured for me, the pleasant scent of a chicken in the oven spreading throughout the house.

"Thanks for doing this on short notice," I complimented as I picked up my glass of wine.

"Well," she said, as she put a container of mashed potatoes in the microwave, "It's Zoltan. Lord knows, it's been awhile."

"Yeah, I don't really understand how we manage to not see one another more frequently."

"Our lives used to be a lot less complicated." There was a touch of sadness in her reply. She paused, turned and faced me. "On another subject, the school called. Ms. Olin, the head, wants to see us about Tommie."

"Already?"

"I'm not sure what this is about. But the meeting is with her and the computer science teacher, a Mr. Diamond."

"That's odd."

"That's what I thought. It feels like something's not right, or more like Tommie's in some kind of trouble again."

"Well, at least he hasn't clocked his classmate, Sharif, with a toy fire engine like he did last year. That's just really strange that they wouldn't come out and say what the problem is. Well, let's look on the bright side. Maybe they've got a computer game for Tommie that provides for behavior modification."

"We should be so lucky."

"Yeah, I don't know. I don't like the sound of this at all." In my mind all the warning lights were going off to go no further with this conversation. I knew that Janet was being gripped by the same cold fear I was feeling, that there might be a chance that this meeting could be about Tommie being expelled, and then what the hell would we do? The next option was a residential school in some other part of the country. Unacceptable to us from all standpoints.

Then Janet actually came out and said it, blurting with determination and anger, "I will never let them send him away."

"Well, let's not speculate. It could be something minor."

"It never is."

"Yeah.... Hey, I saw Sarah's car out front?"

Janet blinked at me, accepted my obvious ploy for distraction, "She's up in her room, changing."

"Tommie?"

She rolled her eyes. "Upstairs, as usual."

"Umm."

Janet looked down and then back up at me with a level gaze. "Honey, I'm going to a conference in Chicago in two weeks, the Moore Psychological Conference. I need a break."

"Don't you need a break from work too? I mean, we could always take a weekend, go to the shore or the mountains."

"I need a break from you and this family."

"Oh … okay…."

"You can handle the kids for three days."

"Yeah …"

The doorbell rang.

Zoltan stood on the front step, beyond him I could see the remnant changing leaves on the maple across the street, his cab driving away, its taillights bright in the gathering dusk. Cool, vibrant air scented with wood smoke from someone's first autumn fire drifted by me into the house. He was carrying a stack of gift-wrapped boxes, his chin resting on the top box to hold them in place. I could smell vodka on his breath.

"What do you have there?" I asked in surprise.

"Ah, it is new computer, a laptop and other parts for Tommie, and I have something for Sarah too."

"How'd you even know he wanted one?" I asked incredulously. "How'd you know what equipment he wants?"

"You not look at Tommie's Facebook page?"

Suddenly I felt completely stupid. "Uh, no. I had no idea he had one."

"I friend him year ago. His page go from fire engines to tech over summer. He and geek friends that's all they post about now, tech, gaming, systems."

"I didn't know he had friends."

"Well, on Facebook, yes. In real life? Who know? Ask him."

Janet came up from behind me as Tommie pounded down the stairs and Sarah followed.

"What on earth is all this?" Janet asked.

"Presents!" Tommie shouted.

"You not know that tonight is very special Hungarian holiday?" Zoltan asked them as he stepped into the hallway and carefully set the stack on the floor beside the hall table while I closed the door.

Janet placed her hands on her hips as if dealing with Tommie, but I could see she was amused, "No, Zoltan, I didn't."

"Yes, tonight is Hungarian Christmas, and I am the, how you say, celeberent of it."

"Celebrant," I corrected.

Janet, Tommie and Sarah began to laugh.

Zoltan raised his right arm, extended his forefinger. "I do hereby declare that tonight be special Hungarian Christmas, name is Zoltanamas and I am the chief celeberant, Zoltana Claus, and I bring presents to good boys and girls." He looked at Tommie and Sarah from one to the other. "Have you been good?" he demanded.

"YES!" they both half-shouted.

"Then I must give you presents."

"These big boxes are for Tommie. And I have a small box here for Sarah. He reached into the inside pocket of his sport coat and pulled out a small, long and thin gift-wrapped box and handed it to Sarah as Tommie began shredding the wrappings on the largest of his boxes.

"Whoa, whoa, whoa, young man. You wait a moment," Zoltan told Tommie. "Let me help you so you do not break any of those things and you wait for your sister to open her present first."

Tommie looked up at Zoltan, a weird quizzical and frustrated expression on his face, but he stopped.

Tommie exhibiting self-control, I thought. What a concept.

Sarah carefully unwrapped her present, revealing an elegant box from the local jewelers and carefully pulled from its inside wrapping tissue a delicate gold chain necklace with a lustrous single pearl on a simple gold pendant.

"You a woman now," Zoltan told her. "You need nice things."

A tear rolled down Sarah's cheek as she examined the necklace, "Oh, thank you so much," she told Zoltan and gave him a hug which was both touching and bit comical because she could not remotely get her arms around him.

She took the necklace, placed the box on the hall table, undid its tiny clasp and gave it to Janet, who carefully pushed aside Sarah's hair and fastened it around her neck. Sarah turned, beaming, the necklace undeniably beautiful on a young woman. She turned to the hall mirror to look at herself and model it.

I glanced at Janet, who was wiping tears from her eyes with a forefinger and could feel my eyes grow moist.

"Thanks, man," I told Zoltan, reaching up to place a hand on his shoulder. "That's incredibly thoughtful."

"You are welcome," he said and then he turned to Tommie, "Now, Tommie, we must open your presents, but must be very careful. What inside is important and expensive. I help you."

He reached into his coat's vest pocket and pulled out a six-inch switch blade knife, held it up for all to see and pressed its button. Its blade snapped into place.

"Where in the *hell* did you get *that*?"

"Pawn shop. Don't you ever go to pawn shop? You find once in a while crazy good bargains there. This here very helpful all-purpose knife. I sharpen it very sharp. You watch.... Now, Tommie, you take off gift wrapping and then I help you open boxes."

Tommie attacked the biggest box, literally ripping at it with both hands.

When he had finished, wrapping paper strewn all around the boxes, Zoltan kneeled and neatly sliced open the tabs on each, the first being the laptop in its Styrofoam packing. Tommie respectfully stood in awe as Zoltan showed him each component and peripheral and read its capacities from each box, while I stood in awe at the controlled respect being shown.

When he had finished, Zoltan said, "Now, Tommie, after dinner I help you set up system. You do not do this yourself. You break something, I take it all back. You understand?"

"Sure Zoltan."

"Then your Dad and I walk Sparky while you play with it."

I looked at Tommie quizzically. This exchange sounded almost normal. It made me appreciate even more Zoltan's role in our family as the virtual favorite uncle. I shrugged. In this day and age friends became family and family for the most part were increasingly strangers.

Dinner was a pleasant exchange, with Sarah and Tommie catching up Zoltan on their lives and Janet and I learning for the first time about their courses, likes and dislikes about their professors and teachers—that Sarah was getting a bit bored with French but would welcome a semester abroad—that Tommie was very engaged and interested in his technology class and very much liked Mr. Diamond.

After dinner, while Zoltan helped Tommie set up his new laptop and peripherals, I helped Janet and Sarah clear the table, stack dishes in the dishwasher, clean the kitchen.

Then I climbed the stairs and peeked into Tommie's room.

Zoltan was working with Tommie, talking with him about what he was doing and why. His experienced dexterity with assembling the components, especially given the size of his hands, was impressive. Tommie was at full attention, rapt with Zoltan's every word and movement.

"Hey," I said gently, "You got a second?"

"Yes." Zoltan stood and came out into the hallway.

"I'll fill you in but we need to tell Tommie and Janet that we need to go to the village shops and buy something for Tommie's new system."

Zoltan looked at me with raised eyebrows. "Like new power cord/surge protector?"

"Perfect."

He turned and spoke to Tommie through the doorway, "Tommie, your dad and I go get new power cord/surge protector in village. Be terrible to have new system without new cord. I come back, we finish."

"Sure. I need to remove some old programs from my old system before we transfer data. But thanks so much for this new stuff."

"You welcome."

On the way down the stairs, I whispered to him, "Give me your cell phone."

Puzzled, he reached in his pocket and gave me his phone. I took mine out of my pocket, put both phones on mute and placed them in the hall table's drawer.

A few minutes later, having told Janet we were going to the

village, Zoltan and I were in the BMW headed toward the county reservoir.

He looked over at me, questioningly.

"All our phones are hacked. They're listening to us. Berger's given me some encrypted burner phones to use to talk with him. I don't want the family or anyone else to be able to listen in on our conversation. I figure driving around the reservoir is good for that. We can go pick up a surge protector on the way back."

Zoltan in a familiar motion reached into his sport coat and pulled out a pint of vodka, uncapped it. "To clear head," he told me, taking a swig and handing the bottle to me.

"Right," I said, taking a swig and handing the bottle back to him.

"So, how Fatso?"

"The same ol' shit cover-up. The next board of trustees meeting is in Washington, the second week in December, being hosted at one of Berger's hotels. Each of us on the executive committee is putting together a report for it. I have to produce and deliver the entire plan for communications of The Global University concept. Same plan, just with Wentz as the centerpiece."

"Umph. He not Fred Astaire, like Fitz-Hugh."

"Yeah."

"More like Fred Astaire skivvies, like maybe three days old," he began to laugh at his own comment.

"Yeah. And something weird is going on with Ramis. Lusby and I both picked up on it. Lusby's looking into it."

Zoltan gave me a sidelong questioning look while taking a swig of vodka and passing the bottle to me.

I took a swig. "I don't know. He thanked all of us for keeping our mouths shut while the university nailed down the patent for your discovery."

"Yes, while he steal it and then blab about it."

"And all these pharmas are approaching the medical center about your work and they're stonewalling them, just giving out a generic paper until you've finished this trial."

"Yes, I know this. So what?"

"Well, he took a seat way the hell away from Wentz when before he always sat next to Fitz-Hugh. I just got an odd vibe. You know how sometimes you just know that something is not right, that there's something going on? I'm not usually wrong about this stuff, and Lusby's never wrong far as I can tell."

"You add paranoia to job description?"

"And now Janet wants to go to some conference in Chicago so she can get away from us. Her words. Real encouraging."

"Hmm, that not good. I thought she okay tonight. On best behavior. But yes, she troubled underneath."

"And finally, I talked to Berger this morning and he told me to see his head dweeb accountant at Sessions after the executive committee this morning. So, his accountant suggests a walk and we go to out to the woods behind the auditorium and he gives me these burner phones."

We had reached reservoir which had an undulating drive around its perimeter. I took a right.

"So, what's going on with you?"

"Ah, I send employment contract to lawyer Berger give me and yesterday lawyer call back and tell me that medical center can award researchers for their discovery but that it at their…" he paused, searching for the word, "discretion."

"Oh shit. That sucks."

"Yes. Big time suck. You know medical center; you know Ramis. I first think of how to do all this experiment, this trial in my old teaching lab by myself on my own time two summers ago. They never want to reward me for it. Cheap sons-of-bitches. Only reason I get own new lab for research is because Fitz-Hugh and Ursula want you and me on their side, be their bitches, buy us off, like with your promotion. Anyway, lawyer say he willing to help me. If Phase 1 trial successful, negotiate."

"Yeah…, damn. Well, that makes sense. You may have to fight for everything."

"Yes. So then, sitting in lab office this morning, being pissed off, I get this call from re-cruit-ter."

"Yeah?"

"She say she represent pharma company, but she not give me name of company. I not sure whether she work for pharma company or recruiter company. Anyway, she tell me that pharma company very interested in me and my research. That if Phase 1 trial successful, they be interested in hiring me to run lab for them to finish research, go from benchtop to bedside."

"Wow."

"That not Wow. Let me tell you Wow. She say they build me my own lab, open budget, whatever I need. And, Thomas, she say they pay me a million a year."

"A million a year! That's fucking insane!"

"They buy me house. They give me car. Big retirement and medical benefits. Long term contract. I set for life."

"Jee-sus. I mean, you think this is real, not some kind of manipulation?"

"I think it both."

"Yeah, right."

"Yes, I don't know what to say. She say I maybe have to move to their headquarters but she don't tell me where that is. She tell me that maybe they are open to building research lab here. Thomas, this fucking crazy. I like what I do. I like where I live. Like being here with you guys. Want to be near Kristina. I don't know what to think, say, do."

"What did you tell the recruiter?"

"I tell her I think about it. What do I do?"

"I'll tell you what we're going to do. We're calling Berger. Open the glove box and get the instructions. Dial his number."

Zoltan opened the glove box, pulled out a phone and the instructions. I turned on the car's interior lights momentarily and he punched in the number, put the phone on speaker and put it on the center console.

Berger picked up on the first ring, "Howaryah?"

"Well, okay, I guess. Zoltan's here with me. I take it our phones have been hacked and that our wireless calls are being listened to?"

"Yeah."

"How do you know this?"

"Well, I keep in touch with folks I know, and it so happens that I give our ol' buddy Bryan a call once in a while to find out how he's doing, or actually, to find out what he's willing to tell me about certain things. I mean, he still has Sessions interests very much at heart, not to mention protecting his own legacy and reputation. For my part I give him my own thoughts and perspectives. So, the other day in a very indirect way he alluded to the fact that it would probably make sense for us to talk securely. The phrase he used was that perhaps our conversations needed to be more "discreet." Subtle hint, huh, coming from a high appointment at our Department of State who is close to Madam Secretary?"

"So, who the hell's listening in on us?"

"The infahrence would seem to be our spooks. It's like the folks doing this just want to be assured that their little imbroglio of last year isn't going to be talked about and thereby discovered. My sense is this: that they really don't want to do anything but just let our dirty little secret die, but should it threaten to get out, they're willing to do just about anything to kill it."

"God damn."

"Yeah, a regular clustah fuck. Anyway, what we gotta do is just keep on keeping on, keep our mouths shut, our internet and phone exchanges all business and nothing else—etc., etc."

"How the hell long does this go on? Forever?"

"Nah, figure until the next election, maybe six months. Even if Greta Hauser were to stay on, they'll be a whole new range of issues and imperatives to deal with. They'll likely just forget about us. Or until they feel like we're all old news and monitoring us is a waste of time and resources. In other words, we put them to sleep."

"So, Blaylock isn't helping matters, is it?

"Nah. Sucks. But I think their inquiry won't amount to much."

"Why?"

"Ah, who knows? Just a feeling. Kinda maybe it won't be productive for them."

"Okay. Whatever the hell you say."

"So, what else you got on your minds?"

We brought him up to speed on Zoltan's conversations with the attorney and the recruiter.

There was a pause while Berger thought about the situation while Zoltan and I drove around the reservoir road admiring the moonlight on water.

"Okay," Berger's voice came back to us over the phone, "So, what'll happen is that providing Zoltan's discovery tests out well in the Phase 1 trial, the university will want to patent it further ASAP and then pahtner through licensing with a major drug company to develop it into a saleable product and treatment. Zoltan, you might get a bonus out of it. If your lawyer is skilled enough, he might negotiate your getting a percent of the action. That could be worth millions.

"So, first, you turn down any of these approaches until the trial is done. When will that be?"

"Umph. Hard to tell. Months."

"Tell the recruiter that she should get back to you after the Phase 1 results are out. Then we'll see what's up. You may get approached by all sorts of folks, some legit, some bogus. I'd be happy to help you figure all that out, but until you've finished your trial, we don't know what we're dealing with. These folks who contacted you about a lab are just trying to get a leg up. All talk; probably all bullshit. Thanks for callin'. This is important shit. Some of these guys, they'll stop at nothing. I want you to keep in touch."

"You think it's Allogenic behind all this?" I asked.

"Ah, it's more complicated than that. We can sniff things out at the board meeting in December. In the meantime, I understand Mr. Barrett committed a big-time gift of stock from the company."

"Yeah. $50 million in stock."

"My God," Zoltan reacted.

"Yeah, I hadn't had a chance to tell you that."

"I bet Mr. Reve did not reveal the terms of that asshole's gift."

"No, he just reported it to the executive committee as a pledge."

"Hah! Yeah, it's a pledge all right—for when Allogenic stock hits a value about 25 percent above its current price."

"Jesus."

"Yeah, so what would cause his stock to increase by 25 percent?"

"Allogenic's partnership with Sessions to develop Zoltan's discovery."

"Egg-zack-ly. You do have a brain. You hear that Zoltan?"

"Yes."

"And Wentz is going along with this?"

"Oh yeah. Fucking assholes. Gotta go. You guys chill. Talk at you soon. Hey, I kinda like this setup. We can say whatevah we want. That's terrific, 'cause I never know what the fuck I'm gonna say. You guys can humor my verbal indiscretions, okay?"

"Sure," I told him.

"Ciao."

We disconnected. I turned to Zoltan. "You okay?"

He took a final swig of vodka, shrugged as if trying to cast off the weight of the world.

"Yes."

VIII

Genius

DESPITE THE BEST of intentions, between the school's assemblies and class trips, Janet's patient schedule and my work schedule, it took two weeks before a meeting could be arranged with Tommie's school. Naturally, the only time available for all of us was the morning I was to take Janet to the airport for her plane to Chicago. Hardly ideal, but we were anxious to find out why the school wanted to see us.

So it was that on a cold and windy November morning we drove up Schossler Academy's narrow and uphill asphalt drive, twisting through now almost bare woods, the car jumping from bumps in the road from tree roots and potholes.

Tommie was in the back seat, staring at the passing scenery, lost in thought. I found it fascinating that he had not even asked about why Janet and I were visiting the school today, while we were trying unsuccessfully to ignore the tension we felt about our visit with Ms. Olin and Mr. Diamond. We crested the hill as the old estate mansion which housed the school came into view, playing fields and a new gymnasium off to the left, auditorium on the right.

The building's ancient brick exterior, covered with ivy, contrasted with its renovated, modern school interior of open spaces and bright colors. Its mansion doors shuttered and quaked with our entry. Children were everywhere, moving rapidly in different directions, oblivious to our presence. The class bell sounded, and Tommie rushed to his classroom.

Janet and I knew all too well from prior visits the location of the head of school's office. Entering its too small reception area we were greeted by the school secretary. Behind a window embedded with wire, Ms. Olin could be seen sitting in her desk chair in conversation with someone out of view, undoubtedly at the conference table in the back of her office. She glanced out at us and beckoned us in, stood and walked to her door to greet us. As usual, she was very professional and pleasant, her brown hair pulled back into a bun, black-framed glasses adding a touch of schoolmarm to her features.

Mr. Diamond was indeed sitting at the conference table. We pulled out chairs and sat while Ms. Olin introduced him.

Rather than the nerd I might have expected, Diamond was a tall, friendly and vigorous young man with close-cut, black hair; bushy, black goatee; corduroy pants, light-green, collared shirt; and an ancient, wool sweater. Sensing his genuine interest in his profession and Tommie, I liked him immediately and intuited that Janet did also.

"Thank you for coming today," Ms. Olin began. "I'm sure you're wondering what this meeting is about, especially given the exchange we had last year about Tommie. This is a bit different, really about Tommie's future."

I could sense Janet clutch at the word *future.*

"But let me have Mr. Diamond brief us on his thoughts."

Diamond put his hands together, fingertips touching. "How do I begin? Tommie is truly a unique entity, isn't he?"

We all smiled, Janet and I with great uncertainty.

Diamond continued. "As part of our normal protocol, to help us better understand each of our students' needs, we run a series of tests exploring everything from intelligence to aptitude to learning disabilities to psychological profile. Tommie, as we all know, exhibits some form of what we today call ASD or autism spectrum disorder, a broader term encompassing what was formerly known as Asperger's syndrome, where he tends to focus on a single area of interest, most recently his computer, technology and coding to the exclusion of social interaction and almost everything else. This kind of behavior makes testing particularly difficult. But I was able to effectively bribe Tommie by offering him free time on our computer in exchange for him taking tests. We got some very interesting results."

Janet and I exchanged a brief look, surprised that Tommie would willingly interact and cooperate with anyone. Diamond's ability to draw him out was impressive.

"First, Tommie is not learning disabled in any way, shape or form. He doesn't do well in his classes because of his monomaniacal focus on other interests, last year in fire engines; this year in technology."

Janet and I looked at one another, a bit surprised, a bit puzzled by this information.

"Well, that's good to know," I commented.

"Second, he has a remarkable working memory, the ability to hold information both mathematical and verbal for extended periods of time.

"Third, when it comes to things he's interested in, he has a ferocious attention to detail. I'm sure you know this from his past interest in fire engines."

I felt myself smile and lightly shake my head, looked over at Janet and found her doing the same.

"Finally, and most surprisingly, Tommie's ability to then take information and work with it creatively and conceptually is off the charts."

Mr. Diamond paused. I could sense he and Ms. Olin were now gauging our reaction. I looked at Janet. She was as puzzled as I was. This was not Tommie he was talking about, was it?

"Okay," I said, "What exactly are you trying to tell us?"

Mr. Diamond smiled. "Well, when it comes to technology, there's no other way to put it. Tommie's a budding genius."

"What?" I heard someone blurt out incredulously, then realized it was me.

Janet and I looked at one another, then looked at Mr. Diamond and Ms. Olin. Had they lost their minds? It was one thing for Tommie to tell us that he was "smart," which we had to some degree assumed was an imaginary proclamation, but to have his technology teacher declare him a budding genius was shocking.

"That is a statement I never thought we'd hear," Janet said evenly, cautiously, certain that another shoe was about to drop. "What *are* you talking about?"

"Well, it's why we wanted to meet with you. Such talent is not without its challenges."

"How do you mean?" Janet asked. I thought, *Uh-oh.*

"Well," Mr. Diamond began to smile, "Your son has hacked the school's computers. From a security standpoint, this is a rather a serious matter."

I thought, *Ohhh shit.* I looked at Janet. Her head was down, small quiver at the side of her mouth.

"To put this into perspective. Any gifted high school student could do this. In fact, it happens with some frequency. Look up "hacking school computers" on the internet and you'll find any number of unfortunate incidents that have already occurred as well as basic "how to" instructions for future hackers.

"But Tommie ..."

"Yes," Mr. Diamond said, finished my thought for me, "Tommie's just entered sixth grade. So, we need to face the fact that in his own very dysfunctional way, Tommie, when it comes to technology, is a genius."

"A genius?" I heard myself say again. "Pardon me, but for years we've been told, or it's been inferred, that he was stupid."

Mr. Diamond laughed ruefully, "Yes, not unusual. Einstein was a slow learner as a child but that forced him into a different learning style that was the foundation for his genius. With children, as the brain matures it's sometimes almost as if a switch is turned on, lighting up a whole new range of capabilities that before had not seemed to exist."

"What damage did he cause?" Janet asked, looking up, significant fear in her voice.

"Ah, that's where it gets interesting. Fortunately, nothing serious. He did not mess with our programming or damage any of our systems. What he did was change last year's grades, fortunately only for himself and for a classmate, Sharif. Ms. Olin has briefed me on last year's incident between the two of the them where they got into a squabble. In any case, Tommie managed to change his grades for last year to straight As and he managed to give Sharif all Fs. We discovered it because of the computer-generated deficiency reports for Sharif. Otherwise it would have gone unnoticed for quite some time. When I confronted Tommie about his chicanery he confessed readily. He's quite proud and delighted with himself, thinks his little trick is hilarious."

Mr. Diamond paused. "And therein lies the problem, the issue being that this brilliance is accompanied by a significantly underdeveloped sense of right and wrong or how his actions affect others."

Ms. Olin said, "As you may know, one of the characteristics of ASD is an insular focus on the self. It actually has some aspects of narcissism to it, where the child or adult sees only a few individuals as being whole and real, like his parents and his sister."

Mr. Diamond added, "And a family friend, a Zoltan? He seems to have great respect for him; holds him in awe."

"Yes," I added, "more or less an uncle to our children."

"Ah, I see. In any case, with the exception of your family and Zoltan, in Tommie's world everyone else is more or less a stick figure, not quite real. Or let me put it another way, other people are no more real to him than his virtual characters in his computer games. He has no sense of their being, their humanity or their feelings. His world is only Tommie; therefore, he has little or an inappropriate sense of right or wrong or the consequences of his actions. He has no sense that his amusing little trick in hacking our computer system is a criminal offense that can result in prosecution for anything from a misdemeanor to felony,"

"Of course," Ms. Olin added quickly, "We have no interest in pursuing such action. What we want is what's best for Tommie."

There was an extremely awkward pause. In my side vision I saw Janet wringing her hands.

Finally, Janet asked, "Well what do you recommend?"

Ms. Olin, placed her hands on the conference table and looking from one of us to the other, said, "Tommie needs the structure of this school and its curriculum. That's important and it is a given. But we also feel that it would be extremely helpful that he be enrolled additionally in a special program that provides advanced course work in technology, allowing him to be engaged by further success, and that also provides counseling to address his asocial thinking and behavior. This would allow him to progress here at Schlossler with our regular curriculum while developing in an outside setting his superior skill set in technology and a better sense of and appreciation for others."

"So, he can stay here?" Janet asked, just to be a 100 percent sure.

"Of course."

I felt a profound sense of relief and I could see Janet's face relax and brighten as I was sure mine was.

"That's wonderful," Janet said.

"As to the program we'd recommend. We think it would ideal if—for one day to a day and a half a week, perhaps with some time over weekends and the summer—Tommie could be enrolled for counseling and some advanced courses at the Sessions Center for Gifted and Talented Youth, he could progress educationally and get the help he needs psychologically.

"Ohhh SHIT!" I heard myself exclaim as I heard Janet gasp.

Mr. Diamond looked at us, his head cocked, a puzzled expression.

Ms. Olin blinked at us. "Somehow that's not exactly the reaction we were expecting," she said.

It took some time to explain to them the dynamics of our household. Sarah's situation, her enrollment in the Sessions Center for Gifted and Talented Youth. Her resentment of Tommie's daily needs dominating all of our attention.

While I could certainly provide some of Tommie's transportation to and from Sessions it would also have to involve Sarah.

Both Janet and I could see how her shepherding Tommie to and from any counseling and course work would cause her to feel that Tommie once again had become her albatross and personal cross to bear, strengthening her resolve to leave our household at the earliest possible convenience. I could already see the transfer applications and first semester transcripts flying across the internet. The problem being that neither Janet nor I were prepared for her departure, for the expense, for the large hole in our lives.

On the way to the airport, we barely spoke to one another, stunned by Ms. Olin's and Mr. Diamond's assessment and recommendation and trying to process what we might say to Sarah and Tommie that would not provoke a family crisis.

I pulled up to the curb at Departures, jumped out of the car to help Janet pull her suitcase out of the trunk. She mumbled a few words of goodbye, gave me a light buss on the cheek, turned and walked toward the terminal door while I slammed the trunk shut and scurried back to the car.

IX

Private Line

BACK AT SESSIONS I settled in at the office. I was trying to focus on the tasks at hand, particularly my draft six month's report and communications plan for the upcoming Washington, DC board meeting, when my desk phone rang with the small, short bursts. I found myself shaking my head again. Whatever, whoever it was, it was not going to be good news.

"Care to join me for lunch at the club?" Lusby asked, his voice unmistakable. "I've also invited Zoltan."

I thought for a moment. Clearly, the inclusion of Zoltan meant that there was urgency behind his invitation. "Yeah, sure."

"Eleven thirty. You okay with that? Zoltan'll be taking a cab over here shortly."

"Yeah, ... I guess so. See you then."

I put the finishing touches on the report, filed it for one last review after lunch, grabbed my suit jacket and overcoat and walked to the club.

On campus the trees and shrubbery were now bare, the wind whipping around corners in gusts, blowing leaves and stray pieces of trash past me.

The club was warm and welcoming. Thanksgiving on the way and the club's October decorations were now completely out of date—pumpkins, autumn leaves, corn husks, colorful gourds in baskets. The general lethargy of the club's personnel was something to be glad about. Unlike everywhere else, we would likely not see Christmas decorations until after Thanksgiving.

Lusby was standing in the front hallway, waiting for me. He looked terrible.

"Let's eat in the main dining room," he said, his voice subdued.

The front door opened and Zoltan stepped in, accompanied by a blast of cold air. He was not wearing an overcoat, just his normal worn sport coat and jeans. He shook himself like a large dog, as if that would help bring some warmth.

"Frank," he said as he approached us. "Bad bowel movement look better than you."

"Yeah, Frank," I added. "You okay?"

Lusby looked from Zoltan to me and then back again. "I'm not okay …." He paused, looked around. "In any case, unlikely there will be any listening devices in the main dining room."

"Guess you've heard from Fitz-Hugh too," I told him.

"Oh yeah," Lusby shrugged.

"It hadn't even crossed my mind they would be listening to us."

Zoltan added, "They missing no tricks."

The club maître de showed us to our table, at Lusby's request in a corner away from anyone overhearing our conversation.

Our waitress came. Zoltan ordered the Reuben and a diet Coke. I ordered an unsweetened ice tea and a club sandwich. Lusby ordered a Dr. Pepper and a bowl of chicken-noodle soup.

When the waitress had left, I asked him, "What the hell is wrong?"

"Fell off the wagon last night."

"Awww, Frank …"

"Well, wasn't the first time. Probably won't be the last. But I will keep trying to beat this."

"You okay? Anything I can do? You want to stay at our place a couple days?"

"Or I move in with you, Lusby. You get near booze, I beat shit out of you."

We both looked at Zoltan to be sure he was joking. Frankly, I wasn't sure, and I could see Lusby wasn't either.

"You'd do that?" Frank asked him. "I mean, everything but the beat the shit out me part?"

"Yes. You friend. You save our ass many times. You need help, companion to keep you straight for couple days 'til you okay. Your apartment much nicer than room I rent. We go my place after work. I get a few things, change of clothes. We go to dinner. Go back to your place for night. It all good."

"There you go, Frank," I joked. "Your own personal bodyguard."

Lusby gave us a pained smile, "Unfortunately, it's not my body that needs guarding. It's my friggin' brain. Anyway, I'm here, so that's something. Don't know where I was last night. Last thing I remember is stopping by the pharmacy in my apartment building, the one next to Burnell's Bar and Grill. Apparently, I went bar hopping. Don't know how I got back to my apartment."

"Damn, Frank."

"Lost my car," he told us glumly. "I called the police, told them it was missing. They're on the lookout for it. Kinda embarrassing."

"Jesus ..."

Lusby gathered himself and looked from me to Zoltan. "But that's not why I wanted to talk to you guys—in total confidence."

"Okay ..."

"Wentz and Ramis. I found out what they're up to."

"What?"

"They're enriching themselves."

"What do you mean?"

"With the pharmas."

"They're shaking down the pharmaceutical companies?"

Lusby laughed at me.

"Well, at least I'm cheering you up."

The waitress came with our drinks as we looked at one another.

When she had left, Zoltan asked, "Why everyone getting rich and I still get nothing?"

"You don't want to get rich like they're trying to. Very, very risky."

"What the hell are you talking about, Frank?"

"It's a little sneakier and more sophisticated than direct pay to play, although the effect may be similar," he told us, taking a sip from his Dr. Pepper, bringing it up to his lips with two unsteady hands.

"How more sophisticated?"

"Well, on the front-end Wentz and Ramis are having meetings to solicit the pharmas one by one for the capital campaign. Nice timing, huh? Of course, the companies are super interested and attentive because they all want in on Zoltan's potential discovery." He turned to Zoltan, "How's that going by the way?"

Zoltan shrugged, "You know, in medicine things never simple, never easy. Some patients in trial doing amazing, others not. Not surprise. Cancer cells in each person express selves differently, so treatment has to account for that. We end up having to design cure for each person. Big bitch to do that. Slow everything down, not always work the way we hope it would. A few patients get worse. So, now we need to figure out how to speed up process and improve results. But I just tell you none of this. Do not be like Ramis, who blab everything. You need to be not telling anyone this. We still working on solutions."

"Got it," Lusby acknowledged. "Can't say I'm totally surprised either."

"We just be persistent and try to be smarter, in-no-vative," Zoltan said, as if he was quoting from something he had read. "We close, but…" he shrugged again. "Some days we seem…" he paused, shaking his head.

"Well, may the gods be with you," Lusby encouraged, and then continued, "In any case, Wentz and Ramis's solicitation of the pharmas is, cleverly, if I do say so myself, not for direct research, which would look a bit like pay to play. It's for a multiyear gift to the Campaign for Progress, the basic message being that Sessions wants them to be long-term believers in the university and the medical center, the whole Global University concept. They're asking the companies to invest in Sessions's future.

"What they are inferring, without it being said, is that such a gift or pledge would make the pharmaceutical company a major stakeholder in the university and thereby would possibly give them an unspoken and unacknowledged priority status when it comes to selecting a future partner for Zoltan's and other future discoveries." He paused to let this information sink in.

"So, now you know the genesis of the Allogenic pledge. Allogenic bought into Wentz's and Ramis's pitch and think their $50 fifty million pledge will give them a leg up, which it probably will, plus with Stanhope Barrett being a board member it makes him look good as hell as a believer in Sessions and as a true leader. Of course, Allogenic tricked us a bit with the terms of their pledge. It doesn't actualize until their stock goes up 25 percent. They aren't stupid."

Both Zoltan and I said nothing, our expressions indicating that this was the first time we had heard this news about Allogenic.

"Man, this doesn't sound like a level playing field," I said, thinking back to our conservation with Mark Berger.

"Because it isn't."

"How do you know all this?"

"I did all the background research, wrote the script and did the briefing and rehearsal for each of their meetings."

"Oh, ..."

"I do what I'm told. That doesn't mean I have to like it. And it doesn't mean I can't share a very deep confidence with a few folks I care about."

"You savior," Zoltan told him.

"Yeah, I don't know. The ol' Titanic here may go down lock, stock and barrel on this one."

"How are their pitches working?"

"Oh, the other companies besides Allogenic are saying all the right things and taking the request under consideration. They have their own bureaucracies and decision-making apparatuses to deal with. So, Allogenic is ahead of the game and of course we're not telling the other companies about the terms of their gift, just that it's a $50 million pledge. So, the other companies are all very well aware of it. Not happy about it. In any case, they've got to figure out whether they want to ante up now and possibly be part of the first tier of companies considered for bringing Zoltan's and the discoveries of others from benchtop to bedside or whether they risk potentially losing out on billions in profits. Given the cash flow of these monsters, it shouldn't be a tough decision."

"But what you've told me about just now—I mean, it's clever brinksmanship. It'll be damn effective, but Wentz and Ramis aren't benefitting personally, they're just doing their best on behalf of Sessions."

Our lunch orders arrived. Lusby took another two-handed sip of his Dr. Pepper, placed it carefully on a university-seal napkin and looked at each of us, his expression knowing and grim.

"Okay, what else?" I asked.

"They have a lawyer ..."

"Wentz and Ramis?"

"Yeah. Who acts surreptitiously as their agent, US-based but who works through a shell company out of the Caymans on their behalf."

"Jesus Christ ..., well, that explains Ramis sitting across from Wentz at the cabinet meeting instead of beside him like with Fitz-Hugh. He wants to appear to be completely independent of Wentz."

"Oh yeah. Interesting that you picked up on that too. No one else did."

"So, they have this lawyer?"

"Yeah. In their meetings with the pharmaceutical companies, once they've made their pitch for a gift to the capital campaign, Wentz and Ramis then extoll this lawyer as an expert in the field of structuring corporate/university business relations—wink, wink. Then she gets in touch with each pharmaceutical company, pitching herself as an advisor/consultant/lobbyist, letting it be known or inferring that she has an inside line into our university.

"So, a few of the phamas have arranged for her to be paid handsome monthly retainers for her 'advice.' And it isn't as if she's not playing a role, providing the companies with inside information she gets from Wentz and Ramis. So, Zoltan, I wouldn't be too forthcoming if I were you."

"I not be. I not trust them from beginning."

"So, the lawyer, she gets a percentage of the monthly retainer, the rest is split between Wentz and Ramis. Over time they're all gonna make a couple million each, especially from whatever company or companies get access to our research discoveries. The payoff will likely continue, if not increase."

"The companies all bought in?"

"A couple of the biggest. And Allogenic."

"I think I'm gonna be sick."

"Join the club. It's enough to drive a man to drink."

"Frank, how you know all this?" Zoltan asked.

"Well, ... one of the things I've learned in consulting is that it pays to be nice to everyone. So, I'm even nice to the maintenance guys—go down to basement once in a while and just shoot the shit. They're good guys. Never know what you might learn. So, I went down there recently and while jawing with them noted how pathetic our antiquated phone system is and that I was concerned that it could be hacked. They completely agreed and even went on to say how it could be done. Funny, they didn't catch on that it might already be taking place. I mean, if you're a spook and you want hack a landline, what better landline to hack than Wentz's. And because of their technology, they can do it after the landline goes to digital, like they all do these days. For someone like me, it's still relatively easy to tap into someone else's lines, particularly if you're in the same office suite.

"So, one weekday evening I worked late. Got on a hardhat with a light on it that the guys downstairs leant me to supposedly help me fix a plumbing problem in my apartment. Took my tool kit, a spool of phone line and *voila*! Working in the dark like some little Disney dwarf—*Hi-ho, Hi-ho*—between the time the cleaning crew left and security arrived to close up our offices I very carefully hooked up a connection from Wentz's private line to my office.

"It was an absolute bitch laying the phone cable. The damn administration building is filthy. I had to very carefully route the new line under the Persian rug in Wentz's office, around the door sills, tucking the line between the carpeting and baseboards in the outer office and hallway. Dust and dirt everywhere. Took forever. Friggin' awful.

"But now, unbeknownst to him, I am recording Wentz's private conversations. Got a voice-activated digital recorder stuck in my desk door where I used to keep the George Dickel Private Reserve." He laughed hollowly. "Maybe I should become a spook. I could call Ursula, ask her where I sign up."

"Not funny, man," I told him, wishing like hell he had not brought up Ursula. "Aren't you worried about getting caught?"

Lusby shrugged, reached over, picked up his spoon, plunged it into his soup and brought a quavering spoonful up to his mouth, chewed, swallowed awkwardly and said, "I don't know," he said with a pathetic, sardonic grin, "If they found out what I'm doing, they could always let it be known over our US-spook-tapped phones that yours truly is a fucking blabbermouth about last year's Kravitz death. Then what would happen?"

"God, I don't want to think about it."

"Yeah, neither do I. But in any case, I've been taping Wentz's private phone calls. Probably not legal, but each week I download his conversations onto a thumb drive and stick it in in a safe deposit box. You mind if I share a key to the safe deposit box with you guys? The box is located in the Safe Deposit and Trust University Branch on the corner of University Boulevard and Sessions Avenue.

"Oh shit, Frank."

"You really getting paranoid, Lusby," Zoltan added, concerned.

"There's no one else I can trust."

"I help you," Zoltan said and held out his massive hand.

"Aw, damn," I heard myself let out a large sigh. "Aww, crap. Well, we've been through a lot together. Okay."

Hell, I thought, now I could worry doubly about boogie men coming after me, US spooks, maybe even pharma mercenaries.

From his suit pocket Lusby pulled out two keys, each stamped with the box number and on a Safe Deposit and Trust key fob, and palmed the first over to Zoltan and the second to me. It was warm in my hand. I stuck it in my suit pocket, imagining it might start burning a hole in it.

"One more thing …"

"You haven't ruined our day enough?"

Lusby sighed, then absently, dutifully, ate another spoonful of soup while staring at our white tablecloth.

"The Washington, DC meeting …"

"Yeah?"

"The keynote speaker is going to be Fitz-Hugh."

"Damn, are you sure? Why would they do that? How come I haven't heard about this?"

"Just happened this morning. Back by popular demand, that is, to continue to fake the smooth transition to Wentz, purportedly to get Fitz-Hugh's inside perspective about the international scene—and let's face it, he's already being groomed for future roles in this administration or in ones to come."

I just shook my head. Ambition is at its essence a behavioral form of cancer, immortal and relentless, ever increasingly aggressive, resistant and rogue. So, what does our noble university do in the face of such a contagion? Fosters it for its own benefit.

"And another thing, don't be surprised if Ursula somehow shows up."

"You're kidding."

"Nope."

"That be interesting," Zoltan remarked. He looked to me, "You need to keep it zipped, Thomas."

"Don't I know it."

I asked Lusby. "How is that possible with everyone on the planet wanting to interrogate her?"

Lusby shrugged. “It’s possible. I don’t know how, but it is.... Maybe with an alias? Diplomatic flight? Who knows?”

“Shit.” I felt totally conflicted. Fear, anxiety, and to my surprise and chagrin, lust. At least, thanks to Lusby, I could prepare myself.

X

Night Calls

THE REST OF the day proceeded uneventfully as I finalized my report draft and before leaving sent it to Wentz in an email as a draft for review.

On the way to Schossler to pick up Tommie, I wrestled with how to explain Janet's and my morning conversation with Ms. Olin and Mr. Diamond to Sarah and Tommie. I was at a loss on how to proceed. Finally, I decided that it would be best to wait until Janet returned before talking with them. At least together she and I could talk the whole situation over, craft the best explanation and present a united front.

It was almost dark by the time I reached the school. Tommie was huddled in his winter jacket at the school entrance, his backpack at his feet, one of the last children to be picked up.

"Geez, Dad," he said, as he got into the car, "I thought you'd *never* get here."

"Yeah, sorry, did the best I could. Traffic was terrible."

"I'm starving."

"Me too. Here ..." I pulled out of my jacket pocket a power bar I'd had the foresight to buy from one of the administration-basement vending machines, knowing that hunger could frequently cause him to go off the rails even more than normal, and handed it to him.

"Aw, thanks!" he said, as he snatched it out of my hand and tore at the wrapper.

"Did you guys meet with Ms. Olin this morning?" His words muffled by his mouthful of power bar.

"Yeah, we did."

"What about?" Interesting that now he was curious. Mr. Diamond must have mentioned it to him.

"Just to catch up on your progress. You seem to be doing better this year."

"Yeah, I really like Mr. Diamond. I'm having fun in his class and he lets me use the computer for different assignments, so when I do that it doesn't seem so much like school work."

"That's great." Wow, I thought. A normal conversation. Have to tell Janet about this.

Sarah had just parked and was walking into the house when we pulled into the driveway. She turned around and walked to my window.

I rolled it down as Tommie got out of the car.

"I just called in pizza," she told me. "Hawaiian Tropical with chicken."

"Okay, you and Tommie get the table set and everything ready. I'll make the pickup."

I watched as they went into the house, then backed out the driveway and drove to the village shopping center. Christmas decorations were already up, Christmas lights on the light poles, each store with Christmas lights, fake wreaths and snow in the windows. The pizza place was near the grocery and the entrance to a small mall of different shops. Our order was ready.

As I left, balancing the pizza carefully as I pushed open the metal door, a woman sitting on a sidewalk bench seat stood and greeted me, "Thomas!"

I did a double take before I recognized her. Alicia McDonald. Tight, worn jeans, a ski parka, beige wool pullover hat with penguin imprints, her blond hair flowing from it over a thick, fisherman's-knit scarf; a red, wool-knit sweater; and black boots with winter soles.

"Uh, hi.... What are you doing here?"

"You have a minute to talk?"

"A minute maybe. Starving children at home. Cold pizza's not going to be popular."

I thought, *Okay, what's worse? Sitting at a table in the village mall where one of our neighbors or Sarah's friends might walk by, or in my car where in this day and age it was possible that I could be falsely accused of sexual assault, a laughable idea given the interior dimensions and obstacles in a BMW 3-Series.* "Let's sit in my car."

We walked across the drive into the parking lot.

"What a nice BMW, an E36 M convertible. They're becoming collectible."

"You like cars?"

"Love 'em. My father collects vintage and classic cars. About the only time I ever saw him, when he took me along when one of his cars was going to win an award. But that's another story."

I put the pizza in the back seat and we got in. The car instantly filled with the smell of fresh pizza and I could feel gastric juices begin to flow.

We turned and faced one another. Strangely intimate, felt like high school.

"What the hell are you doing here?" I asked her.

She shrugged, smiled. "I followed you, a skill they teach in my profession. You didn't see me, did you? I was parked down the street from your house."

"No, I never saw you. Congratulations. But what the hell. Why are you following me? Don't you have better things to do, something else going on in your life that's way more important than traipsing around following a nobody numbskull like me, say a boyfriend, fiancé? Or are you married?"

She looked at me, amused, "No, I'm utterly unattached, Thomas. Unfortunately, men seem to: a.) find me intimidating and b.) find my very transient employment and hours do not make for a very stable or even available relationship. Not a great formula for romantic success."

"Yeah, I can see that."

"Occasionally I envy folks like you, with kids, settled into a suburban lifestyle."

"Don't. It's not that settled, believe me."

She ignored my comment. "Thomas, could I ask you a question or two, unofficially, not part of our work for the Kravitz's? Is that okay?"

"Well, yeah, I guess, depending on the subject."

"Some things have happened at Blaylock that I wanted your perspective about."

"Why would I know anything about your company or have any perspective, or for that matter, interest?"

She ignored my question. "Blaylock is a privately held firm of about seventy detectives and support staff. Our founder, Gregory Blaylock, is in his mid-sixties and still very much running the show."

"Okay …" I acknowledged with a puzzled tone.

"Recently he has, or rather we have, received two almost simultaneous inquiries about whether the agency might be for sale."

"Well, good for Mr. Blaylock. I hope that works out for him, you and your colleagues."

"It's not quite that simple. The first inquiry is from an M&A specialist who's inquiring on behalf of a yet unnamed US conglomerate that apparently feels Blaylock would be a good addition to their portfolio as well as provide ongoing service to their companies."

"Umm, hmph …"

"Would you have any idea who this might be?"

"No."

"Thomas, I can tell when you're lying. I mean, it's kind of endearing. I can understand why Emily Sayzak finds you so attractive."

"Oh, Jesus."

"Sorry. The second offer's from abroad through an investment bank on behalf of one of their clients. We're not sure about the entity, whether it's a business or an individual."

"What country?" I asked as neutrally as possible.

"Germany. Why did that make you start to grin before you caught yourself?"

"Oh, nothing really. Just it would seem that some people or companies in Germany, given everything going on there, might need your expertise," I shrugged, thinking I'd better can this kind of lying before I backed myself into a corner.

"Thomas, you know something."

"No. Wish I did. Thanks. But why are you telling me all this?"

Alicia looked me over, a bold look from a beautiful woman. While in full force denial, I couldn't deny feeling attracted to her in spite of all my internal alarm bells going off.

"So, here's the very strange part of this," Alicia continued. "In both cases, Gregory's been told to name his price."

"Wow, lucky man."

"Don't you think that's a little odd?"

"Would seem so. The pizza's getting cold."

"Can't you help me out here?" she reached across and placed her long-fingered hand on my forearm. *Not fair,* I thought. "Thomas, we—*I* could really use your help if you know anything. It seems everyone trusts you and talks to you."

"Yeah, my friggin' curse." I looked at her, glanced down at her hand. She withdrew it.

"You have no advice for me?"

"Hmmm, okay, I have one word of advice for you, you alone, personally."

"I'll take that as a compliment."

"Take it any way you want—resign."

"What? You're not serious?"

"Totally serious. Get the hell out of there. Tomorrow. Don't look back. Find another agency or something else to do, but get the hell out of there. I'm serious."

"I can see that. The clear impression I'm getting is that the stakes involved here are quite high. Let me ask you this, why haven't you taken your own advice?"

"Contravening circumstances. Life gets way more complicated when you have a family. I gotta go. Pizza's now cold. Kids are hungry. I am too. Takes time for the oven to warm." I laughed a short laugh. "A family crisis is at hand .... Alicia, I appreciate your seeking me out, but understand this, I'm no good to you beyond what I've just said, so I hope you and Emily can leave me the hell alone from here on out .... Please."

She laughed her beautiful, pealing laugh. "We'll certainly think about it, Thomas." She opened the passenger door, got out, leaned back in. "Have a good evening."

"You too," I told her, while I thought, *Ignorance is fucking bliss.*

I was no more than a couple hundred feet down the road when my cell phone rang. Lusby. I felt myself roll my eyes.

"Yeah?" I answered. "On a rush to get home with pizza. Make it quick."

"They found my car," he told me, still subdued.

"Oh, good."

"It was parked right outside my apartment building. Apparently, I never used it on my little misadventure."

"Weird."

"Yeah, I must have just hailed a cab and headed downtown."

"Umm hmm."

"What are you up to?"

"Bringing the kids cold pizza. Mix up at the pizza place. Janet's in Chicago at a conference."

"Okay. Enjoy your dinner. And thanks again for being so supportive."

"You're welcome, Frank. Take it easy, will you?"

"You don't have to worry about that. Zoltan and I are already at the apartment. We had a nice dinner at the Chadwick. Getting ready to watch the Notre Dame game. Got my good luck gold helmet on. Seltzer water is my drink of choice."

"Good for you." I felt myself smile as I thought about him sitting in his apartment living room in his easy chair with the TV on, watching the Notre Dame game and wearing his gold helmet,

Zoltan enduring the game, football being a game he didn't follow, having grown up playing soccer.

We hung up.

Tommie and Sarah practically pounced on me when I entered the family room from the garage.

"What took you so long?" Tommie half-shouted.

"Ah, they mixed up our order, said I had to wait for it when the whole time it was sitting on the counter. I'll put it in the oven and warm it up."

"Forget that, Dad," Sarah said, "Let's just eat."

Dinner was composed of carnivorous and predatory mouth sounds and mild grunts of pleasure. No conversation. A satisfied throwing of paper remnants into the pizza box and Sarah swiftly taking it out to the garage and putting it in the trash.

Afterwards, Tommie went up to his room and Sarah tuned into a National Geographic program on sea otters. Both in school and now college she had rarely had to do any after classes work. She took care of any assignment in the library, plus she seemed to file in her memory everything as it was taught.

I busied myself in the den, checking my email then unobtrusively as possible made my way to the garage as if I had some task I needed to do using my work bench.

In the garage I grabbed a roll of masking tape off the peg board over the work bench, sat in the driver's seat of my car, opened the glove box and pulled out the instructions for the burner phone. I took the safe deposit box key Lusby had given me from my suit jacket pocket and carefully taped it onto the back of the instructions.

I decided that Berger needed to know what I had learned from Alicia.

Then I thought about what Lusby had told me at lunch about Wentz and Ramis and decided it was best to leave that to Lusby to disclose at a time of his choosing.

Better that Berger learn it from Lusby firsthand rather than me betray a confidence.

I went back into the house and told Sarah, "I realized on the way back from the pizza place that I'm almost out of gas. Going up to the village to fill her up."

Distracted, "Okay, Dad."

I put my cell phone on mute and placed it in the front hall table drawer, went back out to the garage, retrieved the first cell phone from the glove box, placed it under the rear wheel and once in the car, backed over it, to the satisfying sound of crunching plastic. I pulled forward, scraped up the remnants of the cell phone and threw them in the garbage can, then headed for the reservoir, the second cell phone lying in the center console, Berger's number dialed, waiting for a push of a button.

Once I was driving around the reservoir, I picked up the phone and activated the number. As usual, Berger answered on the first ring, "Howareyah?"

"You in Boston?"

"Nah, My-Yami. Warmer down here."

"Good."

"So, what's up?"

I breathed out a long sigh. "Been one of those days."

"Yeah? Seems like that's all there is these days, huh?"

"You got that right. So, tonight Janet's out of town at a conference and I went our local shopping center for pizza for me and the kids and who should follow me there?"

"I have no idea."

"The detective from the Blaylock Agency who interviewed me."

"Interesting. Why?"

"So, she tells me that Blaylock has receive two simultaneous name-your-price offers to buy the firm."

"Two? Fuck."

"One's being made through an investment bank. They don't know whether the bank is representing an individual or a corporation."

"Hmm …"

"The bank's in Germany."

'Ahh—or whether the bank might represent a spook holding company for a US covert agency. Ursula could be a busy girl."

"Yeah. The thought had occurred to me. Then the second is from an M&A specialist for an unnamed US conglomerate. I figured that was you."

I could picture Berger smirking. "Beats me. No one ever tells me anything."

"Right."

"So, she wanted your perspective?"

"Oh yeah."

"They know you know things."

"That would be the inference."

"But they don't know what."

"Right."

"What did you tell her?"

"To get another damn job."

"Hah. That's good. Think she'll listen?"

"I have no damn idea. She's her own woman about five times over. Force of nature."

"Okay, man. I appreciate the call. Complicated situation but thanks to you, probably one we can handle." He sighed. "The things I do for my alma mater."

"I for one am very thankful."

"Yeah, appreciate it. Now, I gotta go. Ciao."

I turned off the phone, carefully placed it back in the glove box, drove to the village gas station and filled up. Back home, I retrieved my cell phone from the hall drawer, joined Sarah and watched TV with her for a time.

After ten I was half falling asleep, so I stood and started upstairs for bed when the landline phone in the kitchen rang. I thought, probably a sales call, and then thought again, it's late, walked into the kitchen and looked at the number. Local. Did not recognize it. Instinctively, I picked up the receiver.

"Thomas?" a pleasant, southern voice inquired. A pleasant

southern voice that hinted of inebriation. “I was hopin’ I would find you home.”

“Who’s this?”

“Florence Wentz.”

“Oh, hi Florence, how can I help you?”

XI

A Matter of Circumstance

SCHOOL PREPARATIONS FOR Tommie the second morning of Janet's trip went smoothly. Sarah was on a college schedule now and routinely slept in. I set the alarm for a half hour early and was able to feed Sparky and give her some time in the back yard as well as persuade Tommie to eat some oatmeal and fruit and take his medications before heading off to school, where we arrived on time without him forgetting his back pack.

At the office, just as I sat down in my desk chair with a mug of coffee, the university phone rang in short bursts. I rolled my eyes and picked up the receiver.

"Front desk, Dr. Simpson," the atrium receptionist told me. "There's a Dr. Vastag here to see you."

"What?"

"For your off-campus appointment."

"Um, okay. Tell him I'll be right down."

"Thank you."

I was completely flummoxed. What the hell was this about?

I threw on my suit jacket, grabbed my overcoat and headed to elevator.

When the doors opened on the ground floor, Zoltan was there waiting for me. Behind him, the security guard was eyeing him warily.

"Ah, hello Thomas," he greeted me pleasantly. "You surprised I'm on time?"

"Uh, yeah ..."

"Well, let us go," he said, turning and walking toward the entrance.

I kept my mouth shut and followed him.

Outside we walked toward a white van parked with both passenger side wheels up on the concrete curb, the few students, faculty and administrators looking askance at it as they walked by.

Zoltan leaned over to me, "We must move quickly. I must have your help. You must drive. I almost get killed and kill others driving here from medical center. First time I drive in over twenty years. No license."

"What the *fuck* are you talking about?"

"Frank dead."

"Frank? Lusby? Oh my God, no. What happened?"

"No time for upset, Thomas. You drive over to Lusby's place. I explain."

In the van I was in shock, in suspended animation as I adjusted the seat forward and realigned the mirrors, started the van, pulled it off the curb and drove toward the university's back exit where I could drive to University Boulevard through the park and then to Frank's apartment building.

"Whose van is this?"

"From medical center. I borrow it."

"You took it without anyone knowing?"

"No. Early this morning I take cab to medical center. When van pool office open, I there and tell van pool attendant I need van for morning. He know me. He hungover. Just shrug and give me keys."

"What the hell happened last night?"

"Frank go to bed after stupid football game. He fine, just tired from night before and stress of the day. I stay up and watch movie, then go to bed late.

"I asleep and suddenly I wake up from noise. I recognize sound is vial of pills dropped on Lusby's bathroom floor. No other sound like that. Suddenly I totally awake because I realize, I sure that it not Lusby in bathroom. Don't know how I know this, but I do.

"Very quietly I get out of bed. My door open to living room. You know apartment. Lusby's room down hallway across living room from me, bathroom on right, door to bathroom off hallway and also have door into his bedroom. It dark except for streetlights shining in through living room window.

I sneak across living room, down hall. Heart pounding. Just as I get to bathroom door, guy inside bathroom come out fast and run into me. Just reaction, adrenaline rush, I shove him hard back into bathroom. He fall backwards, crack head on bathtub, out cold.

"Don't hear nothing from Frank's bedroom. Go check on him. Turn on light, check all his vitals. He dead. Gone. He lying there very peaceful. Gold helmet on bedside table beside half-empty bottle of Jack Daniels. Very sad. Nothing to be done.

"I go back into bathroom, turn on light. Guy who's knocked out is wearing all black, black ski mask, black gloves, was carrying a small black bag with draw string. Bag now on bathroom floor. I pull off mask. He ugly fucker. Check him over. He very muscular. Don't want to ever mess with him. I get small bag off floor and I check in it. Roll of adhesive tape, small flashlight, cotton balls, large, partially empty medical bottle of liquid, print label on it says fentanyl, not prescription label, and syringe in plastic box. I open medicine cabinet. Unmarked vial of pills in there, other normal things—antacids, Motrin, band-aids, dental floss—normal stuff. I pick up vial of pills, check it. There are pills inside. I sure they opioids. No prescription. Bottle is clear orange plastic, small chip out of bottom, from where it hit floor. Look on floor. Beside base of toilet is matching plastic chip. Right away, I see what going on. This guy a spook sent to kill Frank. He inject Frank with enough fentanyl to kill him. He then put vial of opioid pills in medicine cabinet to look like Frank self-dosing. Put half-empty bottle of booze on bedside table. I sure opioid pills have fentanyl in them so it look like Frank bought pills and didn't know that. Only problem is that in the dark, even with flashlight spook drop vial. Not know I in guest room. Big mistake.

"I think back. When we park car around the block after dinner, I go for walk, so I enter building after Frank. Spook probably watching. Not figure out we together."

"God damn," I heard myself exclaim. "I can't believe this." I had driven through the park and reached University Boulevard, took a right toward Lusby's building.

"Why would they kill him? Who killed him?"

"I think Frank blab about Kravitz. Maybe last night when he drunk. They probably shadowing him.

"So," Zoltan continued, "I think for a while about what to do and eventually come up with plan."

"Yeah?" I could hear my voice quaver.

"If I call cops, any other authority, odds are all hell break loose, whole thing unravel, blow-up, international scandal, Emily Sayzak see to that, secretary of state, Fitz-Hugh, all of us, families, university, all of us be badly damaged or worse."

"Yeah, you're right there."

"So, here what I do. I inject guy with left over fentanyl."

"You WHAT?"

"I kill him."

"YOU KILLED HIM?"

"Yes."

"OH FUCK!"

"Thomas, do not be drama queen. You must understand something."

I was speechless.

"Zoltan long know Grim Reaper. He and I in many ways work together. How many people die because of what I do, not do or who die of own causes under my care? Many. From ones who die and from ones who live, we learn from both. That what science all about. My involvement with Reaper not one I like, but one that just part of what I do, who I am. Normal for me in my profession.

That I do his work for him last night, a matter of circumstance. And Thomas …"

"What?" I heard myself answer, startled, shocked. This was my best friend talking.

"This spook guy, he assassin. He kill Lusby. Could be he one who kill Kravitz."

"You think he could have killed Kravitz?"

Zoltan shrugged. "It possible. But one thing sure. He alive, he kill again. Now he will not. He will disappear."

"Disappear?"

"Yes."

We had reached Lusby's building.

"See alley there?" Zoltan said, pointing to the alley by the building's side. Pull in."

"Okay."

The alley was small and short, a loading dock and an array of garbage cans at its end. On its right, the brick wall of the apartment building, windowless, wet and algae covered, rose up for several stories. On the left, the wall of the adjacent apartment building did the same. The light in the alley was diffused, greyish. Dank, garbage-smelling air penetrated the van cabin.

Zoltan turned to me. "Pull up to door there. This where spook come into building. No cameras. Door lock still taped. You back van up to door, open back doors. Okay? I be back in a minute. Last night I straighten up, wipe down quickly everything in Frank's apartment, make my bed, gather my stuff into plastic bag I bring with me. Make it look like spooks wanted, that Frank die in his sleep. Poor Frank still there. Folks at Sessions will miss him very soon and call him, then call apartment building. That why we must move fast, just in case. Because of alcohol problem, nobody be surprised he die like that. Hope normal notifications and procedures made with family, his company and funeral home. No reason to involve cops or anyone else. But if unlikely happen, then what do cops or anyone else find? That Frank self-medicating. Got pills laced with fentanyl, plus he a drinker. Double whammy.

And if they search for DNA, they find me. I colleague who been to Frank's before. No one know otherwise. Don't think it will come to that. If they find trace of other guy, what will that tell them? Nothing. If agent, then maybe he not exist. His identity wiped clean."

"Jesus ...," was all I could muster as a response.

Zoltan left through the alley door. I pulled forward and then backed the van up to it, got out, opened the rear doors and got back in. A few minutes later in the rearview mirror, I saw the building door open and Zoltan emerged, his back to me, pulling hard in separate tugs a knotted bedsheet with the body in it, his plastic overnight bag tied to his belt swinging like a pendulum with each effort. He pulled the bedsheet to the back of van and heaved it onto the floor, where it landed with a loud thump, then slammed the back doors shut. I waited for a moment for him to remove the tape from the lock. He vaulted into the passenger seat, holding his plastic bag. I shifted the van into drive and we headed out the alley.

"Next traffic light, plug 120 Forrest Street into your phone GPS. I show you where to go once we there."

"Zoltan," I asked him, as I realized I was beginning feel nauseous, as the faint, odd smell of the corpse, body odor and hint of feces, came into the front section of the van and I rolled down my window, "what the hell have you gotten me into?" Cold air came blasting into the front of the van, but it was better than the smell.

"Ah, Thomas, this all terrible, but be over soon and no one will know."

"I'LL KNOW!"

"Hmmm, yes."

"What the hell are we going to do?"

"Ah—as I think in Lusby's apartment, I frisk this man. He have no identity on him. So, we need cadavers at medical school. That where we take him now. To metal tray among shelves of others in refrigerated embalming room. I fill out paperwork for him. That not justice for this man?"

I shook my head. It was spinning. "Fuck, man, you just killed a US citizen working for our government. He has a family somewhere, maybe a wife and kids."

"Yes, but he evil, he killer who work for our government who cheat on university, try to use it for black ops, now big cover-up and they not stop at killing us."

"Fuck."

"You not worry. Now they worry. What happened? Agent vanish."

"I don't know. I don't know about anything anymore."

"Thomas, just do what you always do."

I thought about what he had just said, "Yeah, keep my mouth shut. Zoltan, I don't know. I don't know whether I can handle this one. I mean, I'm an accessory to murder now. My best friend is a murderer."

Zoltan looked at me, peeved, as if I was a misinformed teenager.

"No murder. I protect us. Self-defense. In this country, like Hungary, like Russia, China, Latin America, like them all, there is no justice, only injustice. We have in this country only injustice system. We must protect selves, family, maybe university. University I not so sure about. But Berger good man."

I sighed, "Okay, whatever you say," I could see that it would quite some time before I could come to terms with what had just happened and was still happening.

Zoltan looked at me. "You know what else I find?"

I shrugged.

"I find microchip embedded in John Doe forearm. They tracking him. He supervised. He suddenly stop moving, they going to show up at apartment and check things out."

"Shit … wait a minute, wait a minute …. What did you just say?"

"That if he stop moving they going to show up at apartment. Check things out."

"No, no, about supervising. God damn it, Zoltan—that's it, that's it!

"That it what?"

"God, the answer was right in front of us the whole time and we never figured it out!"

"What answer?'

"Ursula! That night Kravitz was killed. She didn't kill him. She was supervising an agent or agents who did. Maybe this same guy! She wasn't just an agent coordinating the black ops project, she was the boss."

Zoltan gave this revelation some hard thought for a moment. His eyes widened, "My God, Thomas, … I think you right."

"God damn it!" I said, as another set of thoughts and emotions came flooding into my consciousness.

"Yes, but back to now," Zoltan said, "Thomas, with John Doe, I cut out microchip with my handy, very sharp switchblade, tape up wound with cotton balls and tape from bag, wipe chip and knife off on sheet, put them and tape from bag in my jacket pocket, then wrap him and all his other stuff in sheet and take it to basement. It now past four in the morning. No one around. Figure I must find place to hide corpse while I go to medical center for van. So, I search around and stuff it behind large travel case covered with dust in dark corner way in back. Then I find door where he entered. I go outside. In alley I take out microchip, double side tape it. I see this done in movie. There is stray dog sniffing around, lifting leg on garbage cans at end of alley. I go over to cans, dog watch me with interest. I open lid, find nice end piece of stale croissant and call him. He come over, cautious but I go on knee and am very nice. He come up for croissant. I stick croissant in my mouth while I scratch his head and while scratching head stick microchip on his belly. Then give him croissant. He run off with it. Maybe that slow up spooks. Follow wild goose or dog chase. Maybe not. Best I can do. If they smart, they stay away."

We drove to 120 Forrest Avenue, a low, dark brick building down the street from the medical center. It was probably an old warehouse that the medical center had bought, like almost everything in the surrounding neighborhood, and converted into a medical facility.

Zoltan directed me to the dark alley beside the building and had me pull the van up to a metal door with keypad on it. He punched a code into the keypad, propped the metal door open, opened the doors to the van, lugged the body in the sheet out, dragged it inside and disappeared for a long time. I shut the van's back doors and then sat in the front seat, my palms sweating and my throat dry. Finally, he emerged.

He opened the door and jumped into the passenger seat, a look of relief on his face. "Well, he spook on a tray. Good place for him to be."

"Jesus, this is no time for humor," I heard myself half-whimper.

Zoltan looked at me. Mild disgust mingled with empathy.

"I come back tonight when no one around and do embalming myself, cleanup forearm wound, make him look like all other cadavers."

"What did you do with all his clothes and stuff?"

"Incinerator."

"Okay."

"Drive van out of alley and get out, catch cab back to university. I drive van back to pool two blocks from here. Try not to have accident. Thank you, Thomas. We do right thing."

I had no response but did as he had asked, parked the car by the curb on Rolling Avenue, the street perpendicular to Forrest and got out.

Zoltan walked around to the driver's door, got in the van and drove off, the van weaving as he made mid-course corrections. Suddenly I felt very alone and insecure.

Fortunately, a cab appeared. The driver told me he had been headed to the line of cabs at the Outpatient Center and was delighted to pick up a fare without having to wait. Twenty minutes later I was back in my office. The time was 11:36 a.m.

I sat down hard in my desk chair, my overcoat and suit coat still on, my arms resting on the arm rests, sitting straight up, and gazed at my cold mug of university coffee, flashbacks of the morning coursing through my mind in quick succession, trying to come to terms with what had just happened, fighting an upwelling of mourning for Frank Lusby. As I sat there in the stillness listening to the faint buzz of the fluorescent lights, the heat came on, spilling out dry, urethane and overheated dust-smelling air from the register above. I thought about calling Janet about Frank but, given how the combination of the suicide of her patient plus Kravitz's death last year had upset her, I decided I should tell her about Frank in person. Plus, I realized I should wait until he was discovered and the news was out. It occurred to me only then that I had my weekly meeting with Wentz at 1:00 p.m.

XII

Playing It Straight

I WILLED MYSELF out of my desk chair and, desperate to be out of the administration building, wandered over to the Student Union and managed a fifteen-minute lunch.

As I sat there chewing on the final bite of my sandwich, my mind drifting, the sudden thought of Frank's recorder flashed into my consciousness. I swallowed so rapidly I almost choked. Once the news was out about Frank's death, someone, a secretary or assistant, would be assigned to remove and pack his personal possessions from his office and send them to Indiana.

Undoubtedly, that person would come across the recorder in his bottom desk drawer, report it and the lines would be traced. Wentz would get the recorder and listen to it. Questions would be raised about who else knew about the recorder and where its other recordings were. It was well known that Frank and I were close. An immediate panic welled up in me.

I hustled over to the administration building and took the elevator to the third floor. My presence caused no notice. I walked along the hallway near the president's office and was relieved to find Frank's door unlocked. Security routinely locked and unlocked office doors daily as a precaution. Thank God, I thought.

In his office I pulled open the bottom drawer of Frank's desk, unplugged the terminals from the recorder. Set it on the desk. Then I pulled the wire from the inside of his desk and took it to where it exited the baseboard and wall-to-wall carpeting. I then jammed it between them in a continuing line so that it was hidden from view. It had only taken several minutes but I found myself sweating profusely from the stress of the situation.

Back in my office, I placed the recorder in my briefcase and breathed a deep sigh of relief. Somehow, later, I'd have to go back and remove the wiring because eventually it would be discovered, but for the moment, I was in the clear.

So, Zoltan and I were now keepers of the secret that could bring down the whole house of cards for the Wentz administration. It struck me that if evidence was ever presented to Wentz of his and Ramis's scheme to enrich themselves, he might very well threaten to blow the Kravitz cover-up. Guilty parties use whatever they can to talk their way out of trouble.

On one hand I needed to get the recordings to Berger, but on the other hand, Berger might very well choose a far different path than confrontation, working behind the scenes for whatever outcome would spare the university.

I spent the remainder of the time before my meeting with Wentz at my desk trying to pull myself together, acting as if today was a normal day at work, answering emails and returning phone calls, reviewing again the draft report to the board of trustees that I had emailed Wentz just yesterday, which now seemed in the very distant past.

When I entered Wentz's waiting area, without looking at me, Ms. Bemis said, "He will see you now."

Today she was dressed in a voluminous, wintry-grey, pleated skirt; a light-grey silk blouse, a white scarf; and a white, knit-wool cap with white, hard-plastic snowflake earrings dangling from her pendulous ear lobes. Clearly, she had missed her calling as a weather announcer for Nome, Alaska. I heard the voice inside of me utter, *I'm going to have to do something about you.* But now was certainly not the time.

Wentz was at his desk in his shirt sleeves, cuffs rolled back, behind him a view of the lower quadrangle, brown grass and bare trees but with the symmetry of the walkways, landscaping and Georgian architecture nevertheless still picturesque.

"Good to see you, Thomas," he greeted me, "have a seat."

As I sat down, I found myself looking at the phone on his desk with its private line and thought, *You mother fucker.* He had been given a once-in-a-lifetime opportunity to lead us, a position of trust to do what was right and noble for our university, to lead us away from scandal into a bright future and instead, like so many others these days, he was just another greedy, lying, ambitious pig at the trough with no genuine regard for anyone but himself.

"Are you here, Thomas?" Wentz asked, with a puzzled expression.

"Oh," I said, startled. "I'm sorry."

"You upset about something?"

"No, no, no … just—I have to pick up Janet at the airport after work and I was thinking of how to best get there."

"I always just use GPS."

"Yeah, I'll probably do that."

"So, to the business at hand."

Wentz had a printed copy of my communications plan in front of him. He glanced at it. Looked back up at me. Smiled. His mischievous smile.

"Well, Thomas, you've disappointed me."

"I have?" I could hear my voice begin to fill with panic-stricken fear followed immediately by a pang of angry self-hatred for being so weak as to now care what Wentz thought. Clearly, I was at loose ends.

"You've managed to produce … I don't use this word a great deal … an exemplary report. I can't even think of anything about it to give you shit about. Frankly, I was looking forward to that opportunity, but…"

"Okay," I replied, relieved, "You had me there for a moment."

"Your crafting separate PR, marketing and communications initiatives tailored for each division, that's really good. The deans are going to luvvvv that, especially the podcast angle. They'll now all begin to believe they're media stars, which would be somewhat hilarious if not for the fucking fact that they'll actually believe it.

I trust your board presentation will be a very succinct version of this?"

"Yeah, I just take the major headings as templates for a power point and drop in bullets for the key parts. Worked pretty well last year."

"Yeah, it did." He paused. I could tell something was troubling him. "So, I've been recently informed by the board that Fitz-Hugh will be the keynote speaker at the board dinner the night before."

"Really?" I said neutrally, as if this was news to me. All this damn lying was wearing me out and I could see no end to it, only more of the same and at an increased level.

"I get where they're going with this. A final closure to his rather abrupt departure last year. Transfer of power and all that. As always, he'll say and do all the right things. Give me a ringing endorsement, but as you can imagine, I'm also not thrilled at the prospect."

"Yeah," I said understandingly. It had to be tough being cold, chopped-liver leftovers to Fitz-Hugh's sizzling chateaubriand.

There was an awkward pause where I could see Wentz was reflecting, looking at me but with other thoughts going through his mind.

"The board is also asking that your pal, Zoltan, be there, given his potential for a big discovery."

I shrugged. "That makes sense."

Another awkward pause.

"I believe you got a call from my wife."

"Yes, I did."

"Let me apologize …"

"No need to. She was just worried about you. Didn't know where you were. I calmed her down a bit. At least I hope I did."

"Yeah, I appreciate that."

His intercom buzzed. We both jumped.

He picked it up, listened to what Ms. Bemis had to say, prepared to touch the blinking line button on his phone, turned to me. "It's John Blakum. You know, the founder of Lusby's firm." He raised his eyebrows. "Wants to talk to me. Immediately."

Wentz pushed the flashing button, "John, how are you?"

He listened to the response over the line, an expression of concern building on his face.

"What's happened?"

I watched as Wentz listened ever more intently to what John Blakum was telling him. "Oh, I'm so sorry. He was a wonderful man, a huge help to Sessions University. This is terrible news."

Small beads of sweat had now broken out on Wentz's forehead. I noticed a tremor in his hand that held the phone's receiver. As he spoke his voice grew ever more breathless.

"Oh my God," he said, reacting to something Blakum had told him. "What can we do to help the family, to help you?"

He listened for a time to the reply.

"Done. We'll do our best. In the meantime, my condolences to you, your company, the family of course. It will be a very sad day here, I can assure you. Thanks. Goodbye."

Wentz hung up the phone, looked at me. "Frank Lusby died in his sleep last night."

"Oh no," I heard myself say as if hearing this news for first time, and the strange thing was that, while I had thought that I would have to manufacture my reaction, it was instead a completely genuine expression of remorse.

"What happened?"

"He didn't show up for work today. We called over there to his apartment building, called his cell phone, didn't get a call back. Called Blakum to see whether they knew something about his schedule or whereabouts that we didn't. They called the apartment building management. Management sent the building attendant up to Frank's apartment. He got no response at the door, so he let himself in. We all know Frank was battling alcoholism. Apparently, he had passed away in his sleep, bottle of whiskey on the bedside table."

"Oh God." The worst feelings overwhelmed me. I felt tears welling in my eyes, beginning to run down my cheeks, put my hands to my face. "He was such a great guy, a great friend," I heard myself blubber. My reaction had taken me by surprise. On one hand, it was understandable. On the other, acutely embarrassing, even as a backwash thought ran through my mind that the black ops agents with Zoltan's assistance had successfully pulled off faking Frank's murder as being from natural causes.

Wentz rotated in his chair and stared out at the scene on the quadrangle to give me some privacy and perhaps to keep his own shock and remorse from my view. We sat there for a minute or two regaining composure.

Finally, he turned around and we faced one another.

"Okay," he said, "Let's end this meeting. We were about finished anyway. Look, about Frank, no publicity whatsoever. Let the firm handle things their way, which I believe will be with no publicity except perhaps a press release to his local papers in Indiana without identifying his present assignment."

"Okay."

"John said they'd figure out a replacement and he would bring that person down for an introduction first week or two in January."

"Sure."

Back in my office I sat in my desk chair and turned to stare out the window while the dry heat and smell of indoor air pollution washed over me, interrupted by phone calls as the news of Frank's demise spread and as Wentz and his office dealt with follow-up and details, calling to keep me in the loop.

The sky, as it had been all morning, was overcast, the air grey, the woods beyond the parking lot bare, the trees still, black silhouettes against the sky, brown leaves at their base, patches of remnant snow here and there.

I was ashamed to work for Wentz. What would I do now without Frank as my advisor, as my friend and as my inside source of everything going on at Sessions?

Where had our leaders gone? Men and women of principle who cared more for us than themselves.

I thought back to the last president before Fitz-Hugh, a man of a different era, Gordon Milton, an avuncular widower and former ambassador who had lived in Stewart House and made good use of it as his on-campus presence, using the house for hospitality that served as a touchstone for his presidency.

In those years, students and faculty often convened there, especially toward the end of the day when the president, nicknamed "Uncle Milt," received them with open gentility, often inviting certain constituency groups to dinner during which topics of the day were debated.

Uncle Milt appreciated all people and tolerated all points of view. He nevertheless was not shy about entering into discussions and expressing his own point of view. Given his background as a political scientist and diplomat, he was able often to make his points with interesting stories or illustrations, sometimes citing events known previously only within the administration under which he served. Even his detractors never missed an opportunity to attend those dinners.

For his part, the former president always had a weekly feel for the pulse of the campus and the topics at the forefront of his constituents' minds. He would often arrive at his office the next day and convene meetings to respond to concerns, issues or thoughts he had heard the night before.

He was a man for all seasons and for all people whose love of and allegiance to Sessions University formed his primary purpose in life, our university's betterment. In those days there was a sense that the university faced its challenges as one institution linked by a respect for all points of view but entrusting its president to decide how to best move forward.

In the modern era, that style of leadership had passed us by, supplemented by short-term raw ambition and self-absorption without scruples.

My cell phone, lying on my desk, rang. I picked it up. Zoltan.

"Hey," I answered, "News must travel fast."

"Yes, I hear terrible news about Frank Lusby. What happened?" he said, playing it straight for anyone listening in on our conversation.

"He died in his sleep apparently. That's all I really know. I was in Wentz's office for my normal weekly meeting when he got the call about Frank from John Blakum. Really shook him up. Everyone's pretty much in shock around here. From what I understand since then, arrangements are being made to transport the body back to Indiana. His firm is handling everything with the family. Wentz has designated Don Powers to attend the memorial service and funeral, which are being held during the Washington board of trustees meeting. Wentz wants no publicity about Frank's passing."

"Yes, that figure. How are you?"

"Not real good. Coming to terms with a lot of things here and at home that I'm not happy about and want to change. Don't want to get into it."

"Yes. I been thinking too. We now need to stick even closer together."

"Yeah. I hear you. I understand you'll be at the board of trustees meeting?"

"Yes, they call me this morning."

"Well, let's get together then. Kristina going to join you?"

"Yes."

"Okay, let me get things straightened away here and at home. Take care, man."

"Yes, I do that. Best to Janet and kids."

"Yep. Thanks."

At 5:00 p.m. I walked out of the administration building, intent on getting to the car and driving to the airport through rush hour traffic to pick up Janet. Sarah had very nicely told me that she would pick up Tommie after school.

The temperature was dropping, my breath streaming out before me, the late afternoon grey and darkness closing in.

Halfway to the lower lot I sensed someone walking behind me, felt my eyes begin to roll and turned, expecting it to be Emily Sayzak.

Instead, … it was Alicia McDonald.

I stopped and turned. She was dressed professionally today in a long, tan, cashmere coat; grey pants suit; heavy tan scarf—her blond hair radiating out over her shoulders from a grey, knit cap. There was a relaxed confidence in her walk—authoritative, edging toward insouciance but not stepping over the line. All in all, pleasant to watch.

"What are you doing here?" I asked her.

"Emily told me at one point that this was the best time and place to find you. I have some good news to share."

I looked at her, felt the emotions of the day take over.

"Are you okay?"

"I'm sorry. You've got terrible timing for good news. A dear friend and colleague died in his sleep last night, was discovered this morning."

"Oh my God, I'm so sorry." One hand went to her mouth in shock. In a gesture of sympathy, she reached out with the other and touched me lightly on the arm. "I can always call you. I wanted to tell you that I followed the advice you gave me."

"Calling me is not a good idea," I told her and started to walk toward the lower parking lot while she walked beside. "What was the advice I gave you?"

"I resigned from Blaylock today."

I turned to her and examined her closely. "This news isn't just some ploy to get me into a talkative mood, is it?"

"My, aren't *we* paranoid."

"Yes, *we* are."

There was silence as I thought about her supposed resignation.

"How'd they take it?"

"Shocked and surprised. Offered me a raise and a promotion to head one of our offices."

"But you turned them down?"

"Yes."

"Why?"

"Thomas, in your car that night I saw the look in your eyes. It scared me. It convinced me that whatever is behind the Kravitz death is very dangerous. I had a sense that you were genuinely concerned for my personal safety. So, I wanted to thank you for your advice. Could we have lunch some time? A thank you."

I thought about her invitation as we walked along. The parking lot and BMW came into view. "On one condition."

"Okay?"

"That we don't talk about the Sessions account or anything connected to it or the university."

"I think I can do that."

"One word, one thought, question, innuendo, anything—I'm walking. Understood?

"Lord, Thomas, I was just talking about a thank you lunch. You need some meds or something?"

"Probably. Look, as noted, I'm really hurting right now. If that's all, great, happy to be thanked.... So, has Blaylock made a decision on being purchased?"

I could see her thinking about a smart reply, something along the lines of why I could ask her questions about confidential matters, but she could not ask me. But then she reconsidered, showed some class and gave me a straight answer.

"Leaning heavily toward the American conglomerate. The German offer after a good deal of research is just more and more shadowy. Something not right about it."

I nodded but didn't provide any affirmation that their decision was right or wrong.

"I've got a board meeting coming up in Washington next week. We'll have to get together after that. Best if we meet somewhere." I thought for a moment. "Annamaria's over on 34th Avenue, just the place where no one will have a clue or care about who we are. Just two colleagues having lunch. Say, Thursday after next, noon. Okay?"

"Sure. Looking forward to it. Sorry about your friend." She came forward, gave me a light buss on the cheek. Her hair carried a faint scent of fresh hay. Then she turned and walked away while I watched her and, of all the damned things, felt myself smiling.

XIII

Reprieve

On the way to the airport in rush-hour traffic the day faded into darkness. Traffic from all directions transformed into tentacles of headlights. The temperature dropped. Light snow flurries drifted aimlessly across my windshield and the convertible top was buffeted by gusts of wind.

Glancing down at my phone, I saw that Janet's flight was twenty minutes late, time enough for me to hang out in the cell phone parking lot, check in on Sarah and Tommie, and once her plane had landed, arrange a pickup along the outside lane at Arrivals.

At the curb we scrambled to get her suitcase in the trunk, our breaths streaming out behind us as we jumped back into the car. After weaving through exiting traffic, once we were on the expressway I looked over at her. She looked tired, a bit hassled and distracted as headlight beams passed over her face. I could also sense her checking me out.

"How are Sarah and Tommie?"

"Actually, everything went smoothly, other than a brief crisis precipitated by a lukewarm pizza from the village pizza joint—they mixed up the order. Tommie ate breakfast, took his meds and was generally cooperative. Sarah was nice enough to pick him up at school today. I just checked in on them. Everything's good. But we missed you. Particularly Sparky."

"Honey, what's wrong?"

I sighed, "It's that apparent, huh?"

"I'm afraid so."

"Okay, I wasn't sure how to handle this, but now that you're here—" I felt myself let out a large sigh, "I have some very sad news to report."

Janet looked at me, worried.

"Frank Lusby died in his sleep last night."

Out of the corner of my vision I could see the shock of this news transform her expression. "Oh my God, no," she told me. "Oh, Thomas, I'm so sorry. I know you thought very highly of him." She paused and I watched as now fear and anxiety crossed her features, "Was it…"

I knew instantly what her thoughts were, "No, no, no—natural causes, if you can call a bottle of whiskey on the bedside table natural. Just one of those things. Everyone at Sessions is in shock. I mean, if you were going to choose someone this would happen to, it would be Frank, but that doesn't lessen the shock and the sadness. Frank was good man, someone who helped me out a lot. It's just terrible that he's passed."

I glanced over at Janet to assure myself that she had not picked up on my lying about Frank's demise, and what I saw from her expression was trauma. There was no other word for it. A cascade of death seemed to be stalking us, and it was bringing Janet, who seemed to have an oversensitivity to it, down. I felt myself sinking inside. There was no way to stop her from reacting this way.

"Back to present," I commented as a way of distracting her, "we need to figure out how we best explain to Sarah and Tommie Schossler's evaluation and recommendations."

I glanced over and I could see Janet tamp down and compartmentalize her feelings about Frank's death. No doubt they would be returning. But for the moment she had shifted gears successfully.

"Okay…. Let's stop by the chicken carryout place in the village and get dinner, talk things over with them at the dinner table. Then be prepared to pick up the pieces." She shrugged. "It is what it is."

"How was your conference?"

Another very different set of expressions crossed her face, puzzling me, "Quite interesting, revealing. We'll have to talk about it at some point when we have some clear space. What's, um… happening with Frank?"

"Being transported back to Indiana. Don Powers has been assigned to attend the memorial service, given that Wentz and everyone else will be at the board meeting in DC next week."

"Okay."

"I've been trying to come to terms with it. It's just left a big empty hole. I hadn't fully realized how much Frank was a part of my life."

"Mmmm …. Not easy, Thomas. I'm so sorry."

"Yeah. Thanks."

On the drive home both of us were quiet, lost in our own thoughts, mine being a rumination that there was no one I could tell about what really happened to Frank. Certainly not Berger. Zoltan and I were in way too deep for that. It was a secret he and I would take to our graves. And then it occurred to me that there was one person I could talk to about his death. I felt myself smile a grim, ironic smile. Ursula. If she showed up at the Washington board meeting, that would be a time to confront her about Kravitz and Lusby and about how long her fellow operatives would cast their reign of terror over us. Feelings of resolve and anger began to overlay the depths of my sadness and bereavement. I felt myself straighten up, pull back my shoulders, which I had not even realized were slumped.

We reached our neighborhood, and having the house come into view gave me mixed feelings. First, a sense of stability and comfort, despite our dissatisfaction with the neighborhood. Second, anxiety, given our upcoming dinner with Sarah and Tommie made all the worse by the terrible circumstances of the day.

Sparky greeted us as we came into the family room from the garage, barking and circling and jumping, deliriously happy at our return, particularly Janet's. Sarah was there, watching the news on TV. Tommie, of course, was not to be seen.

I took Janet's suitcase upstairs and checked in on Tommie, who was in his room on the computer.

"We're home, as I'm sure you could tell."

Distracted, "Yeah, Dad. I could hear Sparky and Mom. What's for dinner?"

"Rotisserie chicken and fixings."

An enthused, "Yeah!"

Downstairs again, I helped Janet unpack our dinner, pop containers in the microwave and oven for reheating and then opened a bottle of white wine while Sarah set the table and poured glasses of water.

Tommie came pounding down the stairs as dinner was being placed on the table, his usual impeccable timing.

"Dad," Sarah said as we sat down at the table, "You look exhausted."

"Yeah, it's been a long day."

Janet and I exchanged glances. No need to tell Sarah about Frank. No need to ever tell anyone.

"So, how are things going at Sessions?" I asked Sarah.

"Good," she said as she prepared to eat a forkful of chicken, "They keep ratcheting up the degree of difficulty with the French."

Janet asked Tommie, "And you, young man, how's school?"

"Mr. Diamond asked—did you talk to me about the meeting you had with him and Mrs. Olin?"

"Uh no," I told him, "obviously we haven't been together at dinner since then."

There was an awkward pause. I deferred to Janet, not only the mother but a respected psychologist, a professional colleague of Schossler Academy's head of school. Plus, I felt that it was possible under the wrong circumstances that I could actually crack—my emotions about the day's horror and potential complications were that close to the surface.

"Well," Janet said, clearing her throat. I thought, *This couldn't be easy, having spent the entire day traveling and confronting a conversation that could split our family apart.*

"It was a very pleasant meeting," Janet told Tommie, "And very surprising in all sorts of ways."

She now had Sarah and Tommie's rapt attention. Eating, day-dreaming, thinking ahead of dissembling ways to disarm any inquiry had ceased.

"You remember a couple weeks ago, Tommie, when you told us that, when it comes to computers and technology, you are smart?"

Tommie shrugged, "Yeah," old news, pushing his mashed potatoes around in swirls.

"And then Zoltan gave you a new computer and equipment because he felt the same way."

"Yeah …."

"Well, that's what Ms. Olin and Mr. Diamond wanted to see us about. They think you're very smart."

I thought, *Well done*.

Sarah put her fork, which she had been holding in midair, on her plate. "Really?" she said incredulously, the notion of Tommie's genius dawning on her perhaps for the first time.

We all looked at her.

She looked at Tommie and said, "Tommie, that's great! Good for you."

Janet and I exchanged a look of gratitude and relief, but with some caution for what was about to transpire.

Tommie was now beaming. "Thanks," he said. Although Sarah rarely criticized Tommie, a compliment from his big sister was rare.

"So, Ms. Olin and Mr. Diamond feel that you are learning so fast and doing so well with computer science and technology that you need some special classes."

"Really," Sarah said, "Wow."

I thought, *Oh, shit, here it comes.*

"What's funny about it is—where do you think they recommend Tommie get additional course work?"

Tommie, I could see, had not a clue. Janet and I watched as the truth gradually dawned on Sarah.

"At Sessions?" she squeaked lightly in disbelief.

"Yes dear, once or twice a week and sometimes during the weekend, some tutoring and also some counseling." I noticed how Janet adroitly skipped over the possibility of summer classes.

Tommie said, suspiciously, "Counseling?"

"Well, there's a lot of responsibility that goes along with learning about computers and technology. They also told us about your little trick on Sharif."

I could see Sarah still processing what we had just told them and was relieved to see her not being angry or upset, at least for the moment. "What trick?" she asked.

"Tommie hacked into the Schossler computer system and changed his and Sharif's grades. He gave himself all As and Sharif all Fs."

Sarah's eyes widened. "You did that, Tommie?"

Tommie looked down, his expression one of shame and pride. Perhaps worse, I could tell he still thought what he had done was funny. "Yeah," he mumbled.

"Hilarious!" Sarah exclaimed, then turned serious, "But, oh Jesus, Tommie, you can go to jail for something like that."

Tommie looked up, disbelief. "Naw …"

"Oh, yeah," Sarah told him, "Against the law, little brother."

Hearing it from Sarah was probably much more impactful that hearing it from either of us.

"Now you know," Janet said, looking to Sarah and then Tommie, "why the counseling is necessary."

Sarah wrestled with this for a moment, made up her mind and said, "Absolutely."

I saw tears come to Janet's eyes and felt my own water over.

"So, you're okay with it?" Janet asked.

"Well, not really, but yeah, okay. I really am having a good time at Sessions and it's not like I'm going to see Tommie when I'm there. Yeah, I can take him to some classes but I'm also not going to be your beast of burden. You guys can't dump all of this on me. I'll do it when it's necessary and," she looked at Tommie, "you have to behave."

Tommie looked at each of us, a puzzled, quizzical expression on his face. He certainly had not fully processed what we were telling him, but I was sure that with the proper encouragement from Mr. Diamond and Ms. Olin that he might begin to see clearly that he was being rewarded, not being punished in some way.

Sarah must have been sharing our thoughts for she turned to Tommie and said, "Tommie, this is a big deal. Your school obviously thinks you're really brilliant or they wouldn't be doing this."

Tommie beamed, his eyelids fluttering and his face ticking.

Later, when the dishes had been cleared and the kitchen cleaned up, the kids having gone upstairs to their rooms and their computers, Janet and I, seemingly by instinct, poured ourselves another glass of white wine and returned to the kitchen table, took our seats and stared at one another quizzically.

"That went much better than I anticipated," Janet said, her voice containing hints of awe and amazement.

"Yeah. What the hell were we so worked up about?"

She shrugged, laughing lightly, "I don't know."

"It's nice to see something in our lives turn out well. Maybe we've done an okay job as parents."

Janet laughed. "Don't be too quick to give us credit. I feel like we've struggled every Goddamned day, don't you? So, let's count this as a happy accident. Give the kids most of the credit on this one, particularly Sarah. I mean, she's always been a good kid, almost too good, but tonight she was over the moon. I really admire her. And maybe there's some hope for Tommie after all."

"I don't know. There always seems to be another shoe that's going to drop, but at least for the moment it seems like we're on the right course, a reprieve." I thought about it all for another moment and added, "Whew!"

Janet laughed, "Yeah, that's right." But I could see her mind already drifting back to thoughts about Frank's passing and felt again the helplessness of not knowing how to prevent it.

We rose, and Janet went into the family room to catch up on the papers and mail while I took my glass of wine into my den, closed the door and sat in my recliner in the dark, thinking about the day that now seemed to have encompassed weeks. I was too exhausted to rest and after a time of replaying the last year and a half at Sessions, thinking of all Frank Lusby and I had been through, I began to sob quietly at his loss. Finally, the sobbing stopped. I collected myself, rose, and went upstairs to bed.

XIV

So Washington

"Is it just me, or is traffic today significantly worse than last year's drive to the Beijing Center dedication?" I asked Zoltan as we sat on I-95 on our way to the board of trustees reception and dinner.

Three uneventful weeks had passed since Janet's return from Chicago. The Thanksgiving break had been good for all of us, with Janet and I able to spend time together, Sarah able to hang out with friends at Sessions and Tommie spending most of his time with his computer. Zoltan had spent his holiday with Kristina in Washington, taking in the museums and opera. Perhaps it was best that we had a break from one another after the tragic events of Frank Lusby's death and that of the agent who had caused it.

The day was overcast, grey and frigid, ghost-like plumes of exhaust rising into the air from the cars and trucks in front of us. We had left early and now were at risk of being late.

Zoltan looked out at the dead-stop traffic, shrugged, "Yes."

We sat there for a time lost in our own thoughts. I was still deeply disturbed by what we had done, and Zoltan knew it.

Traffic began to move, haltingly.

We were meeting Kristina at the hotel. She planned to take a cab there with the dean of the School of Foreign Service. The next day I would attend the board meeting and give my presentation of next year's public relations, communications and marketing plan while Zoltan and Kristina took in a matinee production of *Carmen.*

Zoltan turned toward me, searching for a connection. "How family?"

For the next five minutes or so, with some initial hesitation, I told him about the recent developments since before and after Janet's trip to Chicago, about Tommie and his school, about their declaring him a budding genius and recommending that he take classes and receive counseling at the Sessions Center for Gifted and Talented Youth, about Sarah's mature and even enthusiastic reception of this news, notwithstanding her giving us a warning not to let the burden of Tommie's transportation fall entirely on her.

"Amazing," he commented. "She maturing fast. Good girl. And Tommie, it not surprise me that he smart. Odd yes, forever. Smart, very good."

"Yeah, you can't imagine how relieved we are."

"Good.... How Janet?"

I found myself shaking my head. "I'm not sure. Frank's death hit her hard. Too many damn deaths—her patient, Dr. Compton; Kravitz; now Frank. But ever since she's been back from her conference, she's been... what? She seems less judgmental, less disappointed in me, less subconsciously angry, maybe even a little less depressed. I'm not sure what to make of it." I laughed lightly. "Pretty pathetic when those are the positives in a relationship."

"Ummm, yes."

"Hey."

Zoltan raised his eyebrows.

"Hate to tell you this, but I keep thinking about Frank."

"I know."

"I'm having a lot of trouble with what happened."

"Yes."

"Any advice?"

Zoltan turned to me, utterly serious, and said slowly, emphasizing each word, "Buckle Up Buckaroo."

God damn, I thought, *he's pulling lines on me from watching South*

Park with the kids. "Oh, thanks so much, you fucker. I feel so much better now."

Zoltan smiled his rictus grin. "Like I tell you, sometime shit happen beyond what any of us can figure and you deal with these matters as best you can. Then you go on. Leave it in past."

"I know you're right. But I'm having a lot of trouble with that."

"Yes. Leave it behind because what is coming could be maybe worse or maybe not but you better be ready. Paralysis not option if you want to survive."

I let out a large sigh, "God, I hope it's not worse. Okay, that makes some sense. I'll try to get my head around that."

"Get heart around it. That what count."

"Okay, okay …"

The Tribone was a grand old hotel near the White House built in the early 1900s, reputedly from limestone blocks cut from quarries in Indiana and flat-bedded by locomotive to the nation's capital.

In reading its recent history online I had discovered that it had been purchased five years ago by Berger's hotel division, gutted and renovated over a three-year period during which its exterior and interior were brought back to their original splendor while all its mechanical systems were replaced and additional extensive electrical, HVAC and communications systems were installed.

I pulled up front under the massive portico so we could speed up our arrival by using valet parking while calculating what fictious item I might enter on my expense report to cover it. A bellhop greeted us while the valet attendant took my keys. The bellhop grabbed our bags out of the trunk before we could and hustled us through brass revolving doors onto a lush, carpeted hall of immense proportions. An elegant bar was off to our left where a pianist played under potted palms and guests lingered over drinks and snacks, people walking by us from all directions as the bellhop placed our luggage on a brass, carpeted baggage cart and wheeled it with time-is-money rapidity in the direction of the check-in desk across the hall.

"Thomas! Thomas!" I heard a voice call and felt myself close my eyes and try to wish it away. Emily Sayzak.

I kept walking, following our bellhop. Zoltan looked at me curiously.

She came hustling up beside us, her thick blond hair bouncing, her thin legs moving with chicken-like rapidity. She was wearing a sheer, pearlescent, silk blouse which revealed her braless assets and red stretch slacks so tight they left little to the imagination. She carried a leather portfolio—her pleasant, funny, red-lipstick mouth smiling at me. "You're here! How cool."

"What did you expect," I replied hustling along. I looked at Zoltan and then back to Emily. "This is my colleague, Dr. Vastag."

"Pleased to meet you," she replied, giving him a wave.

"Emily, we're trying to check in. Figures that you're here. Maybe we could catch up later?" I thought, *Not a chance.*

"Okay, sure thing. Bye, Thomas," she stopped and blew me a kiss.

"Jeee-sus," I heard myself say under my breath as Zoltan and I joined the line for registration while our bellhop stood to the side.

"That Emily Sayzak?" Zoltan asked appreciatively.

"Oh yeah."

"Yes, I can see, she big problem. Big temptation."

"Oh yeah."

"Hmm … maybe I do you favor and take her off your hands."

"Right. And what would Kristina say?"

"She not have to know."

"You bastard."

"Yes."

"Be my guest."

"Ah …," he laughed, "much better and more fun she be your problem and I watch you suffer."

"You're such a dear friend … I could puke."

"Mess up expensive carpet."

I didn't bother with a response.

In my room I hastily changed into a suit and tie, texted Zoltan and we met in the lobby five minutes later.

He was still unshaven, coils of grey-black hair springing out from his head, an ominous, mustachioed, hulking figure. He wore new black Levis, a black mock turtleneck and what appeared to be a new, black-and-white, herringbone, sport coat.

"A new sport coat. Wow, you went all out for this occasion."

"Goodwill have super good deals in triple-extra-large."

"Ah …"

As we looked to the front of the hotel, Kristina came through the revolving door. She brightened as she saw us, waved and walked to us in her brisk manner, dressed in a pin-striped, grey, pants suit; white blouse; red silk scarf—intricate gold and red cloisonné earrings drawing attention to her mid-length, blond hair.

"A Belarusian beauty is among us," Zoltan commented as she joined us. They embraced.

She turned to me and we hugged. She drew back, "Thomas, it has been too long. How are the children and Janet?"

"The children, growing up too quickly, I'm afraid. Janet's good, dealing with usual challenges of work and home."

"Ah, yes," she nodded empathetically.

"Where's the dean?"

"He decided to drive, the fool. He let me off and will now be searching for a parking garage endlessly."

"For smart man," Zoltan observed, "he stupid."

"True. But I never said that."

"So Washington," I observed, shaking my head, "A sincere word will never be spoken. Let's go."

The reception was in the Palisades Room, around the back of the elevators, down a long hallway. A young woman I recognized from the special events department sat behind a table set up by the door. We checked in, took our name tags with position titles and our table numbers on them, peeled off their backs, put them on and then stepped into the room.

Florence Wentz, Jack Wentz and Fritz Johnson were there to

greet us and shake our hands—Florence demurely and mildly embarrassed, saying, "It's so good to see you, Thomas."

We smiled at one another. "You too," I said genuinely without a hint of awkwardness or disapproval. I could see that my greeting resonated well with her, that she saw that there had been no offense in calling me at home. At least that's what I wanted her to think.

Wentz shook my hand and drew me closer. "Shadow Fitz-Hugh," he told me, his breath stinking of martini and olives, "I want to know who he's talking with, what he's saying."

"Sure." I thought, *Damned odd request.* Well, hopefully he had only one martini which with his body weight would merely calm his nerves.

Fritz Johnson and I shook hands, gently, as mine disappeared in his paw. He was a big man with a big square head; slicked-back, black-grey hair; a flat, football-injury-indented nose; and a fleshy face—wearing a black suit; stiff, white shirt with a string tie fastened by a big, turquoise and silver clasp; a large black belt with a turquoise and silver buckle; and the requisite black, tooled, cowboy boots.

"Good to see yew, boy. You stayin' the hell outta trouble?"

"God damn, I try, Fritz. Not sure I succeed."

"Haw-Haw. Well, hell, Thomas, *nun* of us is *pur*-fect," he half yelled and slapped me hard on the shoulder, knocking me a bit off balance.

I stepped away and waited for Zoltan and Kristina to finish their greetings. I wondered about Fritz—*How is this guy worth over a couple hundred million dollars?* Then answered myself—*Yeah, it's all an act. He's smart and savvy as hell. This is the guy who negotiated Fitz-Hugh's departure from Sessions with the State Department.*

Wentz greeted Zoltan with sarcasm, "Well, hello, Dr. Nobel, it is such a pleasure seeing you this evening."

"Yes, thank you, Jabba … I mean, Dr. Hutt … Mr. President."

Wentz looked chagrinned and began to redden, Kristina surprised, Florence a bit aghast, Zoltan delighted with himself.

"Now, bouys, you be friendly," Johnson told them, stepping in authoritatively, which straightened them up immediately, "I'll be happy to refer-ree mud-wrasslin' at sum other time."

"Delighted to meet you, dear," Wentz said to Kristina by way of recovery, "I'd ask what might motivate you to accompany such a figure as Zoltan, but that would be impolite, wouldn't it?"

"Zoltan is a wonderful man, President Wentz. I love him very much," Kristina told him directly, linking her arm in Zoltan's.

"Whoa!" I heard myself say out loud.

They all turned and looked at me.

"Sorry," I said, with an embarrassed and guilty expression.

Fritz then marveled at Zoltan's size, congratulating him on his research and greeting Kristina with an appreciative look, all things that I knew would piss off Zoltan even more. I watched as he failed miserably in his attempt to be cordial.

They freed themselves and walked over to me.

"How much this bullshit I have to put up with?" Zoltan asked.

"Very normal, this kind of lovely, meaningless talk and repartee" Kristina told him, amused.

"I need drink."

"You guys go ahead. Wentz has given me an assignment."

Zoltan looked at me questioningly.

"Shadow Fitz-Hugh."

"Ah."

We looked around the room.

There were bars on either side with a divider drawn at the room's end that would presumably be opened at the conclusion of the reception to reveal our dinner tables and a raised dais for the various speakers and dignitaries. Between board members, spouses, select members of the university administration, academic division heads and special guests, I guessed there were some seventy or eighty people there. Hotel waitstaff moved between them offering glasses of red or white wine, taking drink orders and serving hors d'oeuvres.

I looked around to see where Fitz-Hugh might be while a

sudden haunting thought hit me that the room seemed empty without Frank Lusby's presence, that today was the day of his memorial service in Indiana that Don Powers was attending. I felt a stab of remorse that I tucked away just as I spied Fitz-Hugh over in a far corner, a crowd of well-wishers surrounding him, surrounding him and—Ursula. My stomach did a flip-flop and somehow miraculously sank out of my body onto the floor, or at least that's what it felt like.

Just as I turned to walk toward them, someone called out my name.

I turned back, looking to see who it was. A gentleman was approaching us, distinguished looking in a black, three-piece power suit with large, chalk-white, pin stripes; a peacock-blue silk tie; grey, swept-back hair; modern, angular glasses with blue frames; handsome leonine face. I knew him. My memory bank scrambled for a place and context. Last year's board meeting, Allogenic, Stanhope Barrett.

He was all smiles, holding out his hand to me. I shook it as he clasped me on the shoulder.

"Wonderful communications report, Thomas," he told me, his voice a hard rasp. "I can see you propelling Sessions into the stratosphere!"

I thought, *He wants to meet Zoltan, doesn't give a rat's ass about my report.*

"Why thank you."

He pivoted to Zoltan and Kristina. "And this must be our researcher of renown," he complimented and held out his hand, which Zoltan took belatedly and with reluctance. "Stanhope Barrett," he introduced himself. "Our company, Allogenic Technologies, is taking a great interest in your work. I'm delighted to make your acquaintance and commend you on your success to date and its future potential. Say, how is your Phase 1 project coming along?"

"I cannot say."

"Ah, certainly I understand." He paused, placed a hand on his chin, posing as if thinking. "My sense would be, given the many, many trials we have witnessed and even supported financially, that for projects such as yours they never seem to be as simple as they might seem, not that you were not aware of that from the beginning. The complicating fact is, of course, that you—we—are dealing with the human genome and that is in fact an extraordinarily complicated entity, not to mention that each individual's genome is somewhat unique to them, so whereas you might find common typologies and address them, each person may present you with a specific different set of needs for a cure, don't you think?"

"What you say true enough," Zoltan replied noncommittally.

"Hmm, I see. Well regardless, we would love to at some point in the future have the resource and expertise of someone of your caliber representing Allogenic, and it goes without saying that we would reward such a scientist/researcher quite generously, perhaps beyond all that person's imagination. Because that person is on the cusp of presenting a remarkable gift to mankind, the prospective cure, or at the very least, the key to future cures of the scourge of our time—literally a modern world plague. Think of how many lives could be saved! Remarkable. And Zoltan, you are, like your colleague here, a relatively young man. You two could work together on your research's refinement and its promotion over the next decades. Just think of that. In any case, I wish you both every success."

With that, before Zoltan could even reply, he turned on his heel and walked away.

"Thomas," Zoltan said as we watched Barrett head toward the bar, greeting several fellow board members as he went.

"Yeah?"

"He slick motherfucker."

"Yeah."

"But all he say, it just like university. Promises. What happen when he gone? Just like what happen when Fitz-Hugh leave or Wentz or even Ramis. One way or another we little guys fucked."

"Right. Unless you've got a great lawyer and/or a great contract. The two go hand-in-hand, I guess."

"Yes. Right now, I need two great drinks."

"Okay. I've work to do."

A server walked by at that moment and I helped myself to a glass of red wine as Zoltan and Kristina walked away. I took a sip. Wow. A Châteauneuf-du-Pape or something like it. It was clear Berger had spared no expense for this occasion. I took another appreciative taste, letting it bounce around in all my senses. Spectacular. I fortified myself with another sip, snatched a hamster-sized shrimp from a passing server, munched it down.

I turned back toward Fitz-Hugh and his admirers, taking in the group as I approached them. On his immediate right was Maggie Garnet, an alumna, former bank CEO, now head of the Federal Reserve in Kansas City. Her husband Frank owned Garnetvision Communications, a significant cable, broadcasting and media enterprise. Given his business interests and lack of affiliation with Sessions, he never attended these meetings. Maggie was hovering in Fitz-Hugh's aura as if she were his spouse. Fitz-Hugh's spouse, Celeste, even when they were in the US, occupied as she was with billable hours and two adolescent daughters, rarely joined him at these meetings. Now in Brussels with the children, where she continued her work with her law firm and with Fitz-Hugh being the former president, it was a foregone conclusion that she would also not be in attendance. So Mrs. Garnet could move right in, just as she had done at last year's board meeting. Obvious to me at least. I could see too that it was obvious to Ursula, on his left, who was looking a bit baleful, or maybe that was because she saw me coming.

How the hell did people like him, luminaries, get away with this kind of behavior—Mrs. Garnet one night, his good friend Secretary of State Greta Hauser, for all I knew, the next—followed by from what Ursula had told me, maid service, alumni wives, whomever wherever? I found myself shaking my head as I walked up to them.

Among the group was also trustee Senator Egon Maxwell, intent on showing his interest in another kind of surreptitious intercourse, typical Washington, DC stuff where campaign contributions, gratis foreign travel for factfinding purposes and other favors best left unmentioned might well be rewarded by favorable access and legislation.

Mark Berger was there too, part of the circle, as was Father Lanier, the university chaplain and Ms. Beatrice Fontaine, a jade-bejeweled, agate-eyed, on-the-make heiress who had practically pawed my pants off under the table at last year's board dinner.

Fitz-Hugh, as always, was resplendent, dressed in a perfectly tailored, dark-blue suit of the finest wool, white shirt that set off the tan he seemed to have year-round, and what I thought was a nice touch, a Sessions University-seal tie. I recalled that last year his tan came from his golfing on weekends in Naples. Now where did he go? Gibraltar? Mallorca?

He was just finishing a conversation with the senator while everyone listened in and I could tell just from the body language that Senator Maxwell had asked a question, more or less a badly disguised request, that should have been made in a more private setting.

"Egon, my friend," Fitz-Hugh responded perfectly naturally as if no problem existed at all, "Yes, of course, I understand your constituent company's need and certainly I'll do whatever I can to assist their representatives but recognize that to a large degree it's up to them to navigate the EU bureaucracy. I can make some introductions, praise the company in certain quarters, help smooth the way, but the real work is up to them getting to know and becoming conversant with the players. But rest assured, I appreciate your concerns."

The senator seemed mollified. "Thank you, suh," he intoned. "I do surely appreciate your worthy assistance."

I resisted the temptation to roll my eyes and could see around me everyone else reacting similarly.

Fitz-Hugh used my joining the group to move on from Maxwell's request and Maxwell himself. "Thomas!" he greeted me enthusiastically, as they turned toward me, "Wonderful to see you!"

"I wanted to congratulate you on your new position," I told him as we shook hands. "We all miss you at the university."

"Thanks so much," he smiled, seemingly genuinely pleased.

Ursula added a politic, "It is so nice to see you again."

We were all posing and on our best behavior.

"Thanks. Needless to say, Sessions is not the same without you," I told her insincerely.

"Yes, I miss it very much."

I took in her sleek combed-back, styled brown hair accentuating her high cheekbones and strong jaw line. No doubt, she was just as beautiful as I remembered. Perhaps a line or two more around her clear, light-blue eyes. Graphic scenes and sound bites of our love making ripped through my consciousness. It was not difficult to understand how I had so easily succumbed to her.

Berger, in the same business suit he had worn at the faculty reception months before, looked at me meaningfully, raised and lowered his eyebrows over his thick-lensed glasses. "Just leavin'. Gotta go check out the dais and talk with the event coordinator. Want everything to be perfect. Good to see you. Ciao."

"See you later," I said, a casual send-off but phrased in such a way that he might understand that we needed to talk.

He gave a small wave as he walked away.

Maxwell followed his exit, no doubt to buttonhole someone else.

Mrs. Fontaine put her hand on my arm. "I hope I have the good fortune to be sitting with you again, my dear. I have made a special request not to be seated with," she looked around meaningfully to our circle, "that *ghastly man.*"

"Umm, yeah. Good."

She was talking about her fellow board member, Allan Gunderson, a former bond company owner. Ursula, who had been charged with the seating arrangements for last year's board dinner, had had great fun placing me between Fontaine and Gunderson, who might best be called a man of the old school—forthright, upright, racist, sexist and homophobic, who found his own jokes hilarious and who had taken a great liking to me. Then Ursula had placed herself on the other side of the table next to Provost Kravitz so she could flirt with him while I watched.

"But I must pay my respects to your *new* president and his *lovely* spouse," Ms. Fontaine told us as she arched her eyebrows deprecatingly, turned and walked back toward the entrance.

"Good to see you, young man," Father Lanier said, extending his hand.

I was sure he didn't remember my name.

I had not seen Father Lanier since the Kravitz memorial service, but he seemed the same, giving me his dead carp hand to shake, his lizard-green eyes in his pocked, tanned and debauched face taking in everything and revealing nothing.

I thought back to the memorial service, young Samuel Kravitz II standing before us at the pulpit and asking for someone to tell him what had really happened to his father, conveying the strong certainty that he had not committed suicide. Ursula in tears after the service. What had than been about? Just window-dressing? Probably.

Lanier excused himself, thankfully. Fitz-Hugh leaned over to Mrs. Garnet and whispered something to her. She stepped out of his aura, gave me her hand and told me how pleased she was to have met me—her lovely, gracious façade stretched thin over the hard alloy of her face. Fitz-Hugh, Ursula and I now had a moment together.

"I trust that The Global University concept moves forward under your steady guidance?" Fitz-Hugh asked, more to fend off any awkwardness than out of genuine interest. The fact was that I was the one person who knew them for who and what they were. That made them mildly uncomfortable.

"Yeah, we continue successfully on the path outlined last year. The board and the deans are fully bought in, so that helps."

"And the president?"

"He has a lot on his plate, doing the best he can. He has a difficult act to follow."

"Yes, that I understand. Well, I hope I can help him a bit with my remarks tonight."

"I'm sure you will."

There was a pause. Ursula and Fitz-Hugh glanced at one another.

Fitz-Hugh looked at me meaningfully, "We want to thank you for your ..." he paused as if searching for exactly the right word, "loyalty. It's greatly appreciated."

"Thanks," I acknowledged, thinking, *My fucking silence,* a matter of self-preservation, not loyalty.

"Hey look, let me warn you both about something," I said.

Their heightened attention and focus came instantly.

"That same reporter, Emily Sayzak, is hanging around again. Zoltan and I saw her in the lobby. Undoubtedly looking to pick off information from unsuspecting participants."

Fitz-Hugh looked concerned but said nothing.

"I can talk with security, see what we can do," Ursula ventured, looking at Fitz-Hugh.

Ursula the operative, I thought. *Well, security getting involved is better than having Sayzak killed, I guess.*

"Let's think about this," Fitz-Hugh cautioned. "Any provocation she can turn into headline news that sends a message that we're trying to cover something up. Let her go. Hopefully, she just keeps running into a brick wall."

Ursula looked at him a long moment, then conceded, "Yes, Bryan, you are right." It struck me that this was a daughter talking with, obeying, her father. It seemed almost too weird to fathom.

Fitz-Hugh turned to me. "Thomas?"

"Yeah."

"I want to apologize to you for thinking that you might be

involved with Sayzak last year. Entirely my mistake and I have been chastised about it." He looked to Ursula.

"Thanks. I appreciate that." All this insincerity and lying was making me feel like I hadn't bathed in a day to two, as if my whole being was now coated with dirt, grease and oil.

"Good man," Fitz-Hugh told me, putting his hand on my shoulder and giving it a small squeeze.

The lights dimmed and came back on, the sign that we were to take our seats for dinner.

Ursula and Fitz-Hugh turned toward the dais. Obviously, she was sitting at a table up front. She turned back to me, "We will talk."

"Yes, we will," I told her assertively, surprising myself.

XV

Luv 2 C U

On my way to my table I found Wentz as he and Florence headed to the dais and told him that Fitz-Hugh was simply being social, no agenda. He was clearly distracted now that his upcoming remarks were close at hand and seemed to take my report at face value. Perhaps he had figured out by now that his request had been a bit foolish.

I then found Berger headed in the same direction.

"Hey," I told him, "We need to talk."

"Yeah? What about?"

"I really can't say. I need to give you some recordings."

"Uh-oh …"

"Yeah. You need to hear them. They're from Frank."

Berger gave me a bug-eyed look. "Okay. Give 'em to Neil. He'll get them to me securely."

"Okay, then I'll give you a call."

"Sure."

"Sorry to catch you like this."

"No problem. All I gotta to do tonight is sit up there on the dais and look stupid. Easy!"

"Hah! Right."

Given that this year the special events department, not Ursula, had made all the arrangements for tonight's dinner, it was no surprise that I was sitting toward the back where a person of my limited importance should be sitting.

Finally, I located my table in a distant corner. I was surprised to see Gunderson there, but then realized he must have been banished to the outskirts at Ms. Fontaine's request. I smiled grimly. This would have as much to do with Ms. Fontaine being far richer than Gunderson as with his objectionable beliefs and behavior.

I glanced back at the dais and saw Ursula at a front-row table with Ms. Fontaine, Mrs. Garnet, Father Lanier and Senator Maxwell among others. Zoltan and Kristina were sitting at a table with some deans and administrators. Yeah, me and my old buddy, Allan, were part of the rear guard. He stood to greet me and motioned to the chair beside him.

"Delighted to see you again, young man," he said with loud Southern enthusiasm, putting out his hand, "It's gettin' kinda lonely and cold out here in the Arctic Circle," he chuckled.

His grip on my hand was rock solid and he gave me that same look of a filial bond that he had last year. We sat down together. His eyes were bloodshot and there was a bourbon on the rocks, undoubtedly not the first, by his table setting. Before us was a first course of a small crab cake covered with a dab of tartar sauce in an equally small bed of greens. Waiters and waitresses were moving around tables pouring white wine.

I looked around the circular table. John "Fine Fine" Fein, our director of public relations, was across from us. A man crippled by inability and low self-esteem, he looked at me, his boss, with the same expression Sparky had when she had accidently peed in the house. I hoped against hope that he was getting good quotes from Johnson, Fitz-Hugh, Wentz and the board members. He was charged with helping assemble an article on the Brussels Center for the university magazine as well as promotional materials to be placed in other publications. I felt myself give a resigned sigh.

Allan picked up on Fein's and my interaction.

He leaned over to me and whispered, "If that boy had an idea, it would *die* of loneliness," he said and began laughing his jolly laugh at his own joke, his face turning crimson, tears beginning to form at the edges of his eyes.

"Yeah," I laughed with him.

"Stuck between floors, iddint he?" Gunderson found this new insult even more hilarious, his face taking on dangerous splotches of purple as he belly-laughed.

"Right," I told him, noticing the others at the table staring at him. They appeared to be special events and School of Foreign Service staff. I could only imagine what they were thinking.

Gunderson finally came to his senses and stifled his amusement, turned to me and asked, "How have you been, Thomas?"

"Another busy year, Allan. How about you?"

"Market's up—feelin' no pain."

"You're the man."

Gunderson leaned close again, spoke softly, his breath coated with bourbon, "You know we had lots of floodin' in our region last year. Terrible stuff."

"Umm ..."

"So we been buyin' flooded land, piece by piece, quietly, a hundred-thousand-plus acres or so, so far. Sellers think we're crazy. De-lighted to sell us their flooded land cheap."

"Okay."

"Then we file with FEMA for flood relief."

"That makes sense."

"And with the Department of Agriculture we file for funding they provide for not planting certain crops. Fact is we have no intent of plantin' much on property that's under water," he told me, his eyes twinkling. "Let's see if the right hand ever figures out what the left hand is doin'. Ain't gonna happin'. By the time our land is dried out, it'll be ready for sellin' at much higher prices to folks from up north."

"Damn, Allan."

He sat back up, looked around the table and reflected for a moment. "Say, that provost who sat with us last year. Got killed or somethin', didn't he?"

"Yeah, suicide."

"Terrible."

"Yeah, we were all in shock."

"And Fitz-Hugh's assistant who was sittin' next to him?"

"Ursula. Yeah. She's here tonight out of deference to Fitz-Hugh I guess, but also works in Germany now for the embassy."

"A fine piece of tail."

"Yeah." I found myself agreeing reluctantly. If he only knew. More images of Ursula and my noisy lovemaking flashed in my head.

Gunderson leaned closer again and lowered his voice, "Speakin' ah which, before the dinner, a couple of us were hangin' out in one the bars and we got to talkin' with this hot mama. I mean, really somethin'. Her pants were so tight I could see her *religion*!" he said, bursting into crimson, tear-shedding hilarity again at the punchline. "A reporter for your local newspaper."

"Oh shit. Emily Sayzak."

"You know her! Well, butter my butt and call me a biscuit!"

"Oh yeah. She's on the prowl. The paper thinks there's something suspicious about the provost's suicide."

"I was wonderin' what she's doin' down here."

"Be really careful, Allan, unless you relish seeing your name in print."

Gunderson pulled his head back and gave me a reproachful look. "No thank you, young man. I relish anonymity."

"Good."

The room now resounded with talking and the clinking of cutlery on plates.

Dinner arrived, a choice of filet, chicken cordon bleu or vegetarian, and Allan and I caught up with one another a bit more deeply. He wanted to know about our family. I was surprised at both his recall and attentiveness. He told me of all his travels in the last year and I asked him more particularly about his trips to Asia and the Middle East.

As we finished our dinner, Fritz Johnson rose from his seat on the dais and made his way past the linen-covered table to the center lectern graced with a Sessions University seal.

He tapped loudly on the microphone which immediately subdued the sound of conversations.

"Thank you, thank you, dear frends," he twanged in his best Texas accent. "It gives me the greatest pleasure to welcome our dis-tinguished board members, faculty and ad-ministration to this important oh-ccasion prior to the meetin' of our board of trustees tah-marrah."

"And," he turned to Berger, sitting a few seats away, "what a splendid setting! Mark, as usual, you have out-done your-self with your gracious and generous hos-spitality by providing your re-markable hotel for our board of trustees meetin'. I commend you, sir!" Johnson began clapping his hands in applause that resounded over the microphone and caused the rest of us to join in.

Berger merely gave a nod and a tipping of an invisible hat gesture in acknowledgement.

Johnson renewed his introduction, "As you know, our State Department kid-napped Bryan and his family last year. Whisked him and his family away to the foreign land they call the EEE-YEW. Nun of us had enough time to say good-bye and to pay our re-spects. So, bein' that Sessions is making significant pro-gress in its growing role as The Global University and that Bryan is at the epi-center of happenin's in Europe and that our new Brussels Center is off and running to great success and that we all wanted to wish Bryan a proper *Bon Voy-yage*, he's with us tonight. Bryan, why don't you tell these folks what you been up to!"

Johnson made his way back to his seat as Fitz-Hugh rose, while everyone in the room stood, including those at the dais, and applauded enthusiastically.

I notice Wentz applauding awkwardly. It was as if Buddha was being asked to applaud, an unnatural movement.

Fitz-Hugh walked to the lectern, unrushed and confident, conveying an expression and body language that told us he was among friends and delighted to be with us.

He paused at the microphone for effect, to draw all of us in while we sat. As always, he had no notes or props and would speak to us extemporaneously.

"At the Harvard Kennedy School," he began and paused again for another moment, "we received a great deal of training on many of the countries that now form the European Union—their histories, ethnicities, politics, signature events, wars, their languages and their diplomacy. Of course, over the years, boundaries and even country names have changed. As president of several higher education institutions and particularly at Sessions with its School of Foreign Service, it behooved me to keep as up-to-date as I could on happenings in the European theatre with the EU and EU countries. This became especially true as we began to conceptualize and actualize plans for a Brussels Center. So, I arrived in Brussels feeling that I was in some ways at least somewhat prepared for the challenge of my new position.

He paused for effect and then said with a strong emphasis on each word, "What a fallacy that was!

"I discovered all too quickly that I was a complete neophyte when it came to having an in-depth, day-to-day understanding of the European Union and an appreciation of its inner workings and perhaps as important, the people and politics of this unique institution.

"Let me provide a brief perspective.

"The European Union is a political and economic union of 28 member nations whose citizens comprise 7.3 percent of the world population but whose gross domestic product constitutes almost one quarter—*almost 25 percent*—of global GDP. EU member states have the estimated second largest—after the United States—net wealth in the world, equal to 25 percent of global wealth. Of the top 500 largest corporations in the world measured by revenue, 161 have their headquarters in the EU.

"The EU therefore is an economic powerhouse, but an extraordinarily complex one.

"For instance, besides the 24 official languages of the EU, there are about 150 regional and minority languages, spoken by as many as 50 million people.

"The actual composition of the EU as a governing body is in essence a cooperative and coordinating but often overriding bureaucracy placed over but also infused into the bureaucracies of its member countries. It is also extraordinarily complex. I won't even begin to tell you about the ins and outs of dealing with its seven major agencies, which include the Central Bank, the Court of Justice, the Court of Auditors, its Parliament and various key commissions and councils.

"Now and in the future, how do we as a nation even make sense of all this complexity, let alone deal with it in a meaningful and productive manner, especially given the economic and nationalism tensions of these times and the giant ugly vulture to the west doing its best to sow discord?

"The fact is that a bright and successful future for us and for the EU will require that we have knowledgeable, well trained US and foreign nationals to work with and work in the EU—whether for the EU itself, different countries, corporations or private enterprises. Otherwise, ignorance, stupidity, fake news, pig-headed nationalistic notions, racial and ethnic bias and mis-informed and uninformed opinions and actions rule the day as they have, all too often, in the past.

"Given these challenges, I'm delighted to tell you that I learned from president Wentz today that the Sessions Brussels Center has a first-year enrollment of 119 students, 78 from our US campus, the remainder drawn from EU countries with the exception of 3 who interestingly enough transferred over from Sessions's Beijing Center.

"Given all the complexity of the European Union and its countries and their relationships, imagine the extraordinary effort it took to navigate, negotiate educational partnerships, housing, the hiring of administration and faculty and to lay all the groundwork for this successful first year.

"And who was the primary leader who accomplished this on our behalf without fanfare or even wishing to take credit—an individual who worked tirelessly, making a superhuman effort for three years while also assisting me in the founding of our Beijing Center as well as managing the progress and growth of one of our most important divisions, our College for Continuing Education?"

I knew what everyone was thinking—*Didn't you do all that, Bryan?*

Fitz-Hugh turned to Wentz. "None other than your new president, Jack Wentz. I must tell you that it was a surprise to me to be suddenly nominated for a remarkable opportunity to serve our great nation at the European Union. But it is important for you to understand that I accepted that responsibility only because I knew that Sessions could rely on Jack's great administrative and leadership capabilities. Jack, I salute you!"

With that, Fitz-Hugh began applauding Wentz, his clapping echoing through the sound system while the crowd slowly and haltingly began to follow his example.

Fitz-Hugh continued, "So, tonight is not just about my now having a moment with you to bid you a fond *adieu*, but to also to formally welcome and pass the bright torch of administration to my successor whom I've watched grow in his abilities, knowledge and experience over the years to the point where he is now ready and eager and fully able and qualified to be a superb president for Sessions University."

Fitz-Hugh began applauding again, and we all stood and applauded, a noticeably more obligatory applause than an enthusiastic one.

Wentz stood, carefully, making sure that his girth did not knock over his chair or his hands, his water glass. He smiled and gave the crowd a self-conscious nod. All and all a quite acceptably humble acknowledgement.

He carried his remarks with him and when he reached the lectern set them down carefully, smoothed them out, removed reading glasses from his breast pocket and put them in place, looked out at us, glanced down at his remarks and began.

Within a few sentences I knew without a doubt that he had had professional coaching for his remarks, not just rehearsing at his desk but in a studio where his whole delivery and bearing were studied and critiqued and where professionals worked with him on the content and delivery of his remarks.

That I was unaware of this as director of university and campaign communications gave me pause. I felt a small bit of anxiety for a few moments until I thought about the situation. Of course, he would not want my or my department's help where university employees were involved and could comment to colleagues, friends and family about his performance.

I looked at Florence, who was beaming at him. Oh yeah, a smart lady wanting the best for her man. Undoubtedly, she had persuaded him to seek professional help outside the university. Perhaps she had even made all the arrangements.

Essentially, Wentz's remarks were a report card on the university's success during his tenure. He commented on each division, with glowing reports that were guaranteed to warm the heart of each dean or division director, then onto athletics and finally to the Beijing and Brussels centers. As well, he also reported on the success of Sessions's Campaign for Progress, highlighting the most prominent gifts, including, of course, Allogenic's $50 million pledge. Across the room, I could see Stanhope Barrett, surrounded by other board members, light up at this acknowledgement, his fellow board members nodding at him, one giving him a thumbs up.

Wentz's delivery was newscaster-like, speaking to us while glancing at his remarks, all and all a solid and professional performance. I felt proud for him momentarily until the creeping realization of his enrichment scheme with the pharmaceutical companies turned my brief pride into shame. His two-faced ability, the same ability of so many others these days, to carry off their professional responsibilities in seemingly aboveboard fashion while conducting criminal acts confounded me.

He ended with compliments for the university's administrative staff, the department of special events for their successful arrangements for the evening's dinner and for the board meeting tomorrow. Then in ending his remarks he thanked the board of trustees for their support and guidance and finally, he thanked Bryan Fitz-Hugh for his years of mentoring and the confidence and support he had provided.

With that appropriate and well-delivered, full-circle ending we all rose and applauded, enthusiastically this time. Jack Wentz had performed admirably. The transition of presidencies was now complete. The lights came up as our applause ended, followed by the great buzzing of conversations.

"Care to join us in a libation?" Allan Gunderson invited over the noise as we stood.

"Allan, I'm sorry, I'm supposed to get together with my colleague Zoltan Vastag and his girlfriend."

"No problem, young man. See you tomorrow, and thanks for your littl' heads up about that mama," Gunderson said, shook my hand, slapped me on the arm, turned and headed toward the bar.

I turned toward the front of the dais. Zoltan and Kristina were gone, as were Fritz Johnson, Ursula and Fitz-Hugh, Berger, Wentz and Florence. I found myself shaking my head, pulled out my phone and then stopped. Pretty easy to figure out that Zoltan and Kristina had gone to either to his room or her place. Okay, that made sense. Johnson, Ursula and Fitz-Hugh, Wentz and Florence? Undoubtedly huddled somewhere reviewing the dinner, deciding next step strategies for tomorrow. Berger reconnoitering with the hotel's staff.

I thought about texting Ursula at her former cell phone number, then decided against it. After a few more minutes of wandering around to make sure everyone was gone, I shrugged and headed to my room, stalked by a very unpleasant feeling of unfinished business.

There, I took off my suit jacket and tie, washed up and sat on my bed, thinking about whether I should place a call to Ursula's room, when there was a light rap at my door.

"Room service," a muffled voice said.

"I didn't order anything!" I half-shouted.

"Oh, yes you did!"

Uh-oh, I thought. I now recognized Ursula's voice.

"Hello, my dear," she said as I opened the door and she slid in, giving me a light buss on the cheek. I felt my body stiffen. The scent of her, her self-assured air, her purebred movement brought back our times together and the emotions that accompanied them. Yet I could also feel myself detached from them, which brought some sense of relief and some confidence that I could navigate my way through whatever was about to occur.

She turned to face me as we walked into the room, anger showing on her face, "What did you do with our man?"

"What are you talking about?" I asked, puzzled.

"You do not know?"

"Know what?"

She started to speak and then hesitated.

"Who killed Kravitz?" I challenged her.

She looked at me, levelheaded and serious, shrugged, "I might as well tell you. We know you and Zoltan will not talk—destroy yourself, take down your family, friends, the university, everything. Plus," she laughed a cold laugh, "by now, perhaps you would not be believed. You might even become the suspect."

She paused for a moment, collected her thoughts, then continued, "With Kravitz there was not a competent team. They told me when to set my meeting with him, to offer him accounting records showing illicit spending and misappropriation of funds. I was doing this, I told him, out of concern for the university. The accounting records, of course, did not exist.

"Our team had not checked the forecast, did not know how cold it would be and the *dummkopfs* did not know the park, had looked at it on satellite and terrain maps, but then it snowed, so they were disoriented, did not know where to go. I had to go out "jogging" and direct them. So, you want to know the truth; that is the truth. Now you know."

"Why? Ursula, I mean, weren't there other alternatives?"

"In hindsight," she sighed, "I suppose so. There was panic at high levels."

"You mean, at the State Department with the secretary of state,"

"I will never confirm that."

"Okay."

"There was panic. It was a mess. I tried to reason with them. No. There were orders."

"So, you assassinate an innocent man, wreck his family to cover up his potential discovery of your scheme."

"Yes, my dear. He would likely have made a very unfortunate discovery. He would not have been so innocent then."

"Murderers!" I spat at her.

"I liked you better when you were a naïve child."

"Oh thanks. I liked you better when I thought you were a decent, loyal person."

"I am, Thomas. Just not as you had hoped."

"Yeah … great."

"You know, we had code names for all of you."

"Really?"

"Do you know what Lusby's name was? Liquor Lips. We befriended your drunken friend. He was very helpful with Kravitz."

"My God, you shadowed him last year?"

"Oh yes, he and Wentz. But we only befriended him when he was by himself and far gone, not knowing even where he was, or who he was talking to. Sometimes, it is sad, he thought he was talking to you when in fact he was talking to one of us."

"Oh Jesus, so you knew everything he was telling me?"

"Yes. We knew about the Faculty Senate vote the evening it happened, thanks to your friend. That is what motivated the action against Kravitz. We knew we had to move quickly."

"Damn …"

"You wish to know your code name?"

"Not really."

"Your name was No Lips."

"Zoltan?"

"Beast."

"Hmph."

"With Lusby, he squealed again recently, when he went on his bender. Agents followed him, befriended him in a bar and, after a while he talked again all about Kravitz and the plan for the international centers, the secret international wire transfers, Fitz-Hugh by name—worse, Greta Hauser by name, and then he launched into a scheme of Wentz/Ramis with the pharmaceutical companies. None of our business but dangerous for you, the university. Are you aware of this?"

"You mean, Wentz and Ramis? Actually, I am, somewhat. Frank was trying to figure out what to do about it."

"Then he should not go out in public places and broadcast to strangers, things that have very serious consequences attached to them."

"Are you trying to tell me that your agents caused Frank's death?" *Good,* I thought, *you're playing this right.*

"We send an agent in to accomplish that, yes. But he disappeared afterwards. You have any knowledge about what happened to our man?"

"I have no idea. I can't believe you murdered him too. How could you?"

"Usually I can tell when you are lying." She paused. "Now I am not sure. You must know."

"I don't know. I only found out about Frank from Wentz at my weekly meeting with him that morning when he got the call from the founder of Frank's company."

"Hmm …"

"What the hell are you doing here anyway?"

"I came to see you." *Bold-faced lie.*

"Oh, come on. Go tell that to Jean-Claude or any of your other partners. I'm no longer a believer."

"Ah, that, Thomas, is unfortunate."

We both looked at each other. Flashes of sex scenes from our liaison were running through my head again. Now what?

"But I understand. You and I were not and could not be fair to your family. They should come first." *Lie, lie, lie.*

"You're right."

Another pause. This one even more awkward.

"Ursula, what the hell's going to happen now with the Kravitz situation?"

She smiled. "My dear, our surveillance is going to go away, I think. There is no longer any point to it. Be patient."

I felt an immense sense of relief, coupled with a backwash of uncertainly. I wanted to believe her.

"Why do you say that?"

She smiled. "With Frank gone, there is little likelihood of a leak. With Blaylock, I believe that a conglomerate, one where Mark Berger has a silent ownership, is buying them."

"Really?"

"Yes. They saved us some money. Their purchase makes it likely that Blaylock's report to the Kravitz family will be somewhat vague and inconclusive. So, there will be no further avenue for the family to pursue."

"Sad."

"Yes. His death was a tragedy. I tried to stop it. Bryan was furious about it. You know, while he was the beneficiary of the funds coming from abroad, our great secret, he had no idea that Kravitz had been targeted for elimination."

"You're kidding. You, his daughter, and Madam Secretary, your mother, didn't tell him?"

"No."

"God damn it."

"Yes. He would have just complicated the operation, perhaps even given it away. It was better he not knowing and as it turned out, thanks to Fritz Johnson and your Berger, he escaped a dangerous situation brilliantly. That has subdued his anger. He now feels he owes Sessions a significant gratitude and will do his best to repay it."

"Just more sleaziness, right?"

"That is not how I would phrase it, Thomas. You know better than that."

"Oh, of course."

"One final thing."

"Yeah?"

"Lusby told our people he had hooked into Wentz's private line, that it was routed back to his office to a digital voice activated recorder."

"Um-hmph."

"Do you know about this?"

"I'm not surprised. He seemed to know everything about what Wentz was doing."

"You must remove any evidence of this."

"Me? Why?" I did not want to tell her I had already disposed of the recorder.

"If they discover the hookup, and they will, maybe soon, they will follow it to the president's office."

"Well, yeah," I shrugged.

"Then they will wonder who he told about this and where the recordings are. They will begin a frantic search. They know Frank confided in you. Desperate situation for them. You must remove the evidence."

My God, I thought, *she's right.* I knew this but had been putting off the task of removing the phone line because I couldn't see how to do it without getting caught. "Couldn't your people do it?"

"Not our concern, and there is a danger we would get caught. You have access to the building and to his office. You will figure this out. I must go."

I felt myself give a resigned shrug. How the hell was I going to remove than line? I put the question out of my mind for the time being and said to Ursula, "I'd say it's been nice, but …"

"Perhaps it will be nice some other day, some other time…"

Before I could react, she leaned to me, slid her hand around my neck, planted her mouth on mine and gave me a hard, probing kiss, then pulled away quickly. I felt my whole body go electric and then become paralyzed with mind/body conflict.

"*Au revoir*," she said as she turned, waved a hand, opened the door and was gone, all the right things working in her stride.

I undressed and went to bed, but it was clear from the moment I lay down that I would not sleep. Every time I closed my eyes, the day's meetings and conversations began playing through my head randomly. I felt as if my mind had changed into some sort of mirrored fun-house maze where at every turn I saw my reflection in some scene and conversation from the day playing back with distorted perspective without my being able to make any sense of it. And then I heard a sound, a singular small scraping noise, something being shoved under the door. Too early for the room bill. What the hell?

I threw off the sheet, rose and padded over to the door in my shorts, flicked on the doorway light. On the floor at the door sill was a room card key holder, a card key inside. I picked it up. On one side the room number had been written by the front desk clerk. On the other in a small, scratchy cursive was written, "Luv 2 C U."

XVI

Mutuality

A BRIGHT, COLD, sunny day with blustering winds and fast-moving clouds as the Kennedy Center came into view. Beyond it was the Potomac River, dark green/brown, full of windswept chop, its shoreline encrusted with ice. Zoltan and Kristina were standing on the corner we had agreed upon, across from the center's northeast side, where the traffic pattern was favorable for a quick entry onto the GW Parkway and home, Kristina huddled up against Zoltan as the wind buffeted them.

They hugged goodbye as I pulled up to the curb. Zoltan made quick work of getting into the car, pulling his seat belt hard across his expanse and fastening it as I shifted into first. We both waved as I pulled away. I watched in the rearview mirror as Kristina waved back at us and then turned to look for a cab.

"So," I asked as we wove our way through traffic over the Memorial Bridge, "How was *Carmen*?"

"Very good! You know, I have seen it many, many times, but it always different, different cast, always interesting to see different interpretation and make you realize your own life, despite all the mess we in, not so bad after all."

"Yeah?"

"Yes. You not get so jealous of Ursula that you abandon university and family, flee to Europe and kill Jean Claude."

I laughed. "You have a point there."

"Things maybe could be worse. So, what happen last night? How this morning board meeting?"

"The board meeting was fine, just an effort not to bore them. They've heard it all before. I revved up my presentation, shortened it. Nodding heads all along. Applause. I made a polite exit once the next presentation from Bernie Reve began."

"Um, good."

"So, last night Ursula showed up at my room."

"My God. You fuck her?"

"Wow. Thanks for the vote of confidence. No. But we had a very, let's say, productive conversation."

"Yes?"

"Most important, she thinks their spying on us will end soon. No one who would talk left to kill. You and I can keep our mouths shut. So can Wentz and Berger."

"Ah, wonderful."

"They are super pissed about losing an agent, but I convinced her I knew nothing about it."

"You save our asses."

"Yeah, I think so."

"She confirmed it was her supervising their first team that did in Kravitz and it was a second team that got Frank.

"Orders came from on high for the Kravitz murder. Bryan wasn't even told about it. How weird is that? Ursula's not only his assistant, she's his daughter. The secretary of state, who presumably at the very least approved the order to terminate Kravitz, is her birth mother and still apparently Bryan's lover. Yet they didn't tell him. That tells you how covert this damn operation was. All this now makes sense to me because Bryan was so shook-up the night of Kravitz's death.

"In any case, Bryan now feels a debt of gratitude toward the university for Johnson saving his ass through negotiating his diplomatic appointment, for Berger zeroing out and replacing the clandestine funds we had received and through their positioning Bryan as a beloved former president at Sessions.

"The worse thing is that, apparently, what led to both Kravitz's and Frank's demise is that each team befriended Frank when he was blackout-drunk and he was the one who told them everything that was happening. Without even being aware of it, he was the one who was responsible for Kravitz's and his own death."

"My God."

"Yeah. Very hard for me come to terms with that. Tragic. He and his alcoholism almost destroyed us all."

"Yes... Now what we do?"

I paused for a moment, thinking everything through. "Well, for starters, I'm going to get the thumb drives out of the safe deposit box and give them to Neil Wexler, Berger's main man on campus. He'll get them to Berger. That's the least I could do for Frank."

"What you think happen then?"

"For a while, maybe a long while, nothing. Can't make a leadership change now. What would be the public reason for it? Plus, it's not impossible that Wentz, if he were confronted about his and Ramis's scheme, could turn on them and behind their backs surreptitiously spill the goods about the clandestine operation, Bryan, Greta Hauser, etc. Try to bring down the whole university and us without him being implicated. So, they're going to have to be very careful. Wentz is not to be trusted."

"Umm … yes, big danger."

"Yeah. So, my guess is, for now they'll probably wrist slap Wentz and Ramis before their scheme goes too much further. Stop it in its tracks. Deal with each of them later as the opportunity presents itself. Doesn't seem right, but nothing does these days."

"Yes."

"Something else."

Zoltan raised his eyebrows questioningly.

Lusby also told the second team about Wentz and Ramis's scheme. Remember, I removed the phone recorder from Lusby's desk the morning you and I disposed of his assassin. But by that point people were in the building; no way I could remove the phone line. It's still there. Ursula warned me to remove everything because if it is discovered then they'll begin to think maybe I know what's going on. Puts us in danger again. This time from Wentz and Ramis. One way or another they could invent reasons to get rid of us, especially if your Phase 1 doesn't turn out well."

"Maybe that good thing. I go work for pharma. You come along."

I shook my head. "I don't think so. At least not right now. Things are just working out with the kids. Timing's not right. Plus, you need to finish your trial."

"Yes. What you do?"

"I don't know. Haven't figured it out yet. Lusby's office is now locked up. I'd have to break into it and get the line removed before security locks up all the other offices up there, which is after the cleaning crew leaves. Not much time in between. But then again, Lusby did it, and removing it has got to be much quicker than installing, so I've got to follow his timing. The big issue is that his office is locked up."

"Yes."

"Anyway, I've got to figure out something."

We both were silent as the miles passed, Zoltan staring at the scenery while I tried to pay better attention to the road and other cars. Traffic was again terrible.

"Oh, yeah, and something else."

"Yes?"

"Look what a little angel slipped under my door last night." I reached into my coat pocket and pulled out Emily Sayzak's room key holder and passed it to him, note side up.

Zoltan read it and his brows knitted. He looked up at me. "You . . . ?"

"Naw. Part of me really wishes I had. I know she would be terrific, but oh my God, the consequences! No, I remain chaste. Given the way things are going, maybe I should seriously think about joining the priesthood."

Zoltan looked at me. "You not right type for church. Not place for ... what they call ... straight shooters. Place for lizards and snakes—perverts."

"Maybe not the best idea I've had today."

"Or this year."

"Yeah. Strike that thought."

"Umph. Gladly."

When we arrived back at Sessions, I dropped off Zoltan in the ancient neighborhood behind the university's stadium where he kept a third-floor room in a ramshackle, dingy-white, clapboard house with black shutters and a large wraparound porch. Then I headed to the Safe Deposit and Trust across from the campus.

I found a parking place about a block down from the bank, opened the glove box and un-taped the safe deposit box key from the back of the encrypted phone instructions.

Initially puzzled by my request, the clerk I encountered at the bank called his manager and only after conferring and reviewing Frank's account did they discover the note to the file that they were to provide me with the contents of his safe deposit box should I show up to claim them. Thus, having cleared me of any possible criminal intent, they dutifully took me to the safe deposit box, which I opened as they stood guard and removed a plastic ziplock bag with eight thumb drives in it. I calculated the thumb drives would represent two months-worth more or less of Wentz and Ramis's calls to one another and presumably two- and three-way calls to and from their so-called expert attorney.

Back at the administration building, I took the elevator to the university's business operations on the fourth floor, an endless space of cubicles surrounded by outer offices. Overhead in the low ceiling, buzzing fluorescent lights and fire-retardant tiles in metal framework stretched into infinity. The place smelled of stagnant, overheated air and new carpet.

I thought about my meeting last year with Ken DePew, the university's comptroller then, to review, as instructed by Fitz-Hugh, my initial draft budget for a new university communications department. DePew had been the secretive keeper of the books detailing the anonymous and clandestine international wire transfers that kept mysteriously showing up at the university. Now I found his former office occupied my Neil Wexler.

He looked up as I walked in, small surprise and irritation registering on his features.

"You're not supposed to be here," he told me in his nerdy voice.

"Yeah, right. Mr. Berger asked me to give these directly to you for secure transfer. Sorry to cut a few corners. I'm outta here. Thanks for your help."

"Okay…."

I turned, walked away.

Back in my office I played catch up as best I could, amazed at how much incidental crap could occur during a twenty-four-hour absence. Finally, I sensed the day's light fading outside, turned around and looked out the window to see the sun low in the woods—a burst of orange amongst dark silhouetted trees, realized that I had stayed over an hour longer than intended, put on my coat and hustled to my car, the wind and cold washing away any warmth retained from the administration building.

By the time I was on the expressway, driving in the dark, I was in deep thought.

Were we still being spied upon? I needed to talk with Berger to see whether he could confirm that the spying had stopped, but I should probably wait a few days before contacting him. Then we could discuss that and the recordings. But if we were now for the first time in almost a year free? I felt my spirits rise. I had begun to feel that the Kravitz episode and its consequences were something we could never put behind us. To be freed of the crushing uncertainty of it, it felt too good to be true, but I was buoyed nonetheless, to the point that Wentz's scheme with Ramis and any possible threat from it began to seem significantly less of a problem.

Then I thought back to Stanhope Barrett and our exchange with him at the board meeting dinner. There were apparently thirty or more pharma company manipulators like him out there, some of them in charge of multi-billion-dollar enterprises, and who knew what they might be up to or what they could bring to bear at Wentz's and Ramis's urging. I found myself shaking my head. More uncertainty and suspicion. I felt an increasing sense of urgency to get rid of the rogue phone line in the administration building.

I parked the car in the garage. On my way into the house I buried Emily's room card key holder in one of the plastic tie bags in the garbage can, waving the stink away as I shut the lid, and entered the family room through the laundry room, Sparky running in circles and barking her delight at my being home.

I reached down to pet her, looked across the room as I patted her head and told her stupid canine endearments.

Sarah apparently had just arrived ahead of me. She and Janet were sitting at the kitchen table, chattering away. Janet with a glass of white wine, a glass for me on the counter, the smell of a chicken casserole in the oven filling the air.

I walked in and they both turned to me.

"Hi, honey," Janet greeted.

"Hey, Dad," Sarah said, "We're just talking about the curriculum for Tommie at the Center for Gifted and Talented Youth. It's awesome. He can not only take courses in computer science, coding and the like, but also over time—applied courses in engineering, aeronautics, business, even physics, robotics, medicine, even languages and the arts. Very cool."

"Wow," I told her. "That's terrific." I had been away for a day and a half and now felt completely behind the curve on Tommie's situation.

"I talked with Mr. Diamond today," Janet added, "and we're all going over to the center next week and meet with Tommie's advisor and work out a program of individual counseling and classroom and online coursework that integrates with Schossler's schedule and courses as well as what Tommie might do over the summer."

There was a pounding on the stairs. The smell of the casserole had obviously penetrated as far as Tommie's room.

"Hey, Tommie," I greeted, as he turned the corner into the kitchen, "How's it going? We're just talking about your different opportunities at Sessions. They have quite a program. I'll have to catch up with their website. Have you looked at it?"

"Yeah, Dad" Tommie said, his face screwing up, his eyes blinking rapidly, "I wanna build a Row-bot!"

I thought, *Oh, Jesus, another mania.* I pictured a robot that acted like Tommie doubling the dysfunction in our household.

"Well, why don't we go through orientation first, huh, and see what the right courses are for you over the next six months or so?"

"Aw, Dad."

At dinner, Janet asked about the board meeting and I told them about Fitz-Hugh's remarks about the European Union and the Brussel Center's success, which Janet and Sarah, I could tell, found interesting while Tommie continued eating.

I conveyed Kristina's best wishes to all of them and commented on the success of Wentz's remarks.

After dinner we cleaned up and put the dishes in the dishwasher. Tommie actually managed to rinse off his plate and utensils and get them into the dishwasher rather than pantomiming.

Afterwards, Tommie went upstairs to his computer. Sarah, Janet and I watched a talent show in the family room until bedtime.

Upstairs, after my nightly preparations and changing into my pajamas, I lay in our bed. Janet was in the bathroom. I pulled the sheet and bedspread over me, placed my head on my pillow and began thinking again about the last two days, the house quiet except for the wind mildly buffeting our windows and the occasional gust and random small ticking of sleet against them.

Janet came in and lay down on her side of the bed and turned off the bedside table light. Silence as we both lay there in the dark.

"Robot." Her voice came to me softly so as not to disturb the household. "Wouldn't you know it."

"Yeah," I answered back softly, "I've been lying here picturing him merging past and present obsessions, programming a bunch of robot firemen to behave like the guys he so admires down at the fire station, every third word being a racial epithet, ethnic slur or sexist remark, you know, machines making comments about rug heads and towel heads and big racks and then snickering to one another."

There was silence for a moment as our imaginations worked to visualize a fire station manned by Tommie's robots, and then we both started laughing quietly, with growing intensity, the bed shaking a bit from the outlet of suppressed anxiety into hard laughter. Tears were forming in my eyes as I thought, *Well, it's not that funny,* which only made me laugh harder.

It was good to feel something mutual.

Our laughter subsided. The room grew silent again and just as I was beginning to drift off there was a rustle from Janet's side of the bed and I felt her hand cross my hip and take hold of me.

In the time that followed we descended into a subconscious realm where our younger and present day selves merged into one another, where the experiences of our lives together, births, deaths, friendships, emotions, children, professions reordered and reloaded, solidifying and confirming our mutuality, our oneness in one remarkably intense, simultaneous climax. At its end, as if drugged, we rolled into deep sleep.

XVII

A Favor

"SO," WENTZ ASKED, "what were your impressions?"

The following week and Wentz and I were having our usual Thursday meeting, the first since the board's gathering at the Tribone Hotel—Wentz behind his desk, white shirt sleeves rolled up, a view of the lower quadrangle behind him, bare trees, winter-brown lawn with patches of snow and mud, students walking briskly on its asphalt paths as they changed classes.

"Morale seemed good. Interesting, Stanhope Barrett made it a point to introduce himself to Zoltan and me."

"He did?"

"Yeah, very high on Zoltan's work. Made noises about his working for Allogenic down the line."

"He really shouldn't be pulling crap like that. I'll mention it to Fritz, who's pretty no nonsense about calling board members out when they cross lines. As for Zoltan, he should be so lucky."

"Let's hope some luck rubs off on his research."

"If it ever gets completed …"

"Umm ..."

Wentz shrugged. "Seems like a real mixed bag of results over there is the impression I'm getting. No date certain about when they'll finish. Well, maybe by the end of the summer. That's got all our potential suitors antsy, not to mention Ramis." He shook his head. "Shoulda known on this one."

"Yeah … back to the board meeting. I thought Fitz-Hugh

did his usual brilliant remarks and segue into your presentation, which I thought was excellent. Just the right touch, delivery and content. I heard a lot of good feedback." *Well, truth was, I hadn't heard any feedback. But what the hell.*

Wentz smiled, "Thank God. Yeah, Thomas, it went well. Florence was very happy. So, was I. Let's hope this turns the corner on the cover-up and that we can get on with the real business of Sessions University."

I thought, *Yeah, the real business of fraud, deceit and underhanded payments, you fucker.*

"Right," I told him.

We went over the board meeting itself. Wentz filled me in with a general overview. The Campaign for Progress was going well. A more in-depth report on the Beijing and Brussels centers progress was positive. On behalf of Don Powers, Wentz reported on academic programs at the university, noting the Powers had used last year's $2 million appropriation from Fitz-Hugh as an incentive for each department to create a long-range plan with impact assessments. This had apparently been very well received by the board. Ramis had given a highlight report on the medical center, mentioning Zoltan's work. The board seemed generally happy. Fritz Johnson had been impressed. Mark Berger seemed happy both with the success of the venue and with the meeting itself.

"Did you and Ursula have a chance to talk?"

While I was surprised by the question and immediately felt defensive, I resisted the impulse to react. "Just in passing," I told him matter-of-factly. "She seemed a bit distant, just saying all the right things but with no real personal connection to them."

"Hmm ... I was wondering what her take on the board meeting and Bryan's new berth were. Typical she'd not give up any information. I guess they'll just go back to Europe, which is fine by me. After this, the less we see of them, the better."

"Yeah, I agree." I felt a great sense of relief. Clearly, whether he had known about Ursula and me or not, it was of no present concern.

"So, what's your PR, marketing and communications follow-up from the board meeting?"

"Full steam ahead on The Global University theme. Your remarks to the board will be broadcast literally worldwide to our alumni, friends and to the national and international press, magazine, publications and periodicals. A podcast is being prepared. Particular focus will be on extolling the importance of the Brussels Center, particularly to our European audiences."

"Sounds terrific."

"I hope it is."

"Thanks, Thomas."

I returned to my office, made follow-up calls to assure what Wentz and I had just discussed was in motion and as the lunch hour rolled around, left the building, walked to my car. The day was overcast with a penetrating humid cold that pierced through my overcoat and caused my breath to steam out in front of me.

I drove south around Sessions Park to the Milton neighborhood.

Several years prior, Sessions had reached an agreement with the city to take over the park, a steep ravine whose trails had become unkempt and overgrown and its dying stream filled with garbage. The university maintenance crew and student and faculty volunteers had now cleaned it up, lights had been installed and it was a far safer place for citizens and students to walk to and from their neighborhoods to the campus and areas to the east.

Beyond the park, toward the expressway, was Milton, a hard-scrabble working-class area, the remnant of what had originally been a mill town, the mill works long gone, and now, captured within the confines of a city that had grown around it, it comprised a grid of wandering streets, broken sidewalks, ancient overgrown or dead trees, corner liquor stores, various warehouses and garages. Small grocery, dry cleaning and hardware establishments resided among a rundown array of brick, clapboard and Formstone houses—asphalt shingled, shoulder to shoulder with small churches representing a polyglot of religions all aiming at a salvation that never seemed to be at hand.

Milton did, however, feature a few refreshingly local restaurants in modest quarters serving inexpensive, home style cuisine, among them Annamaria's, where Alicia and I could dine in privacy of our own booth.

She was already seated when I arrived a few minutes late.

"So, you found the place and made yourself at home," I told her once I was seated. "Before I forget, thanks for doing this. Unnecessary, but appreciated."

"You're welcome. Nice place," she said, genuinely liking the unpretentious ambiance.

She was dressed casually today, turtleneck and corduroys, her ski parka on the booth partition hook. No makeup yet her intelligence, confidence, appreciation of and interest in life around her more than made up for that. I took in her beautiful blue eyes, clear complexion, radiant long hair, graceful long-fingered hands, then quickly prevented myself from too long an appreciation.

"Is there really an Annamaria, or is that just a name?"

"Oh no, she's real, but she runs the place in the evening. The kids run it during the day. A true family enterprise."

"Interesting," Alicia smiled. "Just when you begin to think the American dream is dying, here it is."

"Absolutely. I can give you one good word of advice. Portions are huge. Don't order more than you can eat or one of the kids, who aren't really kids, they're in their twenties and thirties, will be out here asking you if there's something wrong, thinking you don't like your food. I guarantee they already think you're too thin."

"Well, that shouldn't be a problem."

"Really?" I asked. I was accustomed to Janet and me, two white-bread yuppies, ordering salads and unsweetened iced teas.

"Yeah, sorry, but I eat like a horse. One of my least endearing characteristics."

"How do manage that?"

"Oh, I'm really active. Martial arts three times a week. Jogging. Fitness and weight training twice a week."

"Martial arts?"

"Aikido."

"Aikido?"

"You're not familiar with it?"

"No, not really."

"A Japanese martial art encompassing the philosophy and religion of Morihei Ueshiba. In defending yourself you use the opponent's aggression against them."

"So, I take it that I should never get in a serious argument with you?"

"Correct."

"One question …"

"Where's my cape, bracelets and Wonder Woman outfit?"

"Something along those lines. What the hell do you do to relax? Run marathons?"

She smiled, the smile one has when indulging a child, "Transcendental meditation."

"Ohh-kay. I should have known that it would be something like that. Sorry for being an idiot."

"No, no, no," she said, reaching out and touching me on the arm. "It's me. No one has ever accused me of being normal. I've always just followed my own way."

Our waiter came—large, goateed and pleasantly gruff—and told us about the specials, which sounded like way too much food for lunch.

Alicia ordered a large vegetarian pizza with meat sauce, which confused our waiter momentarily, and a Coke, while I ordered a house salad with unsweetened iced tea.

"Have some of my pizza, will you?"

"I may do that."

"So, Thomas, should I ask you how your meeting went in Washington or is that a forbidden topic?"

"Mostly. I'm sure Emily gave you her impressions."

She smiled, "Oh definitely, at length. She's very frustrated with you."

"Good! How about we talk about anything else, like you for instance. You have a place here? Where do you actually live? How the hell did you ever choose private investigation as a career?"

She laughed as a busboy set down our drinks and a breadbasket of Italian bread smothered in hot garlic butter. "My, you are inquisitive, aren't you?"

"Let me tell you. It's been forever since I could actually ask someone questions instead being grilled. By the way, forgot to tell you about the garlic bread. It's to die for."

We both helped ourselves. The bread was magnificent.

"So, you'll grill me?" she asked playfully, after she finished a first piece, wiping her hands on her paper napkin, sweeping her hair over a shoulder as she spoke, leaning forward as if ready for a challenge.

"Nope, just curious."

"I was a Georgetown grad in political science and then law school and didn't want to follow the normal, boring legal career path of joining a big-name law firm, or ..." she paused.

"Or what?'

"Or join my father's company, which is what he was pressuring me to do."

"Hmm ... I see. Rebelling a little."

"Rebelling a lot."

We both laughed.

"Good for you."

She paused again. I could see her making a decision to talk to me. "I might as well tell you. You'll figure it out anyway sooner or later. My father's Gaylord McDonald."

"Okay," I acknowledged, puzzled, searching my memory for some connection to that name.

"You don't know who he is?"

"Not really, although I've got some vague notion."

"That's refreshing."

"Good. Who is he?"

"The founder and CEO of Piper-Hale."

"Oh yeah, Fortune 500 company. Shipping?"

"Among other things, yes."

"So, Daddy hang-ups?"

She laughed her strong, appreciative, beautiful laugh.

"Oh yes. You called it. For many years."

"Growing up, I had a friend in a similar situation, all the material things a child could ever want in a household devoid of any connection, direction or affection. Died of an overdose in college. How come you made it?"

Alicia shrugged. "Well, for one thing I seem to have inherited a very strong desire to succeed, probably from the old man, and for a long while I had a very significant chip on my shoulder, wanting to prove myself as worthy outside of the parental orbit, but at the same time, defensively, I presented myself to the world as little Miss Ice Maiden/Rich Bitch.

"Growing up, my parents seemed to think I was one of their possessions. You know, trot me out to show off some aspect of my upbringing that would impress their friends. That only lasted so long and when I ceased cooperating, they sent me to boarding school. Somehow I survived that and gradually at Georgetown I seem to have worked through most of my issues, have become my own person I'm proud to say—and frankly it was this erstwhile career decision of becoming a private detective that brought that all about, taught me to be self-reliant, gave me a lot of very interesting and useful skills and allowed me to see slices of lives gone wrong that were educational way beyond the classroom, life lessons in every case we had."

"Very interesting. So what do you do now?"

She laughed lightly, shook her head, "I have no idea. I could join another detective agency, but … it just feels to me like I've been there and done that. It's time for a new chapter. I have to figure things out. Maybe it's time to join the old man's enterprise. He's starting to get on in years and is for the first time, I think, seeing the end of his reign. That's softened him up a bit in a good way."

Our orders came. Her pizza was huge. She removed a slice and took a large mouthful. Nothing dainty about her.

"Fantastic," she said, her voice muffled by the pizza.

There was a momentary pause and I found myself wondering why she was not the least curious about my background. Then it occurred to me.

"Hey, you know I was wondering why you weren't asking me any questions, but then it just occurred to me. Blaylock had a file on me, didn't they?"

She put down her piece of pizza on her plate, "Oh yeah, and on everyone else. I came into my interview knowing you had gone to Cornell for undergrad and to Columbia for your PhD, are married, have a wife who is a psychologist and have two children, one of whom is in the gifted and talented program at Sessions and the other at a special needs school."

"Christ."

"I'm sorry, Thomas. It's just the way the world works these days, especially in the detective business."

"I guess. It sucks though."

"I agree with you."

I decided to let it go. "So, Alicia, you have a place here?"

"Yeah, an executive suite over near the airport. Sterile as hell. Need to be out of there at the end of the month. Blaylock's been nice to give me that much time."

"Then where do you go?"

"Oh, I have an apartment in DC. That's more or less home; has been ever since college. I've been spending my weekends there. What about you? What are you going to do?"

"What do you mean, what about me?"

"You are still in some sort of very risky situation, am I not right? Shouldn't I be returning your favor and telling *you* to leave?"

"It's not that simple. Not a subject I'd care to discuss. Okay?"

She held up both hands. "Okay, just trying to help."

"I appreciate that. Didn't mean to sound so put off, but to try to explain might take way more time than we have here today."

"Okay, Thomas. Some other time then."

Hmm, I thought, *I'd like that. Uh-oh,* I thought again. Yet I could feel myself being interested. In fact, there was an idea I had been playing with in the back of my mind that now came forward.

"Um, you know what? I actually need to ask you whether you might do me a favor, or at least give me some advice. Perfectly okay if you turn me down."

Alicia looked at me, puzzled by this turn in the conversation, interested.

"What's the favor?"

"There's an office in the president's suite that's locked up that I need access to for about fifteen minutes."

"Oh ..., so you want me to play detective and pick the lock for you?"

I felt myself smile sheepishly. "Yeah, that would be the idea."

"And how much trouble could we get into with this little caper?"

"Oh, a total shitload of trouble."

"Sounds interesting. Why do you need to get into this office?"

I paused, looked at her. "You know, the less I tell you about why I need to do this the better."

"Okay. Give me a hint."

"The person who used to be in that office was recording some private-line calls. As a final favor to that person, who passed away, not to mention to protect my own ass because I know about this, I need to remove phone line between his office and another office. Won't take long but has to be done in the time between the cleaning crew finishing and security locking up the offices."

"Hmm .... I'll think about it. Okay?"

"Okay, but can you let me know ASAP?"

"Yeah, I can do that."

There was another pause while we ate. I helped myself to a slice of her pizza. Then Alicia said "So, back to an original subject, Emily Sayzak needs to talk with you."

"Oh God."

"Actually, from what's she's told me, this is serious, legit—not about her and you."

I looked at her dubiously.

"Do you mind if I make some observations?"

"Go ahead."

"She does have a crush on you above and beyond her desire to get you to talk. But you not taking her up on her interest in you, particularly in Washington ..."

"You know about that?"

"Women confide in each other."

"Great."

"Anyway, I think she now understands fully that you are off-limits. And something else has come up. I'm not exactly sure what. And she feels it's very important that she show or give something to you. She wanted me to ask you whether you two could meet—wherever you say."

"Something?"

"She wouldn't tell me."

I sighed. "Okay, tell her I'll meet her for a drink at the Intercontinental Hotel. I'll call her to set it up. Okay?"

"Sure."

I looked at my watch. "As much as I'd like to stay here and chat, I gotta go."

"Understandable, Thomas. It's great seeing you."

"Give me your cell number and I'll call in a day or so about your decision on the favor I asked."

"Sure."

She told me her number as I entered it into my cell phone, then she paid the bill and called a cab. I thanked her again and we both slid out of the booth. I held her coat for her and as she turned and put her arm through the sleeve, I could again smell the hay-like scent of her hair. We walked outside into the dank, cold day and she gave me a brief hug. We touched cheeks. Hers was dry, soft and warm. She stood there waiting for her cab while I walked to my car around the corner.

After work, I decided to take the long way home via the reservoir. It was time to talk to Berger. I pulled off into the village center parking lot near our home momentarily, turned off my cell phone, retrieved and booted up a new phone, punched in Berger's number, then drove west. Once I was driving around the reservoir, I reached over, picked up the phone, hit the send button and then speaker.

"Howaryah?" came the usual greeting on the second ring.

"Better, I guess. You tell me."

"Yeah, well I guess we're off the hook with our covert friends. At least that's the strong implication I got from Bryan. Not like he's going to say anything directly. Anyway, that's a help. But, fuck, this shit you sent me with Wentz and Ramis, those two fuckers have lost their fucking minds."

"Greed."

"Stupid greed. Ants in the pants greed. They couldn't wait? You know, they are both in a position where all they have to do is play ball for a couple years and all sorts of remarkahble opportunities will present themselves. They don't have to be doing this kinda crap. It could bring down the entire university, at the very least, besmirch the hell out its reputation. Fritz and I, well…"

"You'll have to be really careful," I said, reading his mind.

"Yeah, right. We'll figure it out. So, more importantly, how's the family?"

"Actually, there's a lot of good news."

I brought him up to speed on all the recent developments with Sarah and Tommie.

"Fantastic. Sometimes things work out, my friend. Let's hope we can have the same happen at Sessions. Without your help, by the way, you and Zoltan, I don't know where the hell we'd be. Pretty well fucked I guess."

"Thanks. Just trying to survive. Glad to be of service."

"Yeah. Well, let me see what the hell we can do about this new development. Those assholes."

"Right."

"Ciao."

At home, when I walked into the family room, Sparky barking and circling me excitedly, I was surprised to see Janet standing there with a glass of white wine for me in her hand, a concerned expression on her face.

"What's going on?" I asked as I took the glass of wine from her hand.

"You had a phone call."

"Yeah?"

"From Natalie Kravitz …"

"Oh …"

"I don't think it was about Sarah baby-sitting."

XVIII

JoAnn

THE NEXT DAY, after morning meetings and lunch, I located Emily Sayzak's card in the rubber banded stack in my top desk drawer and called her cell phone.

"Emily?"

"Yes."

"Thomas Simpson."

"Hey, Thomas, thanks so much for calling."

"So, what's this all about?"

"I came across something, by accident really, that I need to share with you."

"What?"

"Not something we should discuss, believe me. More like, you wouldn't believe me if I told you."

"Uh-oh."

"My thoughts exactly. You need to see this."

"Oh-kay." Being that it was now Friday, I thought about when we could meet. The weekend was out, too long an absence without an explanation, no viable explanation that I could think of. The next week was Christmas week. The earlier I saw her, the better, but Mondays were always a mess of meetings and unexpected developments. "How about the Intercontinental next Tuesday the twenty-first, in the bar at 2:00 p.m. That's a good setting, big booths where we could meet privately at a time where anyone who might know us is likely to be elsewhere."

"That sounds good. See you then."

"Sure."

I put down my cell phone, rotated in my chair and looked out my window. Grey day. A light snow was being blown southeast by a steady wind. The drive was covered, car tracks in the new quarter inch of accumulation. In the woods individual trees had a lining of snow plastered on their northwest side.

I turned back to my desk, picked up my cell phone and called Alicia.

"Hello, Thomas."

"How are you today?"

"Enjoying a relaxing day, catching up with magazines, watching the snow fall outside my window while I listen to planes take off from the airport."

"I hate you, having a day like that."

"Don't."

"Okay. Have you thought over the favor I asked?"

"Yes, I have. I think I've figured out how I can be very helpful. Low risk. My favorite kind. Would this evening work?"

"Actually, it would. Can you be here around six-thirty? The building will still be open then, just come up to my office. What are you thinking?"

"You'll see," she said light-heartedly.

"Why am I always the last to know?"

"Naivete."

"Oh, thanks."

"Don't mention it."

"See you then."

"Thanks. I really appreciate your help. More than I can say."

"Glad to help, Thomas. Bye."

I put my phone back on the desk and turned to the window again.

My next call, which I had been putting off all day, was to Natalie Kravitz. While I recognized her number as having a Chicago area code, I presumed she and her family were in town visiting Joan Kravitz for the holidays.

Her father's memorial service in the university's Patterson Chapel, almost a year ago now, rushed into my consciousness, the weather that day not unlike today's. Natalie, tall, dark brown hair, pale, graceful, dressed in black, holding a single sheet of paper in her long-fingered hands, her grace under duress as she read from the pulpit a passage from the Book of Wisdom—the gathering of family, faculty and university administrators and staff beyond silent as if that was somehow a collective confession of guilt.

All my feelings of sadness and worry from the past returned, from Samuel Kravitz's murder masquerading as suicide, to all the uncertainty and cover-up surrounding it, tinged with the deepest regret and sadness from Frank Lusby's passing. I felt my eyes grow moist, wiped at them with my knuckles, turned to my desk, found a Kleenex in my top drawer, blew my nose, took a deep sigh, composed myself and placed the call.

"Hello?" her answer had some uncertainty to it, almost waif-like.

"Natalie—Thomas Simpson."

"Oh hello, Thomas. Thanks for returning my call." There was a pause as she collected her thoughts. I felt myself close my eyes, slowly shake my head. "I'm in town. Mother is visiting us in Chicago for the holidays this year, so I came down to help her prepare for her visit, to accompany her on the trip and, frankly, to help her with many of the loose ends from my father's death and his estate that are still plaguing her. This has been a terrible year for her."

"I can only imagine."

"As you probably know, or perhaps you don't, we don't have any more answers about my father's death than we had a year ago, so we've been reduced to grasping at straws."

"I'm so sorry, Natalie."

"Yes, we thought it would be nice if, before we left for Chicago, we would catch up with some of those people at the university whom Dad thought highly of ..."

I thought, *He didn't think highly of me. He was totally contemptuous of me. It was his intellectual arrogance and jealously of Fitz-Hugh that got him killed.*

"And perhaps also see whether they might be able to shed some light on what happened to him that evening in the ..." It was difficult for her to get the last word out. "... park."

"Natalie, I really don't think I can be of any help to you. You know, I told the Blaylock Agency much the same."

"Please, Thomas, this is really just therapeutic for Mother and me, just to talk with people about my father. It helps bring him back a little bit and, in a sense, also puts him to rest."

I sighed, felt myself pressing my temples with my free hand, still shaking my head. "Okay, Natalie. How about I come by after work next Tuesday, say five-thirty." I thought, *I might as well totally ruin my day, Emily Sayzak at two, Natalie and her mother at five-thirty.* After that I could go home and drown my sorrows.

"That would be fine, Thomas, Mother and I will look forward to seeing you."

"Yes. Thanks."

I hung up. Put my cell phone back on my desk, waited a beat then picked it up again and called Zoltan.

"Vastag."

I could hear noises in the background, what sounded like a rack of test tubes or beakers being stacked. "Meet me at the club, usual time?"

"Yes."

"See you then. Have to go back to the office after a drink. I'll explain."

"Very good."

After work, I trudged over to the club, snow now having accumulated an inch and a half, dry and windblown in places, wet mush in others where there were sources of heat from the university's underground steam lines and operations.

Inside, the front hall was cheerfully decorated for Christmas. A large, festive, fully ornamented and draped in silver tinsel Christmas tree topped with a lovely white angel, her hands in prayer, was placed in the small alcove where the second-story stairway curved into the hall. Wreaths decorated with small, glossy, colored balls adorning the breakfront between the dining room doors. Pine-bough bunting gracing the hallways.

I found Zoltan already in the bar area at our customary table, nursing a vodka, remnant bar snacks scattered across the table.

"Ah, Mr. Snowman," he addressed me, as I stamped the snow off my boots, pounded my gloves before removing them and shook out my overcoat.

"Yeah, it's coming down, man."

"I sitting here thinking fun thoughts about at board reception the expression on Wentz's face and then Fritz's and Florence's as my insult of calling him Jabba slowly dawn on them. Wonderful."

"Yeah, they were pretty taken aback, you sick fuck. You know, sooner or later Wentz may get your ass."

"Yes. If Phase 1 not successful, that will happen, but truth be, Thomas, Phase 1, even if not success, may point way to future success, which is what I begin to think, so what he do then? Toss big baby out with bathwater. Even he not that stupid."

"Yeah, maybe."

Our waiter came with my beer. I took a long sip and grabbed some of the bar snacks before Zoltan scattered them further.

"So, what going on? What new?"

"Jesus, a lot. So, I do have one piece of good news to share."

"Yes?"

"The campus is open."

"What? Ohhh …, that wonderful news."

"Plus, it's so nice to be able to tell you that without thinking someone is listening in on us."

"Yes. That wonderful too."

"Yeah, and guess who I had lunch with yesterday?"

Questioning shrug.

"Alicia McDonald."

Blank look. "Who she?"

"The detective from the Blaylock Agency who interviewed me.

Remember, she also showed up at our village center, trying to get information about where the unsolicited name-your-price offers for Blaylock might be coming from. I told her my best advice was to resign Blaylock, which to my surprise she did. So, she took me to lunch to thank me."

"Why you do that?"

I shrugged. "I'm not sure."

"Thomas, I sure. You have sparkle in eye. This not good."

"Yeah, I don't know. I may need her help."

"Help, what? Like you needed Ursula's help?"

"Jesus, thanks. No—like in how to get into Lusby's office."

"Ahhh, that may be smart. She help?"

"Yeah."

"Okay. But I still not like how you look—like pimply teenager with crush."

"Yeah, sorry about that."

"We on verge of getting out of big mess. Don't fuck it up."

"I hear you."

We finished our drink, talking about his spending Christmas in Washington with Kristina and our plans at home, which were to take as much time off work as possible and spend time with Sarah and Tommie, go to a few parties.

Then I trudged back through the blowing snow to the administration building, where I could see that the cleaning crew was already at work, vacuums humming, floors being mopped, windowsills and pictures being dusted and took the elevator upstairs to my office. It was now six-fifteen. I turned on my office lights, stamped off snow again, put my overcoat on the back of my chair and waited for Alicia, listening to the near and distant sounds of the cleaning crew, the faint buzzing of the florescent lights above me and in the hallway, noticing how stale the indoor polluted air was compared to what I had just been breathing outside and feeling antsy as hell, my heart pounding a bit, as it had in high school days when I had to give a speech in assembly.

Suddenly the university line on my phone buzzed and I jumped about a foot in the air. Who the hell would be calling me at this time of day from inside the university?

I picked up the phone.

Ms. Bemis's unmistakably baleful voice came over the line, "He will see you now."

"What!" I heard myself say, drawing in a deep, horrified breath. What the hell was she still doing here? Did that mean Wentz was here and wanted to see me? I had not figured on this. Shit! "Wentz?" I heard myself stammer, "About what?" *Oh fuck*, I thought, *he's onto me. He's going to fire me. What the hell do I tell Janet, the kids?*

"He will see you now," Ms. Bemis said again, even more sternly.

There was a pause. I found that I was sweating profusely, my heart now pounding hard. Then came a small, unsuccessfully suppressed snicker, then a half-guffaw through her nostrils and then Alicia's beautiful, uproarious laugh.

"What the *fuck* is going on, God damn it?" I half-shouted into the phone, then looked at it in disgust, slammed it down on its receiver and walked angrily to the elevator and to the president's office.

There in the president's office reception area both Ms. Bemis and Alicia half sat on the front edge of Ms. Bemis's desk, both dressed in after-work clothes, both looking delighted with themselves, Ms. Bemis with what I took to be a master key on a lanyard around her neck. It was the first time I had ever seen Ms. Bemis smile, and now I understood to some degree why. She had big gap between her two front teeth. Not terribly unattractive, but the gap went a long way toward humanizing her. Looking at them in their giddiness, my anger began to fade.

"What the hell's going on? You scared the crap out of me."

They both laughed and Ms. Bemis reached behind her and then, grinning, held out a section of neatly wound phone line. "You lookin' for this, honey?" She tossed the phone line to me. I fumbled my catch but held on.

"Dr. Simpson—I was onto his shenanigans from the beginnin's," she told me in a completely different patois then her normally professional speech. "He and that Ramis. I could tell they was up to no good. And then one mornin' I come in, and I'm always the first person here, and I can see right away there's marks in the rug by the baseboard. I check it out and can see someone stuck a phone line between the rug and baseboard—follow it right into Wentz's office and see it's hooked up to his private line, then follow it down the hallway to poor Mr. Lusby's office. So, then I think, there's maybe one person who I could trust to tell this to who might have some idea of what to do—my friend here, Alicia."

"We got to know each other through her setting up appointments for Blaylock." Alicia told me. "JoAnn was actually the first person I interviewed. We really hit it off."

I had no idea that Ms. Bemis had a first name. I just stood there, feeling myself gaping at them.

"So, Alicia just said to leave that phone line alone. None of our concern and just let shit sink to its own level."

"Except when we met for lunch the other day," Alicia added, "I realized that Frank Lusby had involved you in his eavesdropping and so, I called JoAnn and we decided you deserved some help. Sorry for our little joke."

"Well, I'm sorry too. You really got me. Thought I was a goner."

"Undoubtedly, you'll live," Alicia told me, and then said to JoAnn, "Thanks. You've been a huge help. I'll go buy Thomas a drink if he'll let me."

"You go on ahead. I'll tidy up here. Thomas, from now on, stop bein' so damn chickenshit. I mean, it was fun for me bustin' your balls, but I seen enough of you over the last year to know you okay. Plus, Alicia, she likes you."

I looked at Alicia questioningly and got no response. I felt ridiculous as I thought about how intimidated I had been of Ms. Bemis all this time. "Thanks, JoAnn." It felt very odd to call her by her first name. "But keep up the gatekeeper act. It's really exceptional."

"I sure will. Now," she said, suddenly becoming the professional Ms. Bemis again, and with a nasty stare told me, "Kindly remove yourself from these premises."

"Gladly." I stuck the rolled-up phone wire in my suit jacket pocket while Alicia grabbed her coat from behind Ms. Bemis's desk. We walked to the elevator and I pressed the down button.

We could hear the machinery working and then the door opened and we jumped. The elevator was full of a herd of cleaning crew with their equipment on their way out of the building, Hispanic, together looking oddly as if they were a displaced family reunion. The word *inequality* popped into my head along with the fleeting thought of whether the price I was paying for my executive privilege was worth it, which set off a pang of nostalgia for my former existence as a professor.

"We'll wait," I told them. I looked over at Alicia. No such doubts running through her mind. All the better.

Finally, the elevator returned, empty this time.

"I need to get my overcoat in my office," I told Alicia as we stepped in and I pushed the button for the second floor.

We stood there facing the doors as they closed and the elevator began to move. Then, suddenly, I felt myself turn toward her. Within an instant we were locked in a long passionate kiss, Alicia's hand warm and soft against my face. The scent of her hair and her warmth, her supple lips and probing tongue turned all my anxiety of the day into a sudden surge of passion, immediately interrupted as the elevator stopped and we separated quickly and tried to compose ourselves in the unlikely event someone was standing there when the doors opened. I was stunned.

The doors opened and we stepped out. "What the hell was that about?" I asked her.

"I might ask you the same thing. Spontaneous combustion, I think."

"I guess. You'd know better than I. You always seem to be about ten steps ahead."

She smiled a pleased and indulgent smile, gave a small shrug. "I'm not really sure, Thomas. Sometimes I just live in the moment. That was a very nice moment."

"It felt more than Goddamned nice," I told her as we walked to my office. "I'm a wreck."

She laughed, "I'm sorry. I can only imagine what you felt when we pulled our little stunt. It was a stupid thing to do."

"Yeah, in hindsight I can see that it was hilarious, for you. But the kiss? What the hell."

"As JoAnn noted, I like you. Is that enough of an explanation?"

"No. That was not a casual bussing of the cheek. That was genuine. Meaningful. You're confusing the hell out of me." I had taken my coat from the back of my chair and turned to face her.

She looked at me seriously, paused, considering what she had to say.

"I guess I owe you an apology for that too. I just have a feeling that you and I need to ... how do I say this without sounding trite or bogus? We should stay in contact. Over time we should get to know one another better. Okay?"

"Maybe," I answered speculatively. "Actually, I'd like that. But for now, look, I don't really have time for a drink without raising all sorts of questions at home."

"Okay," Alicia nodded, "I get it. Let's go."

XIX

Family

THE DRIVE HOME through blowing snow was difficult, made more so by distracting thoughts about Alicia, our kiss in the administration building and the following conversation about whether something truly significant had occurred.

Finally, as I wound up the hill to our neighborhood, back tires slipping occasionally, by necessity I refocused on our family and the upcoming Christmas and New Year's holidays. For starters, I still had yet to think of the right presents for Janet and for Sarah and Tommie.

In the dark my headlights shown over three inches of snow blowing into small drifts around tree trunks, on curbs and other obstructions, leaving bare spots in open areas. I drove slowly, in part to be careful, in part to appreciate the Christmas lights decorating the various houses on my way to ours.

The lights caused me to have an upwelling of good feelings for the coming holidays, for the present changing circumstances that made it seem that much of my struggles of the last year were behind me, thankful to be so fortunate in life that we were relatively well off, that Sarah and Tommie had fared well this year, that Janet seemed to be coming out of her depression.

Nevertheless, as I pulled into the garage I thought, *First things first, I still have some unfinished business.*

I pulled the used and unused encrypted phones and instructions from my glove box. Out of the car in the open garage my breath turning to steam in front of me, I placed the phones under my two rear tires and, traveling backwards and forwards numerous times, listened with satisfaction to the crunching noises as they were reduced to smashed remnants. Then I took the dustpan and broom from beside the workbench, swept up the pieces and threw them into the garbage can, adding Frank Lusby's wrapped up phone line and sprinkling ripped up small bits of paper from the instructions onto the top of the pile. It felt damn good to get rid of all of it. Cleansing.

As I entered the family room, Sparky gave me her usual happy greeting and I was delighted to see Janet and Sarah assembling our Christmas tree, a synthetic tree we had bought several years before because of Tommie's allergies, the large boxes for it spread around the floor and boxes of ornaments stacked on the couch while Tommie tried to help or at least pretended to help.

"Hey, Merry Christmas, everyone."

"Thanks, honey," Janet greeted, looking up from the box she was opening.

A distracted, "Hey, Dad," from Sarah as she hung an ornament that was a miniature Sessions University crest, a gift from the annual giving department as part of their end of the year appeal a few years before.

"You remember this?" Janet held up a blue BMW 3-Series cast metal replica surrounded by a green wreath with a red *Merry Christmas* across its side.

"Yeah, the first tree ornament we ever bought, living together in the apartment we had downtown, right after we got married and I got my appointment in the communications department. We had that scraggly little Charlie Brown Christmas tree and that single ornament on it. Hilarious. Those were the days, huh? Not a care in the world."

"Yeah," Janet laughed, "True. Cinder block bookshelves, spider plants, used rug, dust puppies and cheap wine. On the top of the world."

Tommie looked up at us, his face screwed up, "You guys are *weird*," he commented.

Well, I thought, a normal thirteen-year-old response. Not bad.

"And you aren't?"

"Mr. Diamond says I'm *awesome*."

"Well, I do agree with that."

Janet and I looked at one another approvingly.

I went to hang my coat and find a glass of wine in the kitchen, where the scent of store-bought lasagna came from a foil container in the oven.

Back out in the family room, I took off my suit coat and tie and helped with the decorations, many of them causing us to comment on their history and significance to family Christmas's in years past.

Finally, we rescued the lasagna, which was beginning to burn. Sarah set the table with Tommie's meager assistance, Janet brought a vegetable medley from the microwave and warmed some garlic bread she had heated earlier. We served ourselves, passing the food around and settled into a few minutes of silent concentration.

"So, what are the big plans for the holidays?" I asked Sarah.

"Dad, I don't know. A couple parties with my old classmates at my high school. That'll be weird because now they seem so immature. Almost everyone I know at Sessions has gone home for the holidays, so there's nothing going on with them. But the other thing is—I only have three weeks after we get back from the holidays before exams, so I still have studying to do over the holidays." She paused momentarily, holding a forkful of lasagna, as she thought and then said, "Hey, guess what, Sessions offers a summer abroad program in France. How cool would that be?"

"What would be the cost? Aren't you too young?" I replied dubiously, then reflected that it was the typical parent response.

"It'll be chaperoned by one of my professors. Not only do we get to study but also travel around. It'll be in Nice, but we'll travel to places like Paris and to Sessions's Brussels Center. I'll give you the materials."

I looked at Janet. Neutral expression, focused on her plate. She and Sarah had undoubtedly talked this through and plotted on how they might convince me to say yes.

"With Sarah gone," I asked Janet, "how would we handle Tommie's summer classes at Sessions?"

"We can coordinate," Janet began, and I could tell immediately that her response was rehearsed. "If we know in advance, I can always blank out the time in my client schedule. I can take Tommie in. You can bring him home perhaps, or maybe we can find someone to help, another student who lives in the area, something like that."

"Umm ...." I could see this was a done deal. No point in a pushing it. Besides, beyond the expense, it might actually be a good idea. I had to get accustomed to letting our child grow up.

Janet shifted the subject. "Mr. Diamond called. The Center for Gifted and Talented Youth is sponsoring a Friday trip to NIH for families in January. You think you can get off?"

"Yeah, probably. What do think of that, Tommie?"

"I dunno. Yeah, maybe it'll be cool."

"You know what NIH is?"

"Yeah, they study gen-net-tics and the only way to do it is with com-put-ters."

"Well, they do a lot more than that, but yeah, I think that would be an interesting trip."

No response as he shoved too large a portion of lasagna into his mouth.

After dinner, Tommie went back up to his room and Sarah camped out in the family room to watch a Christmas special. Janet and I cleaned up the kitchen and found ourselves sitting back at the kitchen table with a final glass of wine. We were chatting about the neighborhood party at our community center, about whether we even wanted to attend it given the insincerity of the whole event and the people there.

Then we paused and I became aware suddenly that Janet was

preparing to tell me something important. All my relaxation from our evening together vanished instantly.

"I need to talk with you, Thomas," she began awkwardly. "I need to apologize for something I did. I need your understanding."

"This does not sound good," I heard myself say, while my mind started to race.

"It will be what we make of it, like it always has."

"Okay."

"At that conference a couple of weeks ago …" she took in a deep breath, then blurted, "I slept with a colleague. I had to tell you. I've felt terrible about it. I want you to understand why and what I learned."

"Slept with a colleague?"

"Yes."

"God damn it. Why? I mean, I know I've been distant, distracted a lot over the last year, like we've discussed, but … who is he?"

"She."

"She. Oh, fuck, great."

"Let me finish."

I felt overwhelmed, completely surprised and in shock. Just when you think you know your spouse, that things are trending the right direction, she dumps something like this on you. It pulled the rug out from under me. Then I thought about my infidelity with Ursula. I deserved this. I'd listen, but I wasn't sure I would hear. This was too upsetting. Why the hell did she even have to tell me? Ruinous.

"It was very spontaneous, tender and loving. That was the good part. Someone I've known for years, a good colleague and friend."

"Thanks. You're making me feel completely worthless." How was I supposed to deny the possibility of spontaneity with what had just happened between Alicia and me?

"So, the bad part was this: I came to realize later that, even though we'll still be in touch, beyond that it was meaningless, empty. She has her life; I have mine. It made me realize how much our family, you, meant to me and that I'd become numb to that. In short, it woke me up emotionally—shocked me, really. Do you have some understanding about what I'm saying?"

"Yeah, maybe. Awwww Jesus, Janet. God damn it. Part of me wants to go low-life and fly off the handle and smack you around, shake you, beat you to a Goddamn pulp. But that's not me, is it?"

"No, thankfully."

"I don't know. We're going to have to let me live with this awhile. Figure it out. I mean, Janet, what the hell do you want from me? I've done the best I can for you, for Sarah and Tommie. The last year's been a tough one, new job, big responsibilities, lot of pressure, Kravitz's death, Lusby's, having to report to Wentz. What do you want? For us to continue? I mean, can things ever be right or the same after such a confession? Why the hell would you even tell me this?"

"With all my heart I want us to go on, Thomas. Things may be different to some degree perhaps, but we belong together, don't we? Forgive me."

"Well, if you don't mind," I said, feeling a delayed but rising fury, "I think I need to go take a long drive to sort this out."

In a dream, I saw myself stomping into the hallway, grabbing my coat and heading to the garage.

In the BMW I hammered through the gears, fishtailing in the falling snow through the neighborhood. At the bottom of the hill on my way to the expressway, driving blindly, the roads deserted, I took the left hand turn too rapidly, spun the car in a full circle and ended up with the rear of the car facing the curb at the far end of the crossroad. The fear that came with that maneuver brought some caution back to my driving but I nevertheless sped away recklessly in agony, in a fury.

As I entered the expressway, I speed-dialed Zoltan.

"Thomas?"

"Yeah, I'm calling because Janet just told me she slept with one of her female colleagues at the conference in Chicago. I'm taking a long drive to try come to terms with it."

"Bad time to be out, Thomas. You slow down. Be careful... You not tell her about Ursula?"

"No."

"Umph. Good. You at least that smart."

"Yeah. I wish to hell she had just kept her mouth shut about her own infidelity. Now I've got to deal with it. But she felt too guilty. And she wanted to tell me that it made her wake up about the importance of me and our family to her."

"Yes. Sometimes one need to do these things to discover .... Or at least that excuse we use to do what the devil in us want to do. So, Thomas, how can you feel bad about this probably one-time thing with Janet when you fuck Ursula all last year? Maybe this help even things up."

"Yeahhhh. Well, not as if the thought hadn't occurred to me. But I'm still shocked and upset as hell."

"Yes. You must let it go. Family more important than you."

"Yeahhh."

"That she tell you mean she trust and depend on you. Plus, from now on guilty sex be pretty good. She try to make it up to you."

"Oh, great. You are so fucking comforting."

"Yes," Zoltan said with mock seriousness. "It difficult to be this wonderful."

"Asshole."

"That too. But I bring smile to face, yes?"

"You fucker."

"No, you fuck her."

"And such charm and wit."

"I try."

"Why did I even call you?"

"I best friend."

"Yeah. Okay, I'm better now, a little bit. Thanks."

"Call me if you need to talk more. I do my best to maybe make things worse."

"Sure."

We hung up.

I looked around and realized I had no idea where I was, driving blindly in a snowstorm on the expressway, not even remembering whether I had taken a north or south entrance.

My first cue came when out of the cascading gloom the sign coming up was for an exit near the airport.

"NO!" I heard myself say out loud.

I thought about Janet, Tommie and Sarah decorating the Christmas tree and our conversations at dinner, about Janet and our recent lovemaking, about today's kiss with Alicia. There was one thought in the back of my consciousness that I should take the exit, call Alicia and go see her, while another thought overlaid it with concerns for our family, how I could hurt them, that they did not deserve such get-even behavior. Then came the confirming thought that my showing up at Alicia's in my current state of turmoil might very well cause her to seriously reconsider any positive feelings she had for me.

I took the exit, made a left at the light and a second left onto the expressway entrance heading back toward our home, snow now deep and light enough that it came up and over the hood of the car, making for a long, slow and difficult return, the heat and defroster on full blast, my headlights barely penetrating the whiteout in front of me.

XX

Lucky

SHORTLY AFTER I arrived at work the following Tuesday morning, my day for meeting with Emily Sayzak and then Natalie and Joan Kravitz, I received a businesslike call from Ms. Bemis informing me that President Wentz had set a catch-up executive committee meeting for four o'clock that afternoon and that he also wished to meet with me at ten-thirty.

Then she added in her JoAnn voice, "Bad day up here, honey."

"Yeah?"

"Bad day."

"Okay." I wondered what the hell this was about. At least now I had been forewarned.

When I entered the reception area, Ms. Bemis gave me the normal baleful look.

She was dressed, for all I could tell, as one of Santa's elves. Red skirt, white pullover turtleneck, green suspenders displaying fake small clusters of holly leaves and berries—and of all the damn things, on her shorn head she was sporting a brown hat with antlers, complemented by her snowflake-spangled earrings. Any other time I would have laughed out loud.

"He will see you now," she said, shaking her head, her earrings rattling slightly, closing her eyes momentarily, indicating I was in for some trouble.

"Thanks a lot," I told her.

She turned and transformed into the Christmas Sphinx.

Wentz was seated at his desk, behind him a picture post card view of the snow-covered lower quadrangle unblemished by students, proof positive that they were gone for the holidays.

His shirt sleeves were rolled up on his large, white, black-haired arms—elbows on his desk, hands clasped, looking genuinely pissed off.

I thought, *Uh-oh, she wasn't kidding.*

I sat in one of the chairs facing his desk. "What's wrong?"

Wentz looked at me for a moment, weighing his response. The heat kicked on and blew hot, dry, dust and urethane-smelling air on us from the register overhead. The papers on Wentz's desk ruffled slightly.

"Does it ever concern or bother you," he began, his voice angry, a bit breathless, "that we serve at the whim of a board leader, one worth a couple hundred million, who really doesn't have a clue what it's like being in our shoes, what it's like to have to deal with all the crap this university manages to throw at us from disgruntled faculty who argue and fight like children, to students who feel they are oppressed, to interfering egomaniacal alumni, to helicopter parents, to everyone wanting special treatment or a favor with little reward for any of our daily efforts to stave off disaster—and then you have on top of all this our Goddamned cover up, which is killing us, literally."

If he only knew the extent of it, I thought, the vision of Zoltan and me in the white van with a dead black ops agent in the back flashing through my mind. I replied, "Um, yeah, I guess. Comes with the territory."

"Well, Thomas, it shouldn't, God damn it."

"No argument from me there. So, why are you bringing this up now? I mean, what happened?"

"Aw, Fritz is all over my case about some things. Really pissing me off."

"Sorry about that." *Oh,* I thought, *I get it. Fritz just shut down Wentz and Ramis over their lawyer/consultant scheme with the pharmaceutical companies.*

I'd never seen this side of Wentz before, a petulant twelve-year old. Very worrisome.

"Have you ever thought," he continued, poking a fat forefinger at me, "that we might be better off without Fritz leading our board? That with him gone we might be able to run this place without Fitz-Hugh always on everyone's mind like the ghost from Christmas past?"

"No, not really."

"Well, I'm very frustrated with the whole scene here, the whole cover-up. It's crippling our university. Maybe it's time for some of the cover-up to go public, so that fucker gets some blame for the mess he's created."

"Whoa, Jack. Really? I don't know. That could bring us all down."

"Not if it were leaked in such a way that no one knew where such a leak came from, that it was about Fitz-Hugh cooking the books and Johnson covering it up, didn't reveal the covert aspect of things."

Fuck—he was serious. So, here it was, as I had feared, vindictiveness. "Nice trick if you can do it," I told him.

"Well, someone in your position with lots of media contacts, like that blond reporter you're friendly with, could probably get the ball rolling on something like that."

"Oh great. I don't think so. She'd likely see through something like that in a heartbeat."

"Off the record? Anonymous? Thomas, don't underestimate the appeal and power of such information. Could sell a whole lotta papers. Hell, if she's got any kind of ability, she undoubtedly knows that Kravitz succeeded in getting the Faculty Senate to vote for an independent audit of university finances. A little rumor about fiscal malfeasance would play into that. Your reporter friend, she'd probably even go down for you for information like that. It'd make my day, month, hell, my whole fucking year to get that fucker off my back."

"That's not the way I see it."

"You know, the rewards for such assistance could be very substantial. Have you thought about that? Your work here deserves a substantial bonus and I know that Allogenic might well be interested in Zoltan and you somewhere down the line. I could certainly make a strong recommendation when that happens. Who knows? I may go work for those guys in the future. With all the international credentials and contacts I have, it would actually make some sense. Plus, Thomas, one other thing …"

"Yeah?"

"If Fritz were to resign, your buddy, Mark Berger, would be chairman of the board."

I was stunned, speechless. This felt like Darth Vader asking me to come over to the dark side. Finally, it occurred to me that I had to say something. "Well, let me think about it. It would have to be very adroitly done."

"So, you'll do it?"

"I didn't say that. I need to think through how the hell I might pull it off. I need some time."

"You got until after we return from the holidays. Then I want an answer."

I let out a long exhalation. *"Okay."* I thought, *Push comes to shove on this, I may have to resign.* I needed to talk to Berger. No holding back on this one. I knew where my loyalties lay. They weren't with Jack Wentz, especially now.

"Okay," Wentz said, "So onto some other business. I need you to be at the School of Foreign Service the second week in January. They're giving this year's Leadership Medallion Award to Berger. Since you guys are friends, I thought it would make sense for you to cover it, plus I want to be sure the whole publicity and roll out of his coverage is handled perfectly, and that idiot Fein you have working for you doesn't exactly inspire my confidence. You can work with Berger's PR staff."

"Okay."

"Look, Thomas, I know he's your friend but he's also, as Bernie analyzes our prospect potential, far and away the best prospect we have. He really could be a billion-dollar donor over time or all at once, however he wants to play it."

"Yeah, I know."

"I appreciate your need and desire to preserve your friendship. I really do. But if the opportunity ever presents itself, I would hope you'd sound him out about his interests. We're talking about a transformative gift, one that would put Sessions head and shoulders above our peers. I can't stress the importance of that enough. If he were chairman of the board, maybe he'd also feel more invested in making a substantial contribution."

"No pressure, huh?"

My seeming consideration of Wentz's request to leak information to Emily Sayzak had clearly improved his mood. So, my remark actually caused him to laugh.

"Nah," he replied, "None at all."

I returned to my office, tried to get some work done, but was totally distracted. Finally, I headed over to the Student Union, slammed a sandwich while drinking a Dr. Pepper in honor and memory of Frank Lusby, went back to the office, returned a few phone calls, read and replied to emails and then took a taxi downtown.

The Intercontinental was at the heart of our small city, fronting a park which had originally been the village square, surrounded by a mix of office buildings and the hotel.

I found a booth in the quiet and elegant, old style, all mahogany, brass and leather bar and ordered an unsweetened iced tea. Before it arrived, Emily Sayzak appeared, obviously having walked in the cold from her office several blocks away. She pulled a red knit cap off her head and shook out her thick blond hair, put the cap and her overcoat on the bench seat on the other side of the table. She was dressed in too-tight black slacks, a crème-colored silk blouse that was cinched and twisted at the waist, a red silk scarf that was askew. What was it about journalists? No matter what they wore, it was always in disarray. She slid in next to me, shimmying over so that her leg was hard against mine, so her hair was touching my shoulder and so I could smell her overuse of perfume. She set her leather satchel beside her, reached in, pulled out a file folder and placed it in front of me.

"These are," she told me, her funny, expressive mouth so close I could see how thick her red lipstick was applied, "as they say, self-explanatory, and pretty gross. You'll understand why I didn't want to let Alicia or anyone else know about them."

I looked at her, looked at the file, then opened it.

Grainy, blown-up, blurry, black-and-white pictures, obviously taken from security camera footage, hard to make out what was going on, who it was. Pretty clear at the outset that these pictures were from a bathhouse. That set alarm bells ringing. I focused harder.

"Aw, shit," I heard myself say.

"Yeah," Emily sighed sympathetically, placed a hand on my leg.

"That's Frank Lusby."

"Yeah."

"No clothes, just a towel."

"Yeah."

"Back there in the corner. That's Wentz. No clothes. God. Yuk."

"Uh-huh …"

"These other … guys … some of 'em …"

"Yeah …"

"Way underage. Fucking boys."

"Uh-huh. That's what they were up to, I guess."

I leafed through another five photos. Much the same, some worse, fondling, leering, no doubt about what was going on.

"God damn, Emily. Where did you get these?"

She shrugged, moved her mouth around reflectively.

"Damnedest thing," she told me. "Just having a social drink at a bar near here with a friend and there's this big, muscled-up guy sitting next to us. Reasonably well dressed, obviously wants to impress us. So, we start talking, you know, what do you do, who do you know? Well, turns out he's the security for this place you're looking at. After a while, the conversation kinda drifts to things that go on that nobody knows about except people like reporters and security folks. And the next thing we know he drops into the conversation things he knows about some key players at the university. My ears, of course, perk up and after a time, I say, 'I don't believe you. Prove it.' Then a couple days later these pictures arrive in the mail. Little typed note, 'Hope to see you again.'"

I felt myself shaking my head, reached down and removed her hand from my leg which phased her not at all. "These are totally explosive."

"Oh yeah, nitroglycerine."

"Your timing's also pretty damn amazing."

"Yeah?"

"I can't get into to it. Look, you have my word that these will get to the right person. You've done me and the university an incredibly important and significant favor. I really admire and appreciate what you've done, not taking this public."

"It was a big temptation. This is front page news, not just local/regional, but national. Could advance my career. But I thought it over, a lot. This is our university we're talking about. I should give you guys the chance to handle things internally. Otherwise, I/we bring a bad name to the university, our city, this whole area. Not that something like this should, but it will. You know what? I don't want to be responsible for that."

"I owe you big-time. You are one classy lady. Maybe this is one reason we all like living here. Still small enough that we know one another and have a vested interest in our community."

"You owe me enough to let me know what the hell happened over there last year?" Emily asked as her hand returned to my leg.

I laughed. "Look, let me do you a big favor."

"Yeah?"

"Never tell you about that."

"Really? That serious?"

"You bet your life."

"Ohhh … you're not kidding. I was wondering why Alicia

seemed to make a 180-degree turn about her investigation and working for Blaylock."

"Um-hmm. Just take the hint. I like you."

"How much?" she responded, squeezing leg.

"Aww, Emily. I got a family. Let's just leave it at that. Okay?"

She withdrew her hand, looked at me disappointedly. "I guess. But I still like you."

"Like's good."

We slid out of the booth together. She gave me a light peck on the cheek, put on her coat and hat. I watched her walk away and tried unsuccessfully to push away thoughts of what I might be missing. I clasped the folder tightly and made my way to the taxi stand. God, I was a lucky son-of-a-bitch. And Wentz was a dead man walking.

Back at the office I found a large document envelope, slid the file folder in it and sealed it. Wrote "To Mark Berger" and a big, printed and underlined "CONFIDENTIAL" on the top right corner. I placed it in my top desk drawer.

When I entered the president's reception area at 3:50 p.m., Ms. Bemis gave me the slightest of nods, so I continued into Wentz's office. He had already taken his place at the conference table, acknowledge my entry, "Good to see you, Dr. Simpson."

"Thanks."

I sat next to Frank Lusby's empty chair. Two gone, Lusby and Kravitz. Would there be more? Wentz? Very depressing.

Bernie Reve was already there, sitting to Wentz's right in an immaculate black suit, crisp white-on-white shirt and beautiful maroon silk tie.

Ramis sat at his outpost at the other end of the table. He had a very different look than at our previous executive committee meetings. Instead of radiating the hubris of the master clinician and God-like ruler of the medical center, he had an odd, chastened and crestfallen look about him, as if he had been dressed down by Hippocrates or had experienced a close-by strike of lightning or perhaps had been drilled a couple new butt holes by a big, no-nonsense, take-no-prisoners Texan named Fritz Johnson.

Don Powers entered. Sat in his usual seat, greeted us diffidently and smiled his worthless smile.

Finally, Neil Wexler scurried in, accompanied by his large black briefcase. As usual, he sat in Kravitz's former chair.

"Glad you could make it here on such short notice," Wentz told us. "Needless to say, this has been an unusual and unusually busy Fall, but I'm nevertheless remiss in not calling us together before now. Thanks for being here. Let me begin by wishing you all the best of the holidays. I hope each and every one of you takes some good, quality time off to enjoy being with your family and/or significant others."

We all murmured agreement.

"As you know, we had a very successful board of trustees meeting two weeks ago. Very positive feedback and to my way of thinking a significant transition from the old order to the new. My great thanks to those of you who participated."

We all nodded.

"Of course, Don, we're sorry you couldn't be there but convey our thanks for what must have been a very difficult assignment attending Frank's memorial service.

Powers placed his hands in front of him, fingertips touching. "Indeed, it was," he remarked without any real emotional connection to what he was saying, "Tragic. Only a few family members there. John Blakum gave a nice send-off. I spoke briefly on Frank's great work for our university. I get the sense that the company has some life insurance and retirement in place. Difficult, rainy day. Pastor who didn't know Frank or the family trying to say the right things. Wife and his teenage daughter devastated. You know how it goes."

I felt huge amounts of shame and anger well up inside me. Had to compose myself. God damn, that's all there is to a life, a life gone wrong. Meaningless words on a rainy day and gone.

"Thanks, Don," Wentz said, "What do you have to report on the academic side of things?"

"Ah, yes—all good news. Steady as she goes. In the interests of receiving a proper, proportionate share of last year's $2 million Fitz-Hugh allocation to the humanities, the majority of the departments have sent their long-range plans to me. Some are God-awful rudimentary, even ungrammatical in some instances. I've returned those. Political Science's is really quite well-done. With their permission and review, I've blacked out sensitive information and emailed it to departments who are still working on their plans as an example and as a motivator. Of course, no matter what the outcome of the allocation's distribution, the majority of the departments will complain that they have been treated unfairly."

"Sounds about right," Wentz commented. "Bernie?"

Reve perked up, sat forward and began his report in his usual upbeat manner, his hands moving expressively. "The Campaign for Progress continues to move right along. A lotta big asks out there. We're hoping to see some significant action before the end of the year.

"As for real results, there've been a smattering of million-dollar gifts, mostly from alumni, a couple from present parents," Reve moved his eyebrows up and down knowingly, "and even one from parents of a former student in appreciation. Not to be looked down on, but if we're going to make our goal, we need eight-figure, nine-figure gifts, not seven—or we need something transformational." He looked at me.

I thought, *Christ.*

"We're cranking up our regional campaigns after the beginning of the year, setting goals for each one—have leadership teams assembled who are highly placed and motivated and who have already made their own gifts. We launch them one at a time, big to small, beginning with New York, Chicago, LA, Dallas–Fort Worth, Houston and so on. The timelines are set to more-or-less end simultaneously a year and a half from now. We may extend that depending on how things go. A lotta work to do."

He paused, looked around the table for any questions. There being none, he continued, "Our campaign among our corporate supporters is showing moderate progress. The issue remains that we've got to come up with programs and projects that appeal to their specific interests, like biomedical engineering, and that's difficult to do in many cases. We're hard at it though. The pharmas are for the most part holding off despite our entreaties that they should be with us for the long haul and make significant pledges to the campaign. They are, after all, practical mothers. So, we'll see where Dr. Vastag's work takes us."

"Hopefully, not to the cleaners," Wentz remarked.

Everyone but me chuckled at Wentz's cheap shot.

"Thomas?"

I reported on our extensive follow-through from the board of trustees meeting, about how we were working with the Brussels and Beijing centers on specific promotions on their cross disciplinary programs as well as how we were tailoring our communications and marketing to different alumni and parent constituencies. I noted the success of our podcasts, particularly those involving Wentz and then talked a bit about our future plans for the new year, then cut things off before everyone started to become bored.

"Neil?"

Neil Wexler screwed up his face in his nerdy way. "University finances, I'm pleased to say, are in complete balance across the board, for the university and all our schools and international divisions. Having completed our assignment, we're now preparing for the transition to your accounting personnel. I want to thank everyone for your good faith, help and assistance. It's been a great pleasure working with you."

With Wentz taking the lead, everyone around the table applauded in appreciation not only of a job well done but with some recognition that his work and that of Berger's other accountants had played a significant role in saving our university's ass.

"Thanks," Neil said and smiled, genuinely pleased.

"Have the best of holidays," Wentz told us. "Meeting adjourned."

In the hallway outside the president's reception area I caught up with Wexler.

"Hey, Neil!" I greeted him from behind.

He turned and looked at me quizzically.

"Good day for a walk, don't you think?"

He gave me a long look, screwing up his face. "Really?"

"Yeah. Meet you in the atrium in five. Okay?"

"Okay."

So it was that we went walking in the slush and snow around the campus and into the woods on our familiar path, Neil in a heavy overcoat and galoshes, me in my lined boots, my overcoat and cap, both of us looking silly with our briefcases in hand.

When we had finally trudged along the path through the woods, out of view of the university, I pull the large envelope for Berger from my briefcase and handed it to him.

"Please get this to Mr. Berger ASAP and, whatever you do, don't open it. It's for his eyes only."

"Okay. Gotcha."

We trudged on back to campus and went our separate ways.

XXI

Sammie

IN THE ONCOMING gloom of a winter evening I drove into Hampton Park, an old-line, exclusive neighborhood where Joan Kravitz lived. Its august beauty, even in its half-buried, frozen state, was impressive. An icy stream trickled in the wide median of the gently curving two lanes of the main road, running by fallow gardens, bare trees, an ancient snow-covered brick walkway and park benches—mansions in different architectural styles on each side set back on large, rolling, landscaped properties.

I drove up the Kravitz's drive to their Tudor house and parked in their cobbled courtyard to the side of their heavy, mahogany front door.

When I rang the bell, their French poodle, Marcel, began to bark, bringing back all the memories of my visit last year.

Back to the present. Natalie—tall, pale in a dark-blue dress, opened the door.

"Hello, Thomas," she greeted. "Thank you for coming."

I could see behind her, beyond Marcel waiting eagerly to greet me, wooden crates stacked one upon another. Undoubtedly, they were filled with rare books from the dismantling of Samuel Kravitz's library. His pride and joy.

Marcel was a little greyer in the muzzle. He seemed to remember me, was delighted to be petted and pranced beside me as we walked to the living room.

It was a large, beautifully decorated room, oriental carpets in predominant reds and blues, walls painted a soft yellow with large, white, ornate, ceiling moldings; pastoral country scene paintings that I was sure had significant provenance; a mix of lovely ancestral antiques; a large Queen Anne sideboard on the far wall; a grandfather's clock in the corner.

A silver tea set on an ornate silver tray was on a low, leather-topped table between two yellow tableau sofas—the tea set surrounded by thin, bone china cups and saucers, several plates of different cookies and small pastries, thin mints, a small mist of steam rising from the spout of the teapot.

Joan Kravitz was there, standing up from the far couch to greet me. I was shocked at the change in her, a seeming shell of her former self, bent over by arthritis and sadness, trying with all her will for a normalcy that might never return, her life obviously uprooted by the death of her spouse. The whole scene was crushingly sad and I was immediately sorry that I had come. Then on the other hand, somewhere deep down I knew that I had to. Because how could I turn down such a request? This was unavoidable, part of the torture I was destined to endure because of my past and forever continuing role in the cover-up.

"Hello, Thomas," she greeted me with the briefest of hugs. There was a slight quaver to her voice that had not been there before. We sat in the comfortable sofas; all of us, I'm sure, looking totally uncomfortable. Marcel curled up next to the table.

"It's nice to see you again," Joan said as she picked up the tea pot, which began to wobble in her hand.

"I can do that, Mother," Natalie said, and gently took the teapot and began pouring tea.

"How is your family?" Joan inquired against a deadly silence in the room.

"Very well, thank you," I told her, taking an obligatory sip, "Sarah's now enrolled in Sessions Center for Gifted and Talented Youth."

"Oh, isn't that wonderful! How old is she now?"

"Sixteen. Skipping her last two years of high school. Seems that she's gifted in languages."

"That's splendid. You must be so proud."

"Absolutely. It was Sarah's initiative too. Originally, she wanted to go elsewhere. Anything to get out of the old homestead, you know. But we convinced her to stay here, at least for the year. I think for the moment that's she settled in and happy with her choice. Wouldn't surprise me if she wants to continue at Sessions but get an apartment next year. We'll face that when we come to it."

"And your son?"

"Ah, good news there too. He's at Schossler, you may remember?"

"Yes."

"Well, they've discovered that he's gifted in technology."

"Oh, how wonderful."

"Yeah, a major surprise to us." I thought, *Where in the hell do we go with this conversation? Why the hell am I here?* It was as if the ghost of Samuel Kravitz was standing there beside the table, turning his head to look askance at each of us as we spoke. Maybe all that was going to happen was just this normal palaver and I could make a polite escape before too long.

I turned to Natalie, took a sip of tea, "And your children. How are they faring?"

"Thank you, Thomas. Very well. Molly …"

The was a loud opening of the front door latch and then of the door itself and then a loud slam as it was shut. Both Joan and Natalie jumped and looked surprised, concerned.

Heavy, approaching steps sounded in the hall. I felt myself close my eyes momentarily as I thought, *Oh shit.*

Samuel Kravitz II came steaming around the corner, dark haired, compact, fiery dark eyes. He stopped as he saw us.

"Ah, I was wondering whose car that was."

He looked directly at me, "You've got some gall coming here," he said accusatorily

"I *invited* him!" Natalie shot back. "You've interrupted us. Thomas was one of Dad's colleagues whom he liked. We'd like to catch up with him and his family, Sammie."

I thought, *Sammie, a brilliant, self-righteous prig just like his old man, deeply and correctly suspicious that his dad had been murdered.*

"What happened with your trip to the Sessions library?" Natalie asked him.

Sammie threw up his hands in frustration, "Those people! Clueless. I'm going to have to go to Dad's records and submit them. Then they'll research the matter, they say."

Natalie turned to me, "The library had borrowed a number of Dad's rare books for display purposes originally. Now they can't seem to find them and, typically, because of personnel turnover no one seems to have clue about them. We're sure they were accounted for, but no one can find the records."

"Damn frustrating," Sammie commented as he walked toward us, sat in the opening on my sofa and began helping himself to cookies, shoving them into his mouth as he talked.

"Aren't you the communications guy at the university?" he asked between bites.

"Yeah, I am."

"Blaylock felt that there was a big cover-up going on about what happened to my father that night in the park, but they couldn't get anyone to talk. What do you know?"

Oh great, I thought, *an interrogation.* I shrugged, "I was as helpful to their representative as I could be under the circumstances, but you know, I really couldn't be of much assistance."

"Like hell."

I just let his comment lay out there in the space between us. The less I said, the better.

There was a long, extraordinarily awkward silence. I looked at each of them. Sammie in his anger; Joan and Natalie in their mortification, Marcel with a bit of confusion, glancing at each of us for cues. Finally, I thought, *What the fuck,* and stood.

"Well, I better be going," I told them, "Good to see all of you again ..." I almost wished them the best of the holidays, but that clearly was not the right thing to do.

Joan stood, along with Natalie and Sammie and Marcel, "It's

been so nice to see you, Thomas," Joan told me. "Do give our best to your family."

"Thanks, I sure will."

We all walked down the hallway and Sammie opened the front door and stepped out into cold with me.

The last thing I remember was turning to him to say something that I hoped would help defuse his frustration and anger. I do not remember what it was that I was going to say, but that was my intent.

My next recollection was lying on the cold, hard cobblestones of the courtyard, looking up into the winter gloom of the sky, my head resting on something soft, which I realized was Natalie Kravitz's lap, tremulous weeping coming from Joan Kravitz, standing nearby.

I wanted to say something, but couldn't think of what to say, an odd feeling. I wanted to move but could not think how to. Almost unbearable pain was radiating from my jaw and the back of my skull.

An ambulance siren sounded in the distance, coming closer until it cut off as the ambulance reached the drive. Then came the sound of a large engine revving to climb the driveway and the ambulance turned into the courtyard, its flashing red lights reflecting on the surrounding walls, shrubbery, cobblestones and the house.

I caught a glimpse of it as it stopped, the engine continuing to run as two uniformed attendants bounded out, the driver and a medic. The medic—a young, beefy, butch-cut, freckled redhead—walked to me, knelt, looked at me, looked at Natalie.

"So, what's happened here?"

"My brother hit him. He fell backwards, hit head hard on the cobblestones."

"Where's your brother?"

"He left."

"Sucker punched him, huh?"

"Yes."

He looked over at Joan Kravitz, who was still sobbing, turned in on herself, shaking.

"Is she going to be okay?"

"Yes. She lost her husband this year. This has really upset her."

"Okay. Look, you take care of your mother. We'll take care of this guy. He was unconscious for a couple minutes?"

"Yes. He came to just before you arrived. You were here very quickly."

"Yeah, we have a station nearby." He turned to me. "Don't try to talk," he told me gently in friendly tones, "just raise a finger to acknowledge you can hear me."

I heard his request and after a long moment or two it processed. Then I had to think about raising my finger, which I did after another few long moments had passed.

"Good," my attendant told me, "I'm Steve. You've got a concussion. Your jaw may be fractured. We're headed to Wing Memorial."

Steve went to the ambulance, came back and put a pillow under my head while Natalie went to Mrs. Kravitz, took her into the house and after a time, came back out. By then I was strapped on a stretcher and was being loaded into the ambulance.

"I'm so sorry, Thomas. What Sammie did was horrible. I'll never forgive him for it."

I thought, *You will.* Then, *If anything, I probably deserved it.*

Once the rear door was slammed, we were off with sirens blaring. I stared at the white plastic, metal-ribbed ceiling several feet above me while Steve wrapped a blood pressure band around my arm, undid my tie and shirt and placed electrodes on my chest, gently placed an icepack under my head and another on my jaw, propping it in place with two pillows.

"You're stable," he told me, "Are you going to want to press charges? Just give me the thumbs up or down."

I thought awhile about what he had said. There did not seem to be any hurry. My mind was moving ultra-slowly. Wing Memorial was our local hospital, so that was good. Better than going downtown to the medical center. Eventually, I gave him a thumbs down.

"Okay, man—so, what's your name?"

So, now he wanted me to talk. It was funny; I had to think about it, but I mumbled it at him through waves of jaw pain, roaring in my ears, my tongue thick, my voice sounding like I had a mouthful of cotton wadding. "Tah-mous Simp-sun." I realized that I must have bitten my tongue when Sammie hit me. It was swollen and raw on the same side as my jaw pain. "Ouh bit my tong ..."

"Okay," Steve said, "do your best to open your mouth."

I did and all hell broke loose. Steve took a quick look at my tongue using a tongue depressor and a small flashlight.

"You bit it all right. Nothing serious. Where do you live?"

"Sub-bur-bia." We looked at one another, each of us surprised by this response. We started to laugh, which for me hurt tremendously. Our address popped into my consciousness and I gave it to him. More radiating pain.

"What were you doing at the, uh ...," he checked his clipboard, "Kravitz residence?"

I responded without thinking, the pain roaring through my head and in my ears, my enunciation forced and angry but also slow and garbled, "Th-at, my frund, is fuck-king comp-lah-cated. Less jus' say, a hol-li-day miss-understanding."

He laughed. Looked at me directly, "Seems to me you're probably going to be okay, but I'll let the docs confirm that. They'll want to keep you overnight for observation. The two women there were totally blown away by what happened. I thought I might have to call another ambulance for the old lady. Seems like the son/brother is a troublemaker."

"Yea-uh," was all I could muster.

I was wheeled into the hospital through the Emergency Room and put in a temporary bay there, went through more evaluation and testing, had to change under supervision into a hospital gown, was given a pain shot and new ice packs. Then I was transferred to a wheelchair and taken for x-rays and then to an empty double-occupancy room. The wheelchair attendant told me that I must be someone important to get such a nice room. I assured him I was not and for a time was puzzled, until I recalled that the Kravitz's were major supporters of the hospital. Obviously, they had called.

Nurses arrived, settled me into bed, put an ice pack behind my head, propped another onto my jaw with pillows, raised me to a half-seated position, showed me all the bed, nursing station and TV controls.

A short while later an orderly came with a nutritional drink with a straw stuck into the container, a banana and apple sauce, plastic utensils, a napkin and pain meds in a small paper cup—rotated a dining tray in front of me and raised the bed so that I was almost sitting upright.

I had no problem with the drink or the apple sauce. Did not even try the banana, which in my condition took on impossible proportions. Time went by and I dozed, was woken by a tiny, female, Latin doctor who seemed impossibly young, accompanied by the heavy-set, no-nonsense, floor nurse. My dinner tray was gone, the tray table rotated away and my position returned to half-seated.

"So, the good news, sir," she told me with a Latin accent I could not place. "The x-rays confirm that you don't have a broken jaw, just a major contusion. Need to keep ice on it, keep your teeth clenched as much as possible, so as not to aggravate the swelling. Small mouthfuls of mostly liquids: soups, energy drinks until you can handle food. I'll give your wife all the instructions. It could have been much worse. You also suffered a concussion. All signs are that it is transitory, but we'll keep you here overnight as a precaution. If you feel any vertigo, dizziness, nausea or any other symptoms, press the call button beside you and let the nurse on duty know immediately. You will need to take at least several days off work, might as well extend the next day or two workdays into the holidays. That is an order. You must rest, take it easy, keep quiet, stay away from stimulus in a restful setting."

"Yeah," I agreed, my voice heavy and thick.

"Your family is here to see you."

"Okay."

The doctor and floor nurse left and Janet followed by Sarah and

Tommie made their way into the room, looking around and then at me.

"Wow, Dad, you look terrible," Tommie immediately announced.

No shit, I thought. "Thanks."

"Geez, Dad," Sarah added, "Your jaw is really swollen."

"Yeah ..."

Tommie added, "You look really weird in those pajamas."

"Yeah, they're tied on and open in the back so they can stick needles in your butt."

"Eeuww."

Janet looked at me with concern and pity, "Are you okay?" she asked and took my hand in both of hers.

"I guess," I told them and then with difficulty soldiered on with a bullshit explanation, "Beyond stupid, what happened. I went over there to the Kravitz's at Natalie's invitation, I thought to provide some comfort for her and poor Joan. On the way out, I slipped on the ice in the courtyard, knocked the crap out of myself." The kids seemed to accept my lie at face value, which was my intent.

"Wow," Tommie commented distractedly as he was taking in all the medical equipment in the room. "Look at all this cool stuff!"

"You are to touch *none* of it," Janet told him.

There was a sudden diminishing of light from the hallway. We turned toward the door to find Zoltan standing there.

"I interrupting séance of some kind? You try to cure Thomas through voodoo? I can do Hungarian dance, maybe help?"

We smiled at him.

"Dad really hurt himself!" Tommie announced, as if this was the coolest thing that had ever happened.

"On their way here, Janet call me. So, I want to make sure you okay. If you not going to be okay, can I have Bimmer?"

We laughed at the joke.

"Kids," Janet told Sarah and Tommie, "Go sit in the waiting room for a minute. Uncle Zoltan and I want to talk to Dad."

Sarah looked between us, then turned to Tommie, "Okay, Tommie, let's go."

"Awww …"

When they had left, Janet turned back to me, "What on earth really happened?" She squeezed my hand hard.

"Natalie Kravitz invited me to over to Joan's house," I told them. "My read was that they're finding the holidays to be very depressing and are trying to lighten them up by having former colleagues of the provost visit to share some holiday cheer and memories, maybe sleuth out a thing or two about the mystery behind Kravitz's death. I really did not want to go and we were having this awkward as hell conversation when young Samuel—you'll remember him from the memorial service—showed up and started an inquisition about his father's death. You know, I'm the university's communications officer. He thought I might know something. I decided it was best to leave, thought it was all just going to be a bit more awkward but that I could escape. Unfortunately, when we got out to the front courtyard, apparently, he sucker-punched me and falling backward, I cracked my head on the cobblestones in the courtyard."

"Oh, I'm so sorry," Janet said and bending over gave me a light kiss on the forehead while she hugged me lightly as if I would break.

"You want me to take care of young Samuel?" Zoltan asked flatly.

"No, no, no…. Don't you think poor Joan Kravitz has suffered enough?"

"Hmmm… yes. You right."

Plus, I thought, *any roughing up of young Samuel would just add grist to his notion that a cover-up had taken place. He was in retreat now. Let him stay there.*

"Yeah, the ambulance attendant asked whether I was going to want to press charges. I told him no."

Janet said, "You look very tired, honey. We'll leave you. Glad you're going to be okay."

"Thanks."

Within moments I was in a deep, pain-medication sleep.

Much later, deep into the night, I woke, the clock on the wall reading 2:37 a.m., the hospital around me silent. I realized that the pain meds had for the most part worn off, looked around, deciding whether to call the nurses' station for more meds, wondering whether I could just go to sleep again.

As I was thinking, Alicia McDonald whisked into the room silently. She was dressed in blue jeans; a red, heavy-knit sweater; a tartan scarf; and a red, knit-wool, pullover hat.

"Wow," I half whispered, half croaked at her, "What are you doing here? How'd you get by the nurses' station?"

"Would you believe," she half whispered in return, taking off her hat and scarf which let her blond hair cascade across her shoulders, "the nurse on duty is streaming some series on her cell phone. Completely oblivious."

"How'd you know I was here?"

"JoAnn found out from President Wentz. He and Florence were called by Natalie Kravitz. He wanted JoAnn to call the hospital and check on your condition—not bother your family. Just so you know, Wentz and Florence are apparently very upset but didn't want to disturb you tonight either. They'll call you tomorrow."

"Okay."

"You really look bad, Thomas." She reached out and put her hand on my arm.

"So I've been told. Repeatedly."

"I move back to DC tomorrow, so at least I was here."

"Thanks for coming. I've been meaning to get in touch with you. Sometimes life gets in the way."

"Not a problem. I've been busy packing, making arrangements for Christmas with my folks. Move back to DC and before I can unpack, I'm flying off to visit them in Chicago for the holidays."

I found that we were looking into one another's eyes.

"I've been wanting to give you a Christmas present," she told me. "Thought about breaking into your car and leaving something there for you, but that would be awkward, wouldn't it?"

"Sure as shit would."

"Maybe something else ..."

She turned and pulled the privacy curtain around us. I felt her hand slip under my gown.

I was in no shape to resist, nor did I want to.

XXII

Not At All Like That

THE NEXT MORNING, December twenty-second, after some final tests I was released from Wing Memorial.

Janet met me in the lobby and drove us home in the BMW, which she and Sarah had rescued from the Kravitz's that morning.

When we were in the car, she handed me my cell phone, which she had removed from my room and taken home. I turned it on, glanced at it and saw numerous phone calls to return, the one standout being a call from Mark Berger.

There would be no returning of calls for a while. Dressed in yesterday's clothes and intermittently holding a ziplock bag full of ice to my jaw, I was not feeling all that great or put together. I put the phone on mute. Everything from sunlight to the car's movement seemed a bit jarring. My jaw still hurt significantly while the pain from the back of my skull seemed to be subsiding.

"Were you as shocked as I was, seeing Joan Kravitz?" Janet asked.

"Yeah."

"She's aged so dramatically. She's still extremely upset about Sam Jr.'s attack. Natalie told me she can't get her mother to Chicago for the holidays soon enough. All the remembrances here of provost Kravitz and their lives together and the upkeep of the house and library—her mother simply can't cope with it now. They're putting the place up for sale. She's going to move into a townhouse nearby, large enough for her and Marcel. Natalie's talking to collectors and auction houses about the sale of the books in the library. They've already sold some of the collections. The library itself makes the house something of a white elephant, although there's the unlikely possibility that they'd find a wealthy buyer who's a bibliophile who wants to negotiate a package deal. So, everything's up in the air."

"Yeah, tragic. You know, Frank Lusby told me last year that the Kravitzes originally were going to donate the house and the library to the university lock, stock and barrel as part of their estate plan, but then the board appointed Fitz-Hugh president and he was too prideful to ever make peace with the provost, so ..."

"Really?"

"Yeah." I wanted to add something about the perils of pride, jealousy and ambition, but not only was I not up to it, it would lead down a path of discussion best not traveled.

"How are you feeling?"

I thought about her question. "Like shit."

"I'm so sorry, honey." She reached over and gave me a light pat on my leg.

"Yeah … thanks."

At home I discarded yesterday's clothes in a heap, showered, decided shaving could wait another day, felt the large lump on the back my skull gingerly, put on a pair of jeans and flannel shirt, felt almost human.

Downstairs, I saw that Janet had gone to work. Sarah had left a note that she had gone to a friend's house. On my way I had passed Tommie's room where I saw he was lost in space at his computer. Sparky was curled up sleeping on her bed in the family room. The house was blissfully quiet.

I filled an ice pack Janet had left for me and went to my office.

On my desk she had left a notepad with all the calls for me from the home phone recorder, many of them from the same people who had called my cell phone first.

I groaned, took the pad, ice pack and my cell phone to my

office's lounge chair and scanned the list more thoroughly. So much for my doctor's orders for quiet time at home.

"Howaryah?" Berger asked me the moment he picked up on the second ring.

"Been better," I told him, my enunciation still a bit thick, my voice a bit abnormal.

"Yeah, I heard you got your clock rung pretty badly. What the hell happened?"

I gave him the increasingly abbreviated version.

"Damn it, Thomas. Glad you're at least going to be okay. Sessions can't afford to lose you, man."

"Thanks."

"So, you sent me these pictures, which I got via courier last evening."

"Yeah."

"I almost puked."

"Yeah, I understand …"

"Kids …. Horrible. And Lusby."

"I guessing he didn't even know where he was."

"Bad guess, in my opinion. There's no excuse for something like that. He's as complicit, as fucking filthy as Wentz. Or at least he was. I've lost any respect I had for him."

"Okay."

"The more I think about Wentz, the angrier I get. I'm Goddamned sick and tired of Sessions being hoodwinked into hiring greedy, dishonorable buttholes—and I include our former supahstar Fitz-Hugh in that category. Now we got even worse, perverted moral turpitude thrown into the mix. Completely unacceptable.

"You know, Wentz was vetted by the search firm we used for our presidential search, so they fucked up big time, but it's not like we're ever going to bring any attention to that. Anyway, I'm working on solutions as we speak. Just keep a low profile and your mouth shut, as usual."

"I don't think you'll have to worry about that."

Berger snorted an appreciative laugh.

I thought of Wentz's recent effort to have me leak information damaging to Berger and Fritz Johnson. I had wanted to tell Berger about it, but now that seemed like a bad idea. If anything, overkill.

"Have you told anybody about this? Zoltan, for instance?"

"Nope. Haven't had a chance. Was handed those photos yesterday afternoon, just about an hour before my executive committee meeting with Wentz, and then gave them directly to Neil."

"Good. I shouldn't ask where you got these, right? But your source, no one knows about these other than that person?

"Well, my source's source, but I don't think that person particularly cares about or fully understands the photos' significance. All I can tell you is that my source deserves our undying gratitude. Doing the right thing doesn't come easy or often these days."

"Yeah. Maybe someday we can pay 'em back."

"Be nice."

"Okay. Look, you and yours have the best of holidays. I'll be in touch."

"Sure."

"Ciao."

For the rest of the afternoon, I continued to return phone calls with occasional breaks to collect my wits and take it a bit easier than usual.

I returned Wentz's call at the university and he seemed quite concerned about my well-being. We didn't talk business, but the large, angry elephant of his request that I leak information stomped around and trumpeted in the living room of our conversation. I returned Florence's call at the Wentz's residence and she was quite sincere in her "poor baby" sentiments.

Natalie Kravitz was upset and distracted, our conversation brief. What could she say? I wished her safe travels and hoped that Joan was better, asked that Natalie give her my regards.

By the end of the four calls I was exhausted and sat in my

lounge chair, looking around my office and out the window at the sky of another cold grey day and let my mind drift.

I thought about Alicia and tried to come to terms with what was going on between us. The natural, pleasant ease of our strong attraction, the enjoyment of our brief relationship—its simplicity confused and concerned me. Too good to be true in some respects. Untested by time and circumstance. Utterly unlike my lustful escape with Ursula. Having no comparison with the depth of trust, shared experience of decades and family that was the foundation of Janet's and my life together. That was as far as I could get before my mind started to short circuit and shut down.

I sat in silence for a time, then stood, walked to the window and looked out at our snow-covered lawn as it trailed down to the icy and bare-spotted asphalt street.

A sudden concern popped into my consciousness.

Returning to my lounge chair, I called Janet. She was between patients and her assistant put me through.

"What do I do about getting Sarah and Tommie Christmas presents—not to mention you? I feel completely neglectful."

"You and I don't need to exchange presents. The best present we could possibly have is our kids doing well."

"Yeah, I couldn't agree more," I told her.

"As for the kids, I have two magic words for you," she told me.

"Yeah?"

"Gift … certificate."

"Oh, you're a genius. Of course. Great idea."

The next day seemed to fly by thanks in part to the remainder of my pain medications, and I began to feel a bit more normal. I put off any contact with the office, took Sparky on long walks. Caught up with magazines. Made no progress on coming to terms with relationships, my brain freezing at each attempt to the point where I just gave up and let myself lapse into the comfortable flow of our household. Janet was now on her holiday, the kids absorbed—Sarah with her studies and with remaining friends from high school, Tommie with his virtual world of games.

And then came Christmas Eve.

As usual, I was the first to awake. I dressed quietly, went downstairs, let Sparky out into the back yard, brewed coffee, retrieved the paper from the drive, let Sparky back in, fed her. Then she and I sat in my office while I drank coffee, read the paper and tolerated a two-day-old muffin I'd found in the breadbasket until Janet entered.

"Hi, honey. How are you feeling?"

"Better. What's the drill for the day?"

Janet let a small smile slip onto her features. "What would you like?"

"I don't know, stupid Christmas sweaters, Christmas music, a good turkey dinner, open a present or two this evening around the tree, save the rest for tomorrow morning."

Janet began to grin. "I don't think it's going to be at all like that."

"What do you mean?"

"You'll see soon enough."

"Um, okay." I reached to scratch my head in puzzlement but thought better of it.

Janet fixed waffles for breakfast, pulled some actual maple syrup from some secret stash she had. With the smell of waffles, butter and syrup the kids came down and we mumbled at each other pleasantly. I kept looking at Janet and the small secret smile she kept trying to suppress. Something was going on. The kids seemed even more clueless than I.

After we finished breakfast, Janet insisted that we all help dust, vacuum and straighten up the house, a large hint that we would later be having visitors. The kids went back to their rooms. I went back to the paper and magazines, dozed for a while. Time seemed to pass mysteriously. We had a quick lunch.

Just about the time I was beginning to wonder whether I was imagining Janet's secrecy, a car horn sounded from out front.

I walked to the window in my den.

A black stretch limousine had pulled up in front of the house. Behind it was an Intercontinental Hotel service truck.

"Janet!" I yelled, "What the *hell* is going on?"

She came into the den from the kitchen. "Merry Christmas, honey!" she told me as she gave me a hug. "Surprise!"

"Surprise?"

As we watched, the front passenger door of the limousine opened and Mark Berger stepped out, dressed in worn blue jeans; deck shoes; a bulky, bright-red, foul-weather jacket; red scarf; red pullover hat. It was instantly obvious to me that the jacket, scarf and hat were from *Calypso Too,* undoubtedly the kind of "freebie" that came with a boat costing a million dollars or more, and that Mark was wearing them to be sure to get his money's worth.

He made a "get on with it" motion to the driver of the van and his coworker.

There was pounding on the stairs from Sarah and Tommie descending.

"Do you see what's outside?" Sarah announced excitedly from the front hall.

"Yeah," I called to her.

They joined us in the den as the back doors of the limousine opened and Zoltan and Kristina stepped out, looking at our house with anticipation while two hotel delivery men went to the back of the truck and opened its rear doors.

Janet turned to us, "Merry Christmas everyone! I got a call from Mark Berger at the office last week. He decided he'd like to have Christmas with us. Who was I to disagree? And he wanted Zoltan and Kristina to join us. They changed their plans."

"Fantastic!" I told her, giving her a hug.

Sarah jumped up and down and said, "This is so Cool!" while Tommie began grinning from ear to ear, his face twitching.

We rushed out the front door into the cold to the limousine where the driver was helping Berger, Zoltan and Kristina unload presents from the trunk.

Berger turned to us, holding several professionally decorated boxes, his eyes bugging, his eyebrows moving up and down behind his thick glasses, his mustache and connected sideburns bristling in the cold, "Merry Christmas, Happy Hanukkah! Hope yah don't mind, but I took the liberty of bringing an entire Christmas turkey dinner with all tha fixins' with a case of the Intercontahnental's best Chateauneuf-du-Pape, some Pouilly Fumé, some Dom Pérignon, and of course, lots of Chinese carryout. The guys will bring it all in."

Zoltan and Kristina came around the car carrying more presents, "Hey," Zoltan told us, "today even better than special Hungarian Zoltanamas I celebrate with these guys earlier this year."

"Thanks, man," Berger replied. "Let's get the show on the road here."

To help Kristina, Janet and the kids took some of the presents she was carrying. They hugged awkwardly.

In addition to cardboard boxes of food and drink, I noticed the delivery men removing two large hanger boxes from the back of the van, looked at Zoltan and realized he had a laptop tucked under one arm.

I turned to him accusatorily, "You didn't? We aren't?"

He looked at me with mock innocence. "Oh, you mean, have everyone perform scene from opera after dinner, like last year at Thanksgiving. Of course! We all have such great time. This year I have theatre folks I know lend me costumes for *Carmen.*"

"Oh, Christ. Well another reason to drink heavily, I guess."

XXIII

A Carmen Christmas Eve

WHAT A FEAST Mark Berger had brought us!

We set about unpacking, put the huge, still-warm turkey in the oven, unpacked stuffing mixed with apples, onions and parsley, garlic butter mashed potatoes, green beans and broccoli, corn bread muffins, a cranberry roll—and hors d'oeuvres to die for: brie and mushroom pastries, avocado bruschetta, steak and prosciutto skewers with creamy basil-tarragon sauce, small southern-style biscuits with Virginia ham and sharp cheddar—and then boxes of paper containers filled with an array of Chinese food: sweet and sour pork, kung pao chicken, chow mein, dumplings, Peking roast duck. How could we eat it all? Hell, we would give our best shot.

The house began to fill with their fragrances. I turned on the faux fire in our fireplace. Fake flames lit by crimson backlights danced synthetically in the cold air of a recessed blower. I noticed that Tommie gave it no attention and sent up a parent's prayer of gratitude. Perhaps, I thought, in my own private world this might be the best present anyone could give me, the loss of being fearful of dying in our own house's conflagration.

We opened bottles of Chateauneuf-du-Pape and Pouilly-Fumé, celebrated to the pop of the cork when Zoltan opened a bottle of Dom Pérignon. We drank liberally.

Mark Berger helped as we put two leaves in the dining room table, spread a "for very special occasions," family-heirloom, damask tablecloth on it, set out our best china, silver, cutlery, holiday place mats and crystal. Tommie actually made himself useful by bringing items to us as Janet rooted through the pantry and kitchen cabinets to find them. She also brought in from the garage an artificial woven holly and pine bough bunting for the center of the table and silver candlesticks from her parents that I could not remember ever using.

Then we adjourned to the family room where, on Janet's orders, Sarah and Tommie began offering us hors d'oeuvres and we began pouring ourselves more wine and champagne. I noticed Tommie eating an hors d'oeuvre for every three to five we took from his tray. It seemed to me that he was growing a bit taller and more adolescent with each one.

Mark expressed interest in our tree, wandering over to it and admiring the ornaments, zooming in and asking about the BMW.

So, we told the story of our first Christmas together in our first apartment downtown with cinder block bookshelves and a Charlie Brown Christmas tree on the top shelf with that one ornament on it.

Janet turned to Mark and asked, "So, growing up, how did you celebrate Christmas?"

"Ah, interesting question," Berger replied, taking a sip of wine. "My parents were very Orthodox, so, of course, we celebrated Hanukkah, and they didn't want me corrupting my heritage by celebrating Christmas. They were weird that way.

"What is Hanukkah anyway? It's important to remember that bein' Jewish, nobody ever forgets nothin', particularly if it involves our persahcution. So, Hanukkah celebrates our rebelling and tossing out a bunch of Syrians who took over our temple in the second century BC. I kid you not. You might ask yourself, so, what the f—." He glanced at Sarah and Tommie. "What the heck has changed in the last two-thousand-plus years! Same ol' story. Bunch of Arabs trying to annihilate us.

"Anyway, over the centuries Hanukkah's become a Festival of Lights, eight days of reflection and gift giving et cetera, et cetera.

"I always looked at it like this: Hanukkah, Christmas, a

twofer holiday! What's not to like? I had friends who celebrated Christmas; we had family who were married to Christians. What's the big deal? So, gradually, I got my parents to see Christmas as an American holiday, and we're Americans, right? And Hanukkah is a Jewish holiday. We can celebrate Hanukkah at home and Christmas with my buddies and our other family members and friends. So, that's what we'd do.

"Now you didn't ask this, but Hanukkah actually helped me think about what's important in my life." He took another appreciative sip from his glass of wine. "As part of our gift giving for Hanukkah, there's the concept of *mitzvot*, which is that in the spirit of giving, you should give generous gifts to those who are less fortunate than you. It's part of the Jewish belief of helping to repair the world, *tikkun olam*. So, each year around this time I make gifts to organizations that do that, particularly the ones who offer a helping hand, not a handout.

"Sorry to be so verbose. It's the wine. So, tell me about you guys. Zoltan, whaddid you guys do? Roast a commie over a spit?"

Zoltan laughed. "That be fun. Rather just shoot them or put them in work camp like they did to my parents' family and friends. No, our family become Americanized, do American Christmas but keep a few Hungarian traditions. You know, we not want to be outdone by our Jewish friends, so we Hungarians also have a twofer."

"Really?"

"Yes. On December sixth, St. Nicholas, who keep track of good or bad boys and girls, come and leave small presents in shoes they have placed on windowsill. For some, who maybe have not been so good, as a reminder to behave, he leave switches or branches from trees. Big hint.

"Then on Christmas Eve, adults set up Christmas tree, decorate and put presents under tree. Children have to wait until bell is rung before they can go to tree and open presents. They told, bell is angels signaling that the tree is ready and they can open presents.

"Then next day we have great Christmas meal with traditional foods, a lot like here, everyone eats too much. Only then do we roast commies."

We laughed.

"What's Christmas like in Belarus?" Sarah asked Kristina.

"Ah," she replied, "In Belarus, you must remember in World War II we were devastated, lost a third of our population and half our economic resources. After war, we part of Soviet Union, who rule us until 1990 when Soviet Union collapse, so under Soviets there was longtime ban on our traditional celebrations and anything religious.

"Since 1990, even though we are still under a very authoritarian regime, we now have more freedoms, and traditional celebrations are again becoming popular. So, we do things like—on Christmas Eve have hay under the tablecloth as homage to the manger and the birth of baby Jesus, and we have a meal of twelve dishes to signify the Twelve Apostles. We love caroling, so that is also big tradition. Depending on religion and/or preference, gifts are given either at Christmas or New Year's."

"Let's eatttt!" Tommie half-shouted suddenly.

We laughed, brought all the hors d'oeuvres back into the kitchen. Our guests took their seats at the table while Janet, I, Sarah and Tommie brought the Christmas dinner out to the table. Then I carved the turkey to the ohs and ahs and insults of everyone, my state of inebriation seeming to help my dexterity or at least that's the way it seemed. Somehow, we also managed to serve ourselves through the complicated passage of all the traditional and Chinese dishes around the table. There was a moment of silence, and I took the opportunity to stand for a toast, wondering as I did so, what I was going to say.

I spoke from the heart.

"It's wonderful to have all of you here, the most special day of the year, to celebrate it with our most special friends who are more family than anyone else."

Everyone clapped and expressed their approval. I found I did not want to stop.

I saluted, "To my wonderful wife, Janet, who's stood by me and with me all these years."

Everyone applauded, particularly Sarah and Tommie, and I watched as Janet looked away, hiding her emotions.

"And to Sarah and Tommie. I'm so proud of how you both have grown up this year, at your success and your enthusiasm."

"And finally, to Zoltan and Kristina for their support and friendship, and to Mark for the same. Where the hell would we be without you?"

"Already eating!" Berger said loudly. "And I thought I was verbose!"

We all laughed and began our dinner. I felt so much better having made my remarks, as if some burden had been lifted.

For a time, we concentrated on the marvelous meal in front of us, passing more food around, sipping wine and champagne, Tommie working at an impossible amount of food. Then there was a brief pause and Mark Berger looked at Zoltan and asked.

"So, Zoltan, I've been wanting to know. How's it going down there at the medical center with your research?"

Zoltan looked around the table, "You cannot discuss this, what I tell you here. Yes? That include you-young-people, everyone here."

We all nodded.

"I been having exchange with fellow researchers, national and international, and gradually we see the light about cancer vaccine."

"Yeah?" Berger remarked.

"There is none, at least for the present. It like all wonderful ideas, like world peace. Not reality."

"But isn't that what all your research is based on?" I asked.

Zoltan shrugged, held out his hand, palm down and moved it back and forth. "Yes and no. I explain. While different kind of cancers can be classified, how each type of cancer affect each person often different, plus there are many sub-types or variants that add to complications, which is why what we thought might be cure for solid tumors we researching getting mix results.

"As we develop understanding of genetics, we realize these

mix of results come from how each person's cancer cells express selves, have different cell makeup, markers, chemistry. So, finally, light go off. You want to cure a particular cancer for a particular person, you have to custom tailor immunotherapeutic and/or combined other approaches that target, interrupt and kill that individual's cancer cells. Curing cancer then begins with individual, at their level, not with blanket approach to disease. Researchers like me and my lab, others around the world, now developing every month new immunotherapy and other combined delivery, chemical, enzyme and cellular approaches that we know work on different cancer-cell markers and pathways. We begin to build library arsenal of approaches we can use tailored to each person's unique cancer. So, no universal vaccine. We develop vaccine for each person, each person his or her own cure."

The table was silent, feeling like we were being told a very important truth.

"That's remarkable," Berger commented.

"But it tricky business. Cancer very tricky, can change and adapt, so we have to be very alert to that possibility, may have to change approach as we go along. Plus, some cancers made up of multiple different types of cancer cells, like worse kind of brain tumor. To defeat that kind of cancer you have to invent therapy for each different type of cell. How do you do that? All at once or in sequence? What right sequence? How you not kill patient with treatment?"

"Amazing," Mark Berger commented. "So, why are you keeping this a secret?"

"Not really keeping secret but have to figure out each person's cure, apply it, monitor results. But you know what big problem is?

"Haven't a clue?" I told him.

"It be time. All this complexity slow everything down. How you defeat time? You need much greater computerization, artificial intelligence to seek different cures more quickly. We need bigger laboratories and more technicians and scientists to engineer more T-cell, genetic modifications, combined enzymes and antibodies chemistry more quickly. We need cooperative international library for research, enhance communication of discoveries. But even that not help completely. You must understand, all this knowledge of what to do comes as needles in haystack of other research that is not productive—dead ends. How to sort through that big issue. Fast-track what works. Get around FDA approvals or get them to adapt to new procedures."

"Yeah, that makes sense," Berger commented. "But have you told Dr. Ramis about where you are?"

"Yes, we talk regularly. He fellow research scientist so to some degree he understand even though he cheap bastard who try to stealing my research. I just tell him basics. But recently we also decide enough progress been made that we should hold conference where I and my team present our findings, then have them written up in journals. This not only help everyone understand what we dealing with but that if we could partner with pharma researchers, it would be good idea. Then everybody benefit and understand, and we work more quickly toward more trials and novel solutions to different issues with different cancers. Other challenge, which we know, be who owns what, so agreements must be put in place beforehand. I getting smarter, yes? Maybe Ramis figure out that we need more investment of monies."

"Yeah, congratulations, my friend. You have my total admiration." Berger told him.

"Your lawyer …"

"He's not my lawyer."

"Lawyer you tell me about been huge help. On standby. I discuss everything we doing with him. I be prepared as next discoveries made."

"Good man," Berger told him.

As we finished our meal our attention shifted to Sarah and Tommie. We learned of Sarah's interest in a summer abroad in France where she could not only take courses in French but where there were opportunities to travel to other countries in Europe.

From Tommie we got several inarticulate sentences on his work with Mr. Diamond and courses he could be taking at the Sessions Center for Gifted and Talented Youth, no mention being made of his current counseling sessions and plans for their continuance, although we had noticed some subtle changes in his behavior indicating a better awareness of others and their feelings.

Dessert was served—pecan and key lime pies, vanilla ice cream and whipped cream on top.

And then Zoltan rose, as if to give a toast, his inebriation causing him to weave slightly.

"In Thomas and Janet's bedroom you find big box of costumes for women and in guest room we have box for men. We now go there. Of course, you are familiar with plot of Carmen?"

We all looked at him blankly.

"Awk. Peasants! I tell you plot in a minute, but for now, I tell you who you play so you get right costume. Yes?"

Again, we looked at him like deer in the headlights.

"Carmen be played by the one and only beautiful temptress, Janet.

Murmur of approval at this casting choice.

"Michaëla, the also beautiful but innocent and pure first love of Don Jose, be played by the innocent and pure Kristina."

We cheered.

"Don Jose, our main character, who typical stupid male and leave Michaëla for infatuation with Carmen. He a soldier, Corporal of the Dragoons. He be played by Thomas."

Everyone booed.

"Oh, thanks." I told him. This was the second year in a row Zoltan had cast me as the two-timer. The truth hurt. But, thankfully, no one seemed to care about my chagrin.

"I play Zuniga, lieutenant of Dragoons."

We booed again, even though we had only the faintest notion of who Zuniga might be.

"Then we have other love interest of Carmen—big stud bullfighter, Escamillo, played of course by big stud, Mark Berger."

We cheered, then hooted and clapped derisively.

"Finally, we have companions to Carmen, Frasquita, played by Tommie."

We laughed.

"Tommie of course, you have to go with the ladies to get your costume and makeup."

Tommie looked at us, at once flattered to be included and at the same time puzzled by the proceedings, his face screwed up, his tic active, and said, "Naww …"

"Janet," Zoltan added, "he will need help with makeup. And there is nice girly wig in box."

"Oh, this could be fun," Janet commented.

"And then we have other companion, Mercédès, played by Sarah."

Sarah stood and took a half bow.

We rose and slowly clambered up the stairs to the bedrooms.

In the guest room, as we sorted through the costumes, we could hear great hilarity coming from Janet's and my bedroom as the women changed and as they applied makeup to Tommie. I was amazed that he was going along with this prank. A year ago, he might have had a complete meltdown.

For us, the laughter came from the ridiculous look of dressing up in 1800s Spanish regalia, particularly for Berger as Escamillo because nothing fit him properly. His tights were baggy and falling off, exposing his skinny, hairy legs and "tighty-whitey" briefs. His bullfighter waistcoat hung pathetically on him. The belt on his sword's sheath was tightened to the last hole but still falling from his waist to the point that he had to hold it up with one hand, while the sheath and sword dragged on the ground. His feathered hat, too large for him, sat so low on his head that he could barely see under the rim. With one hand he was holding up his belt and the other, his hat, while his tights were falling down and he had to grasp and pull them up every third step. We found ourselves giggling like children at him, tears welling in our eyes.

Of course, Zoltan's costume was several sizes too small, so he gave the impression of a soldier who had somehow been seriously overinflated, threatening to explode.

My soldier's uniform actually fit reasonably well, though it had a strong remnant smell of body odor and moth balls.

We made our way carefully down the stairs, trying not to trip or catch our costumes on the doorknobs, the stair railing or out-croppings of furniture.

We killed time in the family room, making caustic comments about one another until the women and Tommie finally entered.

Tommie brought the house down, marching in defiantly, wearing an oversized peasant's dress with a pinned hem, his face decorated with red lipstick, his cheeks rogued, and sporting a lovely, too-large, goldilocks wig—his face screwed up in frustration until everyone shouted out their enthusiasm and applauded. Then he actually began to laugh and go with the flow of our silliness. Truth was, he loved the attention.

Zoltan stood and cleared his throat, "So, you must understand, this 1820 and final act of normal complicated opera plot. Here what you need to know:

"Don Jose is now fugitive. He encouraged by Carmen to desert army and then she desert him for Escamillo. Don Jose want her back at any cost. He lose his senses over her. So they in courtyard outside of amphitheater where Escamillo about to fight the bull. Each one of you must act and lip sync your part in Act IV as it comes up on screen. I cue you so you know who is who. Alright?"

We had quieted down and now looked at him, ready to act.

On cue Sarah brought up Act IV on the large screen of our TV, and with Zoltan shouting and pointing as the action began, each of us, to much hilarity, imitated as best we could the performance and singing taking place until the final scene in which Don Jose, in a fit of rage at Carmen's rejection of him for Escamillo stabs her to death and then is taken prisoner. Fortunately, the knife which had been provided was rubber. But the act of killing Carmen/ Janet, my wife, even pretending with a rubber knife, felt quite strange and unpleasant.

At the end of the final scene we stood and applauded one another. Janet brought in a tray of Dom Pérignon in flutes and we toasted one another as Tommie tossed his wig across the room, Mark Berger gave a toast while trying unsuccessfully to hold up his tights and belt. We drank our champagne, poured ourselves some more and then headed upstairs to change.

As we did, the doorbell rang and I opened it to discover Intercontinental staff who had arrived to help us clean up. Needless to say, they looked at us strangely while trying unsuccessfully to keep a straight face. While we changed, they cleaned up the kitchen and dining room, taking care to leave the remaining wine and carefully wrap and put the remaining food in our stuffed refrigerator.

When we came downstairs, we discovered that the limousine had arrived for our guests and we went out with them into the dark and cold December evening, hugged and wished them well, all of us telling one another that it was the best Christmas ever. Then we returned to our strangely orderly and tranquil house and were soon in bed.

XXIV

Okay

CHRISTMAS MORNING BROUGHT pain and pleasure.

Pain from a nasty hangover, which announced itself when Tommie shouted, "It's Christmas!" at the top of his lungs from the upstairs hallway.

I heard Sarah talking to him in hushed tones, obviously shushing him and escorting him downstairs to begin some breakfast preparations. Janet stirred beside me, rose, put on her robe and quietly shut the door behind her.

Which left me to focus on—pain. Sunlight beaming in from our bedroom windows bounced relentlessly around the room. Gremlins must have attacked me while I slept, gleefully spraying my open, snoring mouth full of tennis ball fuzz, climbing in through my ears and stabbing toothpicks into the back of my eyeballs, hitting me randomly all over my body with miniature ball-peen hammers. My stomach was filled with acid. I could feel unmentionable disruptions in my bowels. The bathroom called urgently for me and I was almost too paralyzed to respond, but then I had to.

Made it in time. Gave up a small prayer of thanks for having the vent fan in my life. At the sink I drank deliciously cold water from my cupped hands and then for a time pressed my hot forehead directly against the cool mirror in front of me. I dared not look at my reflection. Rooted around in the medicine cabinet for vitamins and all the normal curatives for a massive hangover.

Found most of them. Frank Lusby's medicine cabinet leapt into my consciousness. Shut it out.

Breakfast was quiet in deference to Dad. I looked across the table at Janet and saw that she too was still suffering.

A rule in our house was that stockings and presents were opened only after breakfast. So, thankfully I was able to have some coffee and scrambled eggs and toast beforehand. The sound of ripped wrapping paper otherwise might have done me in.

I was also thankful that the opportunity had presented itself during my concussion convalescence for Janet and me to have a more thoughtful conversation about what to get the kids for Christmas.

Then came the pleasure.

Sarah pulling a small envelope from her stocking, opening it and discovering a Eurail Pass. It helped my recovery immensely seeing her expression as the significance of the card, signaling a summer abroad, dawned on her and watching my daughter jumping around shrieking and waving the card in the air, then hugging Janet and me—Tommie looking on, head tilted, face screwed up and ticking, perhaps not having much of a clue about what Europe meant, its significance to our civilization.

In Tommie's stocking he found a screen shot of the Sessions Center for Gifted and Talented Youth summer curriculum for his age group with the beginning course on robotics circled. This he did find to be very exciting and he leapt to his feet and ran around the room shouting and waving the screenshot while Sparky barked at him.

And so it went, thoughtful gifts from Mark Berger, a beautiful lavender cashmere sweater for Janet and Mont Blanc pen for me. Both, I was sure, from the Intercontinental gift shop.

For Kristina and Zoltan's present, they had arranged a family trip for us to Washington, DC, with Kristina serving as our guide, where we would be staying in her apartment while she and Zoltan stayed in a spare room in her building.

All and all, it was a very good morning, with other presents to be opened and even Sparky getting her share of treats and toys.

And by lunchtime I felt much better, almost back to normal. I could tell because I was beginning to get antsy about work and decided to go into the office the next day to clear up the backlog from my concussion absence, see what new challenges had presented themselves and see whether I might contact Mark Berger's PR folks as well those at the School of Foreign Service about the Leadership Medallion event promotion and planning.

So, the next morning after breakfast, I made the trek to Sessions. As anticipated, the administration building was virtually uninhabited, unlit and cold. I kept my overcoat on as I sorted through email.

My cell phone rang in my jacket pocket. I pulled out the phone and smiled. Alicia. Good timing.

"Hey, how are you?" I answered. "How was your Christmas?"

"Good," she told me. "We had a nice Christmas. Cold and windy as hell, of course. While I thought I knew how bad it could be up here, the reality of it was worse than I remembered, everything frozen, cars, the El, a lot of Lake Michigan. Saw family and enjoyed a relaxed holiday. My mother and I caught up with one another, went shopping downtown, to the art museum, the theatre.

"But something's going on with my father. He's asked me to visit him at the Piper-Hale headquarters downtown this coming week. I have the funniest feeling that something's up, amplified by him being quite cheerful, even solicitous, which frankly has me on guard. At the same time, I notice how much he's aged, losing his hearing, moving slowly with arthritis, beginning to be a bit forgetful. Kind of shocking. I hadn't seen him for several years."

"I'll be very interested to see what this is all about."

"How are you? How was your Christmas?"

I told her I was fine and about Mark Berger and our Christmas Eve with him, Zoltan and Kristina, about the kids and their presents, about getting antsy to get back to work.

"When can we see one another?"

"Welll ..." and as I began, I began to feel guilty. What I was doing was wrong, a bad idea, likely to lead me in a self-destructive direction. With feelings of self-loathing, I went ahead anyway. "As it happens, I have to go down to DC January 12th for an event at the School of Foreign Service. They're giving a Leadership Medallion award to Mark Berger at their board of visitors' annual dinner. So, why don't I come down early and we can have lunch?"

"Wonderful idea. I'll make a reservation for noon at a place I like that's near the school. That work?"

"Sure. Good. Be great to see you."

"Same and in a more temperate climate. Good God—is it cold up here!"

"I can only imagine."

"No, you can't."

"At any rate, see you soon."

"Yes, see you."

I went back to my emails, then checked phone messages and discovered that I had a call from Berger's PR person about coordinating the Leadership Medallion publicity and that she would be in during the holidays. I was just about to call her when my cell phone rang again.

I glanced at the number. It seemed familiar but I could not place it. Decided to answer the call.

"Thomas?" I immediately recognized Wentz's voice. He was calling from home. I felt an immediate impulse to hang up, but instead answered, "Yeah, hi."

"How are you?"

"Good, actually. Fully recovered. Enjoyed a very pleasant Christmas with the family. How about you? I'm actually at the office, playing catch-up."

"We had a quiet Christmas," he told me, his voice a bit breathless. "Just being at home, away from the daily grind was a nice gift."

"Good. I appreciate your and Florence's support during my convalescence."

"Thanks …." Awkward pause, and then he came out with what really on his mind and the purpose of his call. "Say, have you given any further thought to our prior conversation?"

"Yeah, I've actually given it a lot of thought, but I haven't yet reached any decision. It's a tough thing you're asking me to do."

"Yeah, I know. Just hoping you can see your way clear to helping me and the university out."

I thought, *How fucking twisted is that—me helping him bring down Fritz Johnson as a way to "help" the university?*

"Sure, I understand."

"I'll want to see you first thing when we get back on the third.

"Okay."

XXV

Silence Is Golden

NEW YEAR'S CAME and went. Janet and I stayed home and actually went to bed before midnight. Sarah went to a party at a friend's house where we confirmed with the parents that they would be home. Tommie was on his computer—Kristina and Zoltan in Washington.

On January 3rd, I drove into work full of misgivings.

I had just set my university mug of chlorinated and bitter coffee on its coaster and sat in my office chair when my desk phone sounded in quick short rings. I glanced at my watch, 9:07 a.m. A new year, same old shit. It was undoubtedly Ms. Bemis calling to tell me that Wentz would see me now. What the hell would I tell him? I faced the sad fact that I would not cooperate with his request that I leak damaging information about Fritz Johnson and that I would have to resign.

I was not ready to deal with the situation. Couldn't it just go away? Couldn't I ease into the job this morning? Have a nice conversation with someone about their holidays for instance? Have a chance to look out my window into woods and think about our holidays? But no, my university was calling me.

My heart sank when I picked up the receiver and listened as Ms. Bemis said, "Your presence is required."

"Ohhh, Jesus," I responded. "Did he say what this is about, JoAnn?"

"I am not at liberty to say."

"Aw, fuck."

She hung up.

I stood, pulled my suit jacket from the back of my chair, put it on and walked slowly, reluctantly to the elevator, feeling as if I was about to face a firing squad.

On the third floor I made my way down the maze of hallways to the president's reception area and to my great surprise found a pensive Dr. Zoltan Vastag in his usual worn, herringbone, sports jacket and Levi's sitting there, his size making his chair and his surroundings look too small.

He looked pleadingly at me as I sat down across from him.

"What this about? She tell me nothing. Just to be here. Call me on cell phone crack of dawn."

I glanced over at JoAnn. She was in Ms. Bemis Sphinx mode. Interestingly, no costume today, just a grey, businesslike outfit.

"Hell if I know." Now I was totally puzzled. What did Zoltan have to do with this? Did Wentz want to bring him into the effort to besmirch Johnson? Was he going to threaten to fire us both unless we cooperated? I thought about his comments about us being "untouchable." Maybe he was going totally rogue?

So, we sat there, fearing the worst as time went by glacially. My imagination got the best of me as I began to think Wentz had somehow discovered our role in disposing of Frank Lusby's assassin, that a clandestine source had somehow revealed to him what we had done, threatened him and demanded our dismissal, that my family could now again be in danger, along with Zoltan and possibly Kristina. I began to feel deeply afraid.

Then suddenly, without looking at us, Ms. Bemis said, "You may enter."

Zoltan and I rose. Gingerly, I opened the door to Wentz's office and there leaning back in Wentz's double-wide chair, his deck shoes on the desktop, hands behind his head, looking like a Jewish elf, was Mark Berger.

"Howaryah?"

"What the fuck?" I heard myself exclaim as Zoltan shut the door behind us.

"Where Wentz?" Zoltan asked incredulously.

"Sit down. Have a seat. It's a long story."

We sat in the chairs in front of his desk, glancing at one another quizzically, awestruck.

Berger took his feet down, sat forward, leaned his elbows on the desk and clasped his hands together. "I figured I'd let you guys know before anyone else. You're not only closest to this mess, but I'll be frank with you, I've begun to feel almost like we're family. You're my eahrstwhile nephews or something."

Zoltan and I just stared at him.

"Plus, the stakes are really high here, like the whole university's future lies in the balance, and I actually want your input and advice. I trust you guys."

"Okay …" I said, then asked cautiously, a plaintive note in my voice, "what the hell's going on?"

"After Christmas I invited our former President, Dr. Wentz …"

"Former?"

"Yeah, I'll get to that. Of course, I had to share your material with Fritz."

"Material?" Zoltan asked, looking back and forth at each of us.

"Yeah," I told him. "Someone gave me pictures of a bathhouse with Wentz and Lusby in it, along with some boys."

"My God."

"Anyway," Berger continued, "God, was Fritz pissed. So, being closest to the scene, I got the wonderful assignment of breaking the bad news to our president. I was hoping we could come to a more-or-less instant agreement on how to handle his resignation. But fate intervened."

"Fate?"

"Yeah, damnedest thing. I invited Wentz down to the Intercontahnental for a drink. He probably figured out in advance that it wasn't exactly social. So, he arrived with a suitably scared-shitless expression. And then I shared the photos with him."

Berger pointed a finger at Zoltan, "You know none of this."

"I say nothing."

"Right. So, Wentz—it was interesting. When I showed him the pictures, his eyes popped and he started to yammer and suddenly he couldn't get any air, started gasping, went all red and collapsed wheezing right there in the booth, falling to one side right the fuck in front of me. I shouted to the bartender and we got an ambulance there in minutes. Turns out Wentz is an asthmatic. He was hiding this from us. My evidence caused him to go into a full asthmatic attack. The medic there figured this out, gave him a shot and, when he began reviving, an inhaler, which helped him recover enough to get him out of the booth and onto a wheeled stretcher. You can imagine how difficult that was. He was a fucking beached whale. Anyway, he's at the hospital recovering. Then he and Florence are taking a nice, long vacation.

"Vacation?"

"Yeah. Fritz and I came up with a plan. I went to see Wentz yesterday and he agreed to it. He's resigning for health reasons, not only because of his asthma, but the hospital discovered he's got heart disease, high blood pressure and a host of other complications, like the beginning of COPD, that put him hugely at risk. So, now that he's stable, we've arranged for him to be transferred to a spa in Arizona for a month or two, where he'll begin the process of losing a hundred pounds or more and to get him the hell away from here.

"Once he's finished with that, we'll help him find a job, like with one of the pharmaceutical companies or somewhere else he'd fit in."

"Jesus Christ … How did Florence take all this?"

Berger looked at each of us, chagrined. "Very badly."

"Oh, man."

"From what we can figure, Florence, despite her lovely persona, is a closet alcoholic, and this sent her off the deep end. Unmitigated rage and grief and drunk as a skunk. Completely out of control. Had to intervene and get her into a facility, get Wentz's permission, which didn't help his recovery a whole lot, notify her family, get them involved. Long story short, once she's in decent enough shape, she'll be transferred to the same place in Arizona for a thirty-day program, or longer if need be."

"Damn."

"What happen now?" Zoltan asked, shaking his head.

Mark Berger unclasped his hands and sat back in Wentz's chair, grunted a half laugh, "Funny you should ask that."

"So," Zoltan asked, "who president?"

"Interim. Don Powers."

"Awww—shit," I heard myself exclaim.

"Hey, best we could do under the circumstances, and when you think about it, he's perfect. Will always say the politic thing, strategically smart, follows orders, not motivated by greed or ambition as far as we can tell."

"I don't know," I said, "Not my favorite guy, and now I've got to work for him."

"Yeahhh, maybe …"

"What do you mean, maybe?"

"Let me fuckin' finish. Okay?"

"Um, sure."

"We'll go through another search process, hopefully find a successor worthy of Sessions University this time. Powers can be a candidate if he wants. If not, he goes back to being provost or segues into another university presidency somewhere."

"Okay."

"What happen with Ramis?" Zoltan asked.

"Ah, we'll keep him in place. He's been suitably chastised. And he's not a pedophile."

"Umph," Zoltan responded, clearly not thrilled with the prospect of continuing to deal with Ramis.

Berger leaned back toward us, elbows on the desk again. An expression came over him that I had not seen before, a sharpening of the eyes behind his glasses, a sudden flatlining of his mouth. For the first time since I had known him, I felt firsthand that I was dealing with a self-made billionaire. "So, more important, let's talk about the futcah of Sessions University."

"What you mean?" Zoltan wondered.

"What the fuck role can I play that does the best for Sessions and for you guys?"

I found that I was looking at Mark Berger very intensely. "You want to give us a little better idea of what you're thinking?"

"Yeah. Bernie, that charming SOB, has been talking to me about my legacy here and what I might do to advance our university. And you know what? He makes some sense. So, I've been talking with my guys, all my sycophantic lawyers and accountants, and I been talking to Neil, who actually tells me the truth and gives me straight answers. And I want to talk to you guys, 'cause you'll do the same."

"Okay," I said, "So, you're thinking of making your gift to the capital campaign?"

The smirk came back. Berger put his fingers together and looked at us. "Not quite. For stahrters, I gotta a problem that goes back to my days as a poor Jewish kid scrapin' my way by, livin' on wurst sandwiches and doin' laundry in coin machines, which is that I hate the unnecessary or wasteful spending of or investment of money. A phobia, if you will. A phobia that has in fact been a factor in making me a fortune. So, what happens if I give the university some money? And you know, I'm thinkin' of maybe an initial investment of say $600–650 million."

I looked over at Zoltan whose eyes were as bugged out as I felt mine were. This was a real conversation we were having. Holy shit.

"BUT, let me ask you this. Given what's happened around here the last two years with the presidency, would you give your hard-earned dollars to Sessions University?"

"Fuck No," Zoltan blurted out emphatically. "You tossing money into sea full of bullshit self-dealing."

"Yeah, you catch my drift. Plus, being on the board finance committee with Fritz and having Neil give me a bird's-eye view of how the university manages and invests its money, I got another set of problems handing money over to it.

"Fahrst, the endowment is encumbered by all sorts of bylaws regarding expenditure and investments that I don't particularly like or agree with. Okay, let's call them what they are: stupid. And I really don't have it in me to fight the rest of the board to get them changed.

"Second, Sessions's endowment's return on investment is more-or-less in the middle of the pack when compared to its competitors. I find such returns appallingly low, and the idea of giving my money to Sessions to manage and having them earn such a niggling return is totally unacceptable.

"Third, besides investing in other entities—businesses, real estate, commodities, etc.—how do I invest my loose change? You might ask that question. The answer is: I am the key investor in a hedge fund owned by one of my companies and managed by some of the biggest studs in the business. You take a couple billion and invest it in a hedge fund, which has the capacity to invest that money in whatever entity that's going to make the most money in the next twenty-four to thirty-six months and damn if you don't have some real money to play around with after a decade or two.

"So, here's what I'm gonna do: form a charitable foundation to which I will contribute my initial $600–650 million. The foundation's assets will be invested in the hedge fund I favor, the annual returns will greatly exceed the required minimum distribution to charity of 5 percent annually. The fact is that I intend to give away way more than 5 percent in the short term. Of course, the foundation will have a board that I would be happy to chair, and it'll need an executive director to staff it properly, make sure it follows the letter of the law, to consider requests for support, to award grants and check on their success. Of course, Sessions University would be a very favored recipient.

"Now, it has occurred to me that I know someone who might well be a good fit to become executive director of The Mark Berger Foundation."

Mark was looking directly as me,

Out of nowhere, Zoltan erupted in a mighty, roaring laugh,

"*Ahhh-Ha,ha,ha! Ahhh-Ha,ha,ha! Thomas! Thomas!*" he half shouted, slapping his knee. "All those people who think you two-faced, little-man asshole. *Ahhh-Ha-ha-ha!* They now going to be your *best friends! Ahhh-Ha,ha,ha!*"

I was looking back at Berger, "Me?" I squeaked at him. "Why?"

"Aw, come on. You're brilliantly politic. You're loyal. You keep your own counsel. You can spot a phony or anything that isn't on the up-and-up a mile away. You're not afraid to tell the truth to friends. Among others, you keep your mouth shut. Best, perhaps, are your professional credentials. You know how to successfully launch and shape a brand and all the PR, communications and marketing surrounding it."

I could not necessarily disagree with him, despite not feeling worthy of such praise, and, yes, this was a good time to keep my mouth shut.

"So," Berger said, "I'll double your salary. We can base the foundation here, say downtown. You might have to drive another ten to fifteen minutes. What the fuck."

"You're serious?"

"Oh yeah. I've even started thinking about my, or rather our, priorities. Need a couple other initial board members, say Fritz Johnson for instance."

He paused for a moment while he shifted his attention to Zoltan. "To my way of thinking," he told him, "the foundation's first priority should be to fully fund your research annually, Zoltan, for the next decade. That's how long I think it's gonna take for you to be successful. Once we announce the foundation, say a month or two from now, I want you to meet with my main numbers man, Neil Wexler. Thomas knows him and, like me, trusts him. I want Neil to work with you to figure out what you need operationally each year to be successful. How many people; how much money; how much equipment, technology, space etc., etc. Don't be fucking shy. Get it out there, what you need and how much. Be bold. You and Neil will cost it out. Then you and I and Neil will meet with Dr. Ramis and tell him what the foundation is underwriting for you, overhead included. We'll then make a restricted gift to an account we will suggest strongly that they set up specifically for your project. I don't want them dicking around with my money. Okay?"

Zoltan, awestruck, his eyes wide, could not respond.

"Second priority will be student debt relief through an endowment reducing undergraduate tuition and for a merit scholarship program. Thomas, I'm going to want you to interview all the experts and other best-practice programs at other universities and work to design my foundation's program for Sessions.

"The third program is to award student innovation. I want to see proposals from our next-generation entrepreneurs. If they are really promising, the foundation can grant them some support for their projects, then I may invest some of my own venture capital in them. Thomas, again, this will fall under your command.

"Fourth, Zoltan, my company's initiated a negotiation with the university to buy your patents. Hard to know what they're worth at this stage. I'm hoping to get them cheap before it occurs to Stanhope Barrett to buy them. Then I want you to have some ownership of them. What Ramis has done to you is more-or-less in my mind, criminal, even though you are when it comes to practical matters, a stupid schmuck.

"Finally, I'd like to begin working with interim president Powers on structuring a meaningful gift to the humanities. Perhaps we would get the Kravitz family to join us for something in memory of our former provost, although I realize that might be a problem for them emotionally. In any case, I wouldn't mind talking with them.

"And you know, I think it's about time to replace that dinosaur of an administration building, raze it and build something more in keeping with today's values in its place."

I looked over at my friend. Berger's remarks had so overcome him with emotion that tears were streaming down his face. I felt my own eyes grow wet. The magnitude of what Mark Berger was proposing for me was also overwhelming. To escape the politics of Sessions, especially to escape having to work in the administration building, yet still be involved with the university and not have to move, was an outcome too good to be true—but there it was, all because of Mark Berger, a man who wanted to do what was right and was willing to sacrifice for it, who appreciated honesty and welcomed our friendship.

"Now, look guys, straighten up."

Zoltan and I did our best to pull ourselves together.

"Not a word about this to anyone. No celebrations, no telling family or significant others. For stahters I gotta go from here to the medical center and drop Wentz's news on Ramis, no mention of the pedophile stuff of course, just the health problem, leave of absence and Powers as interim. Then I turn my attention back to the foundation. The IRS has just approved it, but we got all this compliance work and other setup stuff to do. So, keep your asses quiet for the next six to eight weeks. Okay?"

"Got it," I said emphatically while Zoltan added an equally emphatic, "Yes."

"Thomas, you know that the School of Foreign Service is giving me some dumb schmuck award about ten days from now. Bernie, Wentz and others are thinking I'll be so touched that I'll be persuaded to make a huge gift. Fantasy Land. But I'm gonna accept it because it would embarrass everyone if I turned it down and make me look way too much like the asshole I actually am. In any case, I understand that Wentz wanted you to work with my PR folks on coverage. Go forward on that basis. And we'll need your help writing the press release about Wentz's illness and Powers's interim appointment. Fritz is already preparing his statement for your review."

"Sure."

"Now, you guys get outta here. I got work to do."

As we left the president's office, I glanced over at Ms. Bemis and saw that she had morphed into JoAnn.

She looked at me with an expression of concern on her face, "You okay?" she asked.

"Never been better." I told her and gave her a smile, winked.

"It's just, I know what happened the last time Mr. Berger sat in the president's office."

"Yeah. Just go with the flow on this one. Super Sphinx time. Okay?"

Her expression changed back to the baleful Ms. Bemis instantly. "You may leave the premises," she ordered.

I laughed. "Beautiful. Thanks."

"Let's get outta here," I told Zoltan.

We walked together down the hallways of the third floor, took the elevator to the atrium and walked outside into the bright sunshine of a very cold, windless day.

We turned to one another, our breaths steaming before us in great puffs.

Zoltan looked over to me, a puzzled expression on his face, "When Bemis become human?" he asked.

"Long story. Couple drinks long. Did that really just happen in the president's office?"

"Yes, Thomas. It miracle."

"More like Berger's a miracle. Look, I gotta go batten down the hatches. All hell's going to break loose over the next few days."

"Yes. I go to lab. Pretend nothing happen."

"Good. Silence is golden, my friend."

"Thomas …"

"Yeah?"

"I love you."

"Oh Jesus, don't go all weird on me, okay?"

"Yes, but we going to be good. That wonderful, is it not?"

"Yeah, I don't know. After that two years of a Goddamned mess, I always feel like there's another shoe about to drop."

"Then before that happen let's enjoy while we can."

"I'm with you on that, man."

Zoltan turned and walked toward the university gate where it would be easier for a cab to find him, the few professors and students who passed him giving him a wide berth.

XXVI

Alicia

THE LEADERSHIP MEDALLION Award ceremony was the centerpiece of the School of Foreign Service's board of advisors' dinner following their annual meeting.

As Alicia and I had agreed, I drove down that morning early to have lunch with her, spend the afternoon assuring that the logistics for the dinner were in order and meet with the school's and Berger's public relations personnel. Thankfully, the weather cooperated. The day was cold but windless and filled with bright sun. And for once, the mid-morning traffic moved steadily.

The restaurant Alicia had chosen was in the K Street corridor, close enough to walk. So, I parked in the depths of the school's underground, dimly lit and noxious-smelling parking garage, thinking as I descended its serpentine ramp about Zoltan and my trip last year to the dinner Frank Lusby had encouraged us to attend, celebrating a $150 million gift to name the new Beijing Center.

The Chinese Ambassador, an eminence, had made very wise and cogent remarks. Fitz-Hugh's remarks had been, as usual, friendly, brilliant, perceptive and kind. Madam Secretary Greta Hauser had been in attendance and in her brief remarks had underscored the importance of the new center to future international relations. Then, as the dinner ended, she and Fitz-Hugh had disappeared together, as had Zoltan and Kristina, leaving my dinner partner, Ursula, and I to initiate our affair in her hotel suite. I sighed and felt myself shaking my head. It all seemed a lifetime ago.

My ten-block walk to the restaurant was pleasant as I took in the post-holiday store fronts, the different buildings and their architecture and other walkers, from the self-important lawyers and lobbyists, to smug academics, to hollow-eyed street people. The highlight was the emergence from a blank alleyway door of a well-known columnist and TV personality, face alcohol-flushed and filled with guilt and anxiety, who looked right and left warily and then walked away, head down, coat collar up. I glanced at my watch. Eleven fifty-three. Interesting.

The restaurant was upscale Chinese, high-ceilinged, open and airy, potted trees surrounding support columns, waiters and waitresses in fancy cutaway uniforms, white tablecloths on small tables laden with heavy, stainless silverware and white cloth napkins, with fresh orchid blossoms in cut-glass centerpieces. Ornate reproduction chairs graced with oriental tapestry cushions were at each place setting, seating an array of corporate, policy-organization and non-profit-expense-account clientele.

I heard a voice in my head go "*Cha-Ching!*" and saw dancing dollar signs. I briefly calculated whether my petty cash for the trip could possibly sustain such a luncheon hit, even if we split the bill. One thing for sure, the lunch expense was in no way going on my university or personal credit card.

I was shown to our table and provided with a Chinese pot of hot tea almost immediately. A few moments later Alicia entered, scanned the restaurant, spotted me, smiled a big smile, gave a quick wave and headed to our table.

I watched with interest and growing pride as patrons, servers, everyone there glanced her way or even stared openly. Yes, certainly she was attractive, but her presence was something else, and admirably so. Everyone there sensed it and I could see some whispering to their tablemates, inquiring—who is that, as if she was a television, media or movie star, as if they should know who she was but could not place her.

I thought to myself, *And I'm the one she's having lunch with.*

Oblivious to the stir she was causing, or choosing to ignore it, I could not decide which, Alicia reached our table. I stood. We had a brief hug and bussing of cheeks as we greeted one another. I held her chair. As she took her seat she stroked her hair off her shoulders, settled herself and said, "You were early."

"Yeah, I walked here. No real predicting how long that would take. Didn't want to be late. So, you're looking even more fantastic than usual."

"I should," she told me. "I have a new job."

"Really? That's wonderful. Tell me about it. But let me ask you one question first."

She shrugged, "Okay."

"Have you talked to JoAnn lately?"

"Yeah."

"What did she have to tell you about what's going on at Sessions?"

"Not much, just that your president is seriously ill and has had to take a leave of absence—that for the time being she'll be reporting to the provost who's a hard guy to read. May be okay, may not be. Difficult to know."

"That's it?"

"Yeah."

"Good. I was hoping that was the case."

"Major goings-on at Sessions these days?" she smiled.

"Yeah, you better believe it. I'll fill you in at some point, but for now I can't talk about it."

"Okay," she shrugged. "Same old story, right?"

"Exactly. So, tell me what's going on with you."

"Let's order first. I'm starving."

We were able to signal our waiter and place our orders, mine the cheapest entrée salad, Alicia ordering a specialty I had never heard of and which I was sure I'd never be able to pronounce.

Once he had left, Alicia began,

"After Christmas, ever alert to my former days when my father liked to show off 'little Alicia', I put on my most serious power suit, which for some clairvoyant reason I had brought with me, mainly because it's the warmest clothing I own, and rode with my father downtown to Piper-Hale.

"There we went through all the security and took the elevator, which goes up very rapidly and forever to the point where there's this wave effect of noise which is actually from the building moving in the wind as the elevator goes straight up. Your ears pop along the way. And, finally, we reach the executive offices and his suite.

"He very kindly introduces me around and then we go into his office and he closes the door and we sit down at a nice little hospitality area by a floor-to-ceiling window looking out over the city to infinity, and he tells me how proud he is of me and asks me about how things came to an end at Blaylock, whether I have a boyfriend or significant other, to which I reply no, not really, and he's interested in what plans I might have for the future.

"I tell him I'm completely undecided, a lot of different options, but I was not of a mind to pursue any of them at the moment, just biding my time."

Our lunches arrived, hers an array of different seafood, scallions, chopped spring onions, cashews and walnuts bathing in a hot broth emanating wonderful fragrances. Our water glasses were refilled and a new pot of tea set in place. Alicia picked up her chopsticks expertly. I, my fork, much less expertly.

She continued, "My news, I can see, is encouraging to my father. He gives some thought to what I've just said, taking a long, cogitating look at the cityscape beyond the window, and then turns to me. I get a sense, perhaps the first time I've seen this in him, that he's anxious. I could see how much he cared about what he was about to say to me. That was a shock—that he cared so much. What was at stake, I realized, was his relationship with me, and that he would be crushed if he lost it, even though he's been distant to me most of my life. I realized this wasn't about his being a big, powerful CEO but about me being his daughter and him being my father. Kind of blew my mind."

"Yeah, I can see why."

"My father says, 'I have a position to fill that I would like you to consider.'"

"Wow."

"Yes. So, here's what's happening. He's getting ready to retire. As part of that, he's dealing with both his exit from Piper-Hale, first by appointing a CEO and holding only the title of Chairman, and then shortly thereafter, becoming Chairman Emeritus and in essence retiring. Well, retiring as much as anyone like him can retire. While he's ceding a great deal of day-to-day management responsibility, he'll still be involved. What would you expect, right?"

"I guess."

"Of course, he'll keep his preferred shares which allow him a significant voting say in how the company moves forward.

"But the interesting part is that over the next year he'll be transferring a significant portion of his common shares and stock options over to a foundation he's creating, The Gaylord and Helen McDonald Family Foundation.

"The new role he sees for himself is to become a major philanthropist and for me to be his partner in that endeavor. We had a long discussion about all the good that the foundation could accomplish funding sustainability, new technologies, private and public sector initiatives for the environment, for education and training for the disadvantaged."

"Jesus ..."

Alicia stopped and looked at me, concerned, "Are you okay? You look ... What? What did I say that was so shocking?"

"He wants you to run the foundation," I blurted out hollowly, the shock sounding in my voice.

"Yeah. What's wrong? I thought you'd be happy for me. What's even better is that while the foundation will be headquartered in Chicago, he's fine with setting up a branch office of the foundation here in Washington. This gives us the ability to have conversations with many of the organizations he wants to support and have me do due diligence and make recommendations on others we should be funding. Isn't that terrific?"

"Absolutely. It's just ... Hah!" I laughed abruptly, so loudly that people at the tables around us turned to stare. "Oops, sorry."

"Thomas, I thought with my new position, with its flexibility, that we might have an opportunity to see one another more often."

We looked at one another—a long, very connected and caring look. I felt my heart begin to thump.

"I'm not sure whether someone up there likes me or doesn't like me." I told her.

"What do mean by that?" she replied, looking at me, puzzled.

"That I think you're probably right."

"Really?" She reached out and took my hand.

"Yea-ah," I responded, feeling utterly conflicted.

At that moment my cell phone vibrated in my pocket. I hesitated, then thinking it could be the School of Foreign Service, or even Janet or one of the kids, I reached in and pulled it out halfway so I could glance over and down at the screen.

It was my conscience calling. Zoltan.

CPSIA information can be obtained
at www.ICGtesting.com
Printed in the USA
FSHW021125250620
71448FS